Their Love

VALERIE TAYLOR

ARSENAL PULP PRESS
Vancouver

ARSENAL PULP PRESS
341 Water Street, Suite 200
Vancouver, BC
Canada V6B 1B8
arsenalpulp.com

Little Sister's Classics series editor: Mark Macdonald
Editors for the press: Robert Ballantyne and Brian Lam
Text and cover design: Shyla Seller
Front cover illustration from the Crest Book edition published by the
    Fawcett World Library
Photograph of Valerie Taylor courtesy of the Division of Rare and Manuscript
    Collections, Cornell University Library
Research assistance: Rima J. Turner
Little Sister's Classics logo design: Hermant Gohil

Printed and bound in Canada

*This is a work of fiction. Any resemblance of characters to
persons either living or deceased is purely coincidental.*

*Efforts have been made to locate copyright holders of source
material wherever possible. The publisher welcomes hearing
from any copyright holders of material used in this book who
have not been contacted.*

Library and Archives Canada Cataloguing in Publication:

Taylor, Valerie, 1913-1997
        Whisper their love / Valerie Taylor.

(A Little Sister's classic)
ISBN 1-55152-210-1

        I. Title. II. Series: Little Sister's classics.

PS3570.A97W45 2006   813'.54   C2006-
903147-9

ISBN-13: 978-1-55152-210-4

Whisper

LITTLE SISTER'S CLASSICS

Whisper Their Love

Contents

Preface

In 1957, amid a torrent of sordid and sleazy pulp novels that exploited every aspect of American melodrama, _Whisper Their Love_ appeared, and stands today as a beacon of an emerging lesbian consciousness. Valerie Taylor, by any standard, can be said to have been one of the true pioneers of American lesbian fiction. Her first lesbian-themed novel is simple in structure, but sophisticated in the nuances of its content and delivery. It is also filled with frank discussions of taboo themes, but from a feminist perspective that is refreshing and surprising. It is a gem in the rough of 1950s pulp fiction.

In many venues that celebrate lesbian and gay history – including the Little Sister's Classics series – the word "pioneer" gets thrown around a lot. It applies, in varying degrees, to nearly all aspects of our recent culture given the challenges we have faced as writers and publishers and readers. Certainly, today's young lesbian author faces a rather different set of challenges and expectations from both the industry and her readers than lesbian writers of the mid-1950s. But, in too many ways, traces of ingrained and institutional homophobia remain: Will bookstores embrace and publicize her work? Will her novel travel freely across borders guarded by bureaucrats steeped in the tradition of combing through fiction for traces of obscenity?

In other ways, the term "pioneer" seems more apt. As we go to press with this, the seventh addition to the series, we cannot contact Valerie Taylor for her insights into the book's creation. During the production of this edition, the execution of the Valerie Taylor literary estate has changed hands due to circumstances that shout out the urgency of recognizing our pioneering sisters and brothers while we can. That legendary dynamo of lesbian American arts and letters, and a pioneer in her own right, Tee A. Corinne, has faced both the loss of her partner and a health crisis of her own during this time, and has lovingly passed the torch of the Valerie Taylor estate to the Cornell University Library's Division of Rare and Manuscript Collections.

Yet it is with jubilation, not sadness, that we unveil a book that has slept for too many decades. To reproduce this novel, with the complimentary archival material about the author, is a joy. This edition is further enhanced by a compelling new introduction by Barbara Grier, co-founder of Naiad Press and long-time champion of lesbian fiction, and yes – a pioneer.

As we cherish and pay tribute to the past, so we look forward as writers, publishers, and readers to the future. Little Sister's Classics is very pleased to present *Whisper Their Love*.

– *Mark Macdonald, 2006*

Introduction

Barbara Grier

Theirs was the kind of love they dared not show the world....

Desire and torment swept through Joyce's trembling young body at the gentle touch of Edith's cool hand upon her face. She had never felt like this before. It frightened her ... and filled her with a terrible excitement!

– Jacket copy, Fawcett World Library Crest Original Novel edition of *Whisper Their Love*, 1957

The Pulp Phenomena

Published in the 1950s and 1960s, "Lesbian pulp" was one of many subgenres of pulp novels that also included westerns, romances, and detective fiction, named for the cheap wood pulp paper on which they were printed. While the paperback novel was not new, previously it had been used by publishers solely as a means of cashing in on residual markets by reprinting books that had been successful in hardcover editions. The practice of publishing an "original paperback" forever changed the publishing industry's (and the public's) idea of a "book." The often lurid subject matter of the pulps and competition within the industry made it necessary for mainstream publishers to create a safe distance from their hardcover sales with a long list of imprints. Increased demand for what we would now call "content" brought new opportunities for aspiring writers, many of whom earned their rent money in clerical positions within the publishing industry.

One of those clerical workers-turned-author is hailed as one of the first lesbian pulp writers. One evening in the early 1950s, Mary Jane Meaker, a secretary and editorial slush pile reader at Fawcett Publications, was having drinks at the Algonquin Hotel in New York with her boss, Dick Carroll, the editor in charge of a new line of paperback originals called Gold Medal Books. She mentioned her desire to write a love story "with a twist," one that was inspired by the unchecked homosexuality she encountered (and embraced!) during her boarding school days. After a discussion of whether or not she had been "cured," she was invited to submit an outline and receive an advance, provided she set the story in a college and agreed not to make homosexuality attractive. Not only could the story not have a happy ending, the character had to eventually reject her homosexuality. The reasons behind Dick Carroll's directive were legal, not moral. Paperback books needed to travel through the mail and pass inspection. If even one book was censured because it proselytized for homosexuality, all the other books accompanying it en route to distributors would be returned. He wasn't concerned with sexual preferences; he simply wanted to make the new publishing line a success. In the end it was a success, and so was Meaker, who would go on to write dozens of pulps about lesbian life, many under the pseudonym Ann Aldrich. Her novel *Spring Fire*, considered one of the very first lesbian pulps, and written under another pen name, Vin Packer, was published by Gold Medal in 1952 and sold more than 1.5 million copies.

And that was only the beginning.

The Golden Age

The standard definition of lesbian pulp fiction is any mid-twentieth century pulp novel with overtly lesbian themes and content. While Meaker wrote hers based on her own personal experiences, many of these "lesbian" pulps were written by male writers writing for "one-handed" male readers who saw the lesbian theme as the stuff of classic heterosexual male masturbation fantasies. To appeal to this audience's voyeuristic demands, there had to be more sex than plot or characterization and of course, at least one of the women had to fall for a man in order to make her a "real" woman. The other was often killed off.

Susan Stryker, in her book *Queer Pulp: Perverted Passion for the Golden Age of the Paperback* (Chronicle Books, 2001), notes that it was Ann Bannon, Paula Christian, and Valerie Taylor who ushered in the Golden Age of Lesbian Pulps. In the early 1960s, these three women began to slowly and courageously overhaul the overly sexualized and exploitative images of lesbians prevalent in pulps written by men. In hindsight, this approach now appears as a brave, possibly unconscious attempt to reclaim lesbianism for their lesbian readers and to bring them some sense of hope that they weren't alone, through more realistic plots, stronger, more credible characters, and relatively happy endings. Lesbian readers spotted the difference immediately.

According to Ann Bannon, the bestselling of the three:

I was aware that more men than women were writing lesbian pulp paperbacks, but most of them were pure titillation – a wild ride from one sexual set-up to another, a way to lure male readers into buying the books and enjoying that most perdurable of male fantasies: two attractive women making love, usually ending with a male stepping in to show them how it's "really" done.

> As for the women authors, we were groping our way
> toward an affectionate portrait of real human beings
> … I can't speak for my fellow writers, but I was too
> naïve, too young and dumb, to give much thought to
> the effect I was having on my women readers – at least
> not until I began to get hundreds of letters from them,
> begging for reassurance and information.[1]

Paula Christian was the second most popular author of the three. Her work, which includes *Twilight Girl, Another Kind Of Love*, and *Love is Where You Find It*, juxtaposes the "glamour" of pre-feminist urban working women with the seedy gay bars of the urban underground. Her characters are worldly yet uncertain, fiercely independent, and seek to define themselves outside the context of a relationship. Christian's women are looking for the "real" thing, but often pass the time in trysts that are lucky to last the evening, let alone a lifetime.

Valerie Taylor was the third author of the Golden Age and, frankly, the least popular in terms of sales. There is a political edge to her work, a serious side not often found in pulps; she dealt with the economic realities of women's lives, examined issues like race and class, and traced so-called anti-social behaviors to a variety of family dysfunctions, in a voice that must have seemed too intellectual, too critical of normal mores, and too shrill for most one-handed readers.

Who was Valerie Taylor?

> I rather resent being thought of as a pulp novelist …
> a pulp is a little more melodramatic than real life, the
> characters are not as fully developed as they would
> be in a really good book … I thought we should have

---

1. "Sleaze, Trash, and Miracles: How Ann Bannon Changed Lesbian Fiction by Writing About the Butch of her Dreams." Joy Parks, "Velvet Park," Fall 2003, pp. 42-43.

some books about lesbians who acted like human
beings.[2]

Lesbian novelist, poet, feminist, and social activist, Velma Nacella
Young was born on September 7, 1913, in Aurora, Illinois. She attended Blackburn College in Carlinville, Illinois, where she was
first exposed to grassroots activism. Velma taught at several country
schools in the state from 1937 to 1940, and in 1939, she married
William Jerry Tate. When the couple divorced in 1953, Valerie went
to work to support herself and her three sons. That same year, she
published her first novel, *Hired Girl*, a heterosexual pulp which was
sympathetic towards those in the grip of poverty and dealt openly
with adultery, abortion, drug dealing, blackmail, and class issues.

Her first lesbian novel, *Whisper Their Love*, was published in
1957 under the pen name Valerie Taylor, and as a result she became
widely known by this name. *Whisper Their Love* was followed by others including *The Girls in 3-B* (1959), *Unlike Others* (1963), *The Secret
of the Bayou* (1967, under the name Francine Davenport), and the Erika Frohmann series: *Stranger on Lesbos* (1960), *A World Without Men*
(1963), *Journey to Fulfillment* (1963), and *Return to Lesbos* (1964).

A member of the Daughters of Bilitis, Valerie contributed stories, reviews and criticism to *The Ladder.* Writing became her career
and her means of supporting her family; she wrote for Chicago trade
publications while penning confession stories and popular novels.

A prolific poet as well (often under the name Nacella Young),
Taylor published at least fifty poems before Womanpress published
Two Women Revisited in 1976, which paired her poetry with work by
Jeannette H. Foster. She continued to write novels and poetry into
the 1990s. Banned Books published a revised and expanded version
of *Two Women Revisited* in 1991. In her later years, she wrote *Love Image* (1977), *Prism* (1981), *Ripening* (1988), and *Rice and Beans* (1989).

---

2. March 30, 1991 interview with Valerie Taylor, in *Happy Endings: Lesbian Writers Talk
About Their Lives and Work*, Kate Brandt, Naiad Press, 1993.

Her writing also appears in numerous anthologies, and an interview with her can be found in Studs Terkel's 1995 book *Coming of Age: The Story of Our Century by Those Who've Lived It.*

Taylor was a life-long activist for peace and justice, and a gay rights pioneer. In the 1960s, she met Pearl Hart, a civil rights lawyer twenty years her senior, whom she described as the love of her life. She lived in Chicago, where she co-founded Mattachine Midwest, the city's first successful gay and lesbian organization, in 1965, and was one of the driving forces behind the Lesbian Writers' Conference in 1974. From 1975 to 1978, she took part in grassroots organizing of seniors in Margaretville, New York, then Tucson, Arizona, where she became active in a Quaker society, environmental activities, and advocacy for the elderly. In the 1980s and 1990s, despite health problems, she gave public talks, lectures, and interviews. In 1992, she was inducted into the City of Chicago's Gay and Lesbian Hall of Fame. She also identified herself as the founder of Lesbian Grandmothers of America.

In 1980, Taylor had established a Sisterhood Fund to aid writer/scholar Jeannette Foster. This kindness would be returned to her in her time of need. In 1993, she suffered serious injuries in a debilitating fall, and author/columnist Lee Lynch established a similar fund, through Antigone Books in Tucson. Because of this, the community she helped to build would make her later years more comfortable.

Taylor was eighty-four years old when she died on October 22, 1997 in a Tucson hospice following another fall.

Why *Whisper Their Love?*

Whisper Their Love is a contradiction. Despite being penned by one of the writers of the "Golden Age," it is an early pulp, and as such, adheres closely to the expected formula, particularly in its ending. Formulaic, too, is the girls' college setting that creates an isolated women's community, as is the age difference between the two engaged in the affair, with the older, more knowledgeable woman initiating the innocent younger girl.

The book also contains a quaint earmark of the early pulps, a seemingly "scientific" warning to readers that the behavior described in the novel is rampant in society, and that by reading this book they will immediately gain the knowledge necessary to guard against such perversities. Taylor once joked that the officious warning, supposedly written by a Dr. Richard H. Hoffmann, was quite possibly penned by the office boy.

As she would continue to do in later books, Taylor begins the development of her main character with an analysis of her family life. Joyce was born to an unwed mother who was too young and too wild to take on the responsibility. She ended up being raised by a repressed country aunt who makes her feel ashamed about her maturing body. Her vulnerability to the affections of headmistress Edith Bannister is, in part, the result of being starved for a mother's affection. On the one occasion that she feels wanted by her mother, when she is invited to her wedding, Joyce is violated by the groom-to-be while her mother sleeps in the next room.

Joyce speaks of the incident as something that has "dirtied" her, something she needs to wash away. Rape appears in many of Taylor's books, but she refuses it as an excuse for someone to "turn lesbian," speaking more to how the real sickness lies in a culture that makes it acceptable for women to be victims. The idea of male sexuality being something "dirty" is found throughout the book, including Joyce's first encounter with her roommate. The girl has been with her boyfriend, and has to go and "clean up" before something bad happens.

Through much of the book, men are a source of evil, and Joyce speaks of the bruises, pain, and discomfort of heterosexual sex, blatantly comparing it to the wonders of spending the night with her new female lover Edith, who tells her:

> All men think about is their own pleasure. A man wants
> to relieve himself, like an animal. There's no tender-
> ness in them. If they do anything for you first, it's only
> to get you all worked up so you'll be more responsive
> and they'll have more fun. Ugh!

The sexual relationship between the two women is isolated, safe from male reach. While Joyce is in bed with Edith, she experiences a wonderfully pure female sexuality not in any way colored by the attitudes of the world outside.

> Joyce wasn't sure what was happening or going to hap-
> pen. Whatever it was, she liked it. This had no relation
> to being with a man, the touch and smell of a man....
> There was no fatigue or worry left ... no world beyond
> these night dark walls. Nothing but the stroking hand
> and Edith's accelerated breathing at her ear, and the
> feeling that flooded through her.

Still, Joyce has trouble dealing with the "real" world conventions that even a woman as independent and clearly lesbian as Edith must contend with. Joyce is upset that Edith occasionally dates men simply because she wants a night out, and is scandalized at Edith's suggestion that she too occasionally date a boy and let him make a pass at her, simply to continue a necessary façade of heterosexuality. In obvious foreshadowing, Edith makes it clear that the two of them cannot have a public relationship, that what is between them will always be in hiding, and that it will not last. She speaks of a previous relationship in which she was the seduced ingénue, and the other woman's suicide in response to being outed. In turn, Edith creates a fierce loyalty in Joyce by justifying the need for secrecy and hiding in a world that hates and misunderstands "our kind."

The muted yet tender and passionate sexuality found in *Whisper*

Their Love is not only characteristic of the "Golden Age," but also of Taylor's tendency not to write extraneous sex scenes or explicitly erotic descriptions: her refusal to have her words, her images of lesbians, turned pornographic and exploited by men. The innocence (and wonderful female-centricity) of the sexual acts described in her books was no doubt another reason why she may have failed to sell to the "one-handed readers," but qualities that must have sent a clear message to her lesbian readers:

> "A woman can do this for you because she knows what it means, she sees her own pleasure reflected in it. This is what matters. The rest is nothing but a trap nature has figured out to keep the human race going. What counts is here."

> She moved her hand again. "This is where the thrill and the meaning are."

In a remarkably daring subplot, Joyce assists her roommate in securing and recovering from an illegal abortion, only to have the girl turn on her when Joyce admonishes her for sleeping with the father following the ordeal and risking a second pregnancy. It's important to note that the abortion issue would have been as equally scandalous as the lesbian theme, and through it, Taylor dealt her pre-feminist audience an interesting analysis of the contradictory messages young women received in that era, and the legal and social controls placed on women's sexuality. For Taylor, the young lesbian of the 1950s is like some sort of queer Cassandra, pointing out the evils of heterosexuality to no avail, while being punished for not participating in it.

Taylor deftly foreshadows the beginning of the end of the lesbian affair with Joyce's night out with Edith. During this era, "nice" women didn't frequent bars of any kind and the stilted lives, the loose morality, the proximity to other anti-social behavior (drugs and prostitution) all weigh on Joyce's mind, hinting at the future that waits for her as a lesbian.

In the pre-Stonewall, pre-liberation lesbian pulp universe (and equally for actual lesbian relationships at the time), models for a happily-ever-after ending were rare, almost non-existent. As contemporary readers looking back at a frighteningly repressive period when so many lesbians lived their lives hidden not only from the world, but also from each other, we can intellectually rationalize the necessity of the book's conclusion; we can brace ourselves for its inevitability, but even so, it is impossible to read the ending and not suffer to some degree over Joyce's capitulation to heterosexuality. Perhaps what's most emotionally wrenching is to speculate on how heavy these endings must have weighed on scared, sad, closeted lesbian readers of that era.

But one has to wonder if perhaps Taylor was skilled enough, visionary enough, even angry enough to create an ending that can be read nearly five decades later with more than a small degree of irony. Not only is the rapid (and no doubt superficial) transformation to heterosexuality "the answer," but also Taylor's version of the man who would set Joyce "straight" seems to have all the answers, including a textbook understanding of female homosexuality. Like the *deus ex machina* he is, John patiently explains to her (but really to us, the readers) how her lesbianism is a merely manifestation of her infantile sexuality, a desire that will evaporate once she matures into a real (read heterosexual) woman. He's a patient soldier who has no problems waiting for her to grow up, as long as he gets benefit of her experimentation along the way. But perhaps even more unsettling is his theory that heterosexuals don't hate homosexuals; most just feel sorry for them, a view that negates the nascent sense of unity and stirrings of community Joyce had learned from Edith. He is gallingly proud of his liberal understanding of her "problem" and seems to view having sex with Joyce as some sort of public service.

John leaned across the table and laid a hand on her
arm.

"Be honest with yourself, kid. If you're getting any real
satisfaction out of it, then okay. I can wait for you to
grow up. But if you're past it, then for God sakes, put it
behind you and move on...."

"It's not just me. I couldn't let her down. Everyone's
down on people like that anyway."

"Not half as much as they're down on normal people,"
John said. "That's a lot of hooey, that propaganda they
give you, how persecuted they are. Most people simply
feel sorry for queers. They're sort of handicapped, like
someone with an artificial leg."

John is so one-dimensional, so woodenly unreal and resigned not
only to bedding Joyce into being straight, but also doggedly explaining to her (and the rest of us) why her lesbian experience wasn't all
that important or special. In doing so, he invalidates all lesbian relationships, marking them as merely a phase on the road to maturity.
While it's hard to imagine how bitterly the 1950s reader might have
resented this character, today he seems tragically pompous, comically
so, more caricature than character, and certainly fodder to be cuck-
olded the moment Joyce has the chance.

Was this Taylor's way of "sticking it to the man"? Was she expecting this ending to be read ironically at some point? Is this some
sort of code? The ending of *Whisper Their Love* reads so obviously as
"fiction"; it is so different in tone and pacing from the earlier parts of
the book that one can't help but wonder about the author's real mo-
tives, beyond ending her story in a way that would allow it to legally
pass through the US mail system.

Why do we need this book now?

What can possibly be gained by reprinting yet another novel that is clearly a historical artifact, one with a view of lesbianism that can best be described as archaic? Especially now, when collection after collection of explicit lesbian-created erotica is easily available, when lesbian families dominate our literature, when lesbians write about all kinds of lesbian characters freely and openly in every literary genre; a time when our political writings go beyond mere homosexuality, to consider questions about the very fabric of gender itself.

While it sounds trite, it is true that you can't know where you're going if you don't know where you've been. To forget the past is to risk repeating it. No gay or lesbian activist can afford to ever forget how it was before. Especially now, particularly in the US, when rights and freedoms for gays, lesbians, women, and minorities, long fought and hard won over decades, are now in serious danger of being lost. A time when at least one state can, with the sweep of a pen, obliterate the freedoms made possible by Roe vs. Wade; a time when the refusal to open the institution of marriage to gays and lesbians is used to distract Americans from the real evils that threaten their rights and freedoms. Books like *Whisper Their Love* belong to an era we too often believe is comfortably in the past. It speaks of attitudes we tell ourselves no longer exist. Could we be wrong?

Whisper Their Love, like all pulps, is of its time and place. It is a reminder of the kind of oppression, fear, and invisibility that inspired our fight for the freedoms, self-respect, and community we now enjoy. It is the work of a woman who wrote from a lonely place, knowing the story she needed to tell, but having to, like so many others, tell it slant. It's daunting to consider the kind of creativity and risk it took to bend and code this novel into something both she and the United States Postal Service could live with. Even more so that it has continued to capture our interest and our attention for nearly half a century.

Little Sister's bookstore has long shown us the importance of the fight to write, to read, to think, and by extension, to love, as we choose. Valerie Taylor, with her serious literary ambitions, her rebellions large and small, her courage, her life-long struggle to make our lives better and her desire to tell the truest tale she could, was a reconnaissance soldier in that fight, and this series will be stronger for her inclusion.

Thanks to the Rare and Manuscript Collections at the Cornell University Library, particularly the biographical information found in the online selections of the Valerie Taylor Collection (donated by Tee A. Corinne, former executor of the Literary Estate of Valerie Taylor).

Whisper Their Love

All parents should read this book. Those who do must leave it with the conviction that they are derelict in their duties if they abandon their responsibilities toward immature girls and boys, and expose them to the indifferent care of outsiders without sufficient moral preparation or mature direction.

Whisper Their Love is a tragic but touching portrait of a conflicted younger generation, and the painful consequences arising from sexual disorientation and adolescent rebellion.

That youth is normally in a state of rebellion most adults come to accept. But without genuine concern and understanding – without the means of communicating love and acceptance to those lost in the bewildering jungle of adolescent feelings – the destructive congeals into behavior patterns which can lead only to isolation and perpetual mutiny. The crushing loneliness of those who have set themselves apart from the world is dramatically illustrated in this story.

– Dr. Richard H. Hoffmann

Chapter One

She took a taxi from the railroad station to the campus. That was the last thing Mimi had told her, in the drugstore where Ferndell people waited for the bus. "Take a taxi, sweetie pie. This isn't any Community High School you're getting into; this place has class." She looked wistful, as if she had been the daughter and Joyce the mother. "It makes me feel good, you getting a break like this."

It didn't make Joyce feel good. Not at this stage of the game, anyhow. The meter registered thirty cents before they even started. Thirty cents was a lot of money to throw away. The rear-vision mirror gave back a small pale face with big eyes and an unfamiliar mouth, Mimi's Pink Passion smoothed on with a brush. Somebody else's face. She caught the driver's cynical eye in the glass and leaned back, trying to look as if she rode around in cabs every day. He grinned. "You going up to the Female Factory?"

"Pardon me?"

"The Louisa Henderson Hicks Junior College, kid." He turned halfway around. "Any time you want a hack, call and ask for Scotty. Any time at all."

"Thank you."

If this was the town of Henderson, it didn't look like much. But then, railroads always ran through the dirtiest part of town. Streets away, there were probably tree-shaded lawns and big white houses with pillared porticos. She had lain awake in the farmhouse bedroom nights, picturing it. The streets they were passing through now were more citified than Ferndell, but dirtier too, and mostly given over to small taverns and cheap eating places.

A small kid on a bike skidded to a stop in front of them. Scotty rode his brakes. "Little bastard wants his neck broke," he said. The kid made the sidewalk all right and thumbed his nose at the cab.

Railroad arch. Out in the sun again, Scotty ran the red light at a four-way stop and pulled up alongside a stretch of sunburned grass and fall-browning trees. "This is her. Take a good look."

This was her, and how urgently she wished it weren't. There was the library, stone, with ivy or something crawling up the front of it. All the other buildings were of dark red brick, set among clumps of trees and tied together with red brick sidewalks. There was the Civil War cannon pointing at the railroad arch which for some reason cut one corner off the campus. There was the marble statue of a Confederate general on a horse. For all the neglected grass and encroaching train tracks, the place wore a look of what she considered historical elegance.

Scotty came around and jerked the door open. The meter read eighty-five cents. She dug in her new handbag with slippery fingers and unwadded a dollar bill. "Keep the change."

"Thanks, Miss Moneybags."

The gravel was hot and gritty under her thin soles. Scotty, sliding back under the wheel, pointed. "That there one over there."

"Thanks."

Up the drive was as far as from Atlanta to the sea, and her feet felt glued to the ground, but there was nothing to do but plod toward the three-story building with pillars and the wide circular steps so overlaid with sitting and sprawling girls that she didn't see how she was going to get to the door. Nobody stopped talking, or batted an eye her way, or indicated by the turning of a head that her approach had been noticed. And she knew that nobody was missing a thing, from the way Mimi had cut her hair to the shiny toes of her new pumps.

They were all beautiful, or carried themselves as if they thought they were, as if they'd spent hours every day since the age of twelve just practicing up on being beautiful. Blondes, brunettes, a smoldering redhead in purple shorts. The new girls stood out from the rest, chic but hot in suits. The redhead looked at Joyce without a flicker of interest, as if she couldn't possibly offer any competition, and then moved over the least possible bit. Joyce had no choice but to edge past. It was a relief to get indoors, out of the hot sun and the cool stare of glamorous Southern womanhood.

There were more stairs inside, with a long hall at the top, chintz-curtained windows and cushioned seats at both ends. The inside steps were marble too, or almost. At the top was a woman in sheer black, whale-shaped and whale-sized; if she came unzipped she would have spilled over. She had pneumatic-drill eyes in a face creamed and massaged, rouged and powdered almost into youthfulness. Her voice was so elegant and cultured Joyce wouldn't have been surprised if she had taken it out like an upper plate when she went to bed at night.

"Good evening, dear. I am Mrs. Abbott, your housemother. Now may I have your name and home address?"

Joyce told her, and she recorded notes in a small, neat hand.

"Joyce Cameron, what a delightful name. Let's see, you're in with Mary Jean Kennedy, one of our sweetest girls. I just know you'll love her, she comes from Charlottenorthcarolina." Her eyes gimleted into Joyce's face, which felt as if it had Ferndellillinois printed all over it. Me and Abe Lincoln, she thought, then remembered that this was a Southern state and it might be more tactful not to mention Lincoln down here. "All of our girls are high caliber," Mrs. Abbott said. "Very high caliber, indeed."

Joyce smothered a giggle and followed Mrs. Abbott past an empty lounge with flowered curtains, a fireplace and a concert grand; past a row of doors with typed name cards; up another flight of stairs, wood but carpeted. Her new pumps were pinching badly. She damned narrow toes and pinpoint heels. The dirty loafers that had seen her through her senior year in high were in her closet at home.

She'd write tomorrow and ask Aunt Gen to send them.

Room 205, three doors from the stairs and almost across the hall from the bathroom, had been hit by a cyclone. It was a boxlike room looking out on the front campus and the railroad arch. Bleached wood furniture in pairs: two single beds, two chests of drawers with metal pulls, two desks, two straight chairs. Now a trunk stood open in the middle of the floor and somebody had evidently been interrupted in the midst of pulling out the contents and throwing them around.

Mrs. Abbott ignored the mess, like a lady. "Make yourself at home, dear. I'm sorry you are seeing our lovely campus when it isn't quite its prettiest, but you know we've had a dry summer. I'm sure you'll just love it here."

Joyce pushed back a white buck flat and a pair of pleated nylon panties off the nearest bed and sat down, a little dazed.

After Mrs. Abbott left, Joyce walked to the bathroom. So this was what it would be like. The door stood open and she went in. An unstoppered bottle of nail polish was drying out on the window sill, wet footprints crisscrossed the tile floor, and tiny hairpins sprinkled over the basin suggested that someone had been combing out a home permanent. I wish Aunt Gen could see this, Joyce thought. Uncle Will had put plumbing in the farmhouse during the early years of the war, when corn and hog prices were high, and one of Aunt Gen's maxims was that you could judge a housekeeper by her bathroom and kitchen.

The room door was shut when she got back. She hesitated, then pushed it open and walked in. A naked girl was bending over the trunk, back to her, throwing more things out on the floor. She turned. "Hi. Are you the perfectly delightful character Abbott put in with me?" She threw a net crinoline on the bed. It slid off with a whispering of ruffles. "Were you in the john? Anybody else in there?"

"No, it's empty."

"Good. Gotta do some first aid, but quick." She scowled, dark eyes angry under black arched brows. "I told the fool I wasn't fixed, we'd better wait, but no, he can't hold off till tonight." She bent over the trunk again, sweat beading her back. "The little monsters travel an inch every six minutes or something, Butch told us in Hygiene, though I don't know how she'd know." She found what she was after and straightened up, draping a terry robe around her. "Be right back."

She can't mean what I think she means, Joyce reassured herself. There wasn't anything to do but stand there, looking at the cream plastered walls, until Mary Jean came back into the room.

"I didn't mean to be rude," Mary Jean apologized. She pulled off the robe and dropped something into a gaping drawer. "The big lug makes me so mad, coming at me like he's been starved all summer." Her cheeks creased into a dimple. "I can't say no to him either."

"Well –" Joyce could feel her face getting red. Of course she had sat in on enough washroom sessions about whether a girl should or not, and whether you would if you really loved a boy, and whether certain other girls had. The consensus at Community seemed to be that it was pretty darn sophisticated to Go All the Way but simpler if you waited, especially if you ended up marrying a man who wanted his wife to be without experience. Certainly it was better not to admit anything, except maybe to your best girl friend.

Mary Jean was simmering down now that she had fixed things, or hoped she had. She began taking piles of clothes out of the trunk and laying them in piles on her bed, slips here and balled-up nylons there. She moved quickly and well – tennis or maybe ballet lessons. "Excuse me," she said politely, "are you a Vee?"

"I don't know –"

"Virgin, silly. One of the girls Kinsey missed."

"I guess so," Joyce said, humiliated. If you could believe the little blue-paper booklets Aunt Gen left on her bed, the autumn she was thirteen, *not* being a virgin was something to blush for. And according to the copies of romance magazines the girls bought at the corner drugstore and passed around at school, as soon as you quit being one you got pregnant and full of remorse. Only to wind up with forgiveness and the pure love of a good man, which evidently took up all your time and energy for the rest of your life, since that was where the stories ended. She guessed the truth was somewhere in between.

"Don't let it get you down." Mary Jean had finally reached the bottom layer of the trunk. Jewelry, gloves, a wad of tissues. The room looked liked a rummage sale. She stepped into a doll-size puckered panty girdle, found her wristwatch and put it on, pulled on flat beaded moccasins. "Now where in hell is my pink honan?" She found it under a pile of books and put it on, shaking out the pleats. "Abbott likes us to dress up for dinner. Our delightful dinner. The first night doesn't matter, though; your suit's all right."

"My trunk isn't here yet, anyway."

"I love your hair," Mary Jean said dreamily. "It's the exact color of molasses taffy." She moved over and made a place at the mirror for Joyce. Her own hair was ink-black, cut short and feathered against her cheeks.

"My mother cut it," Joyce said proudly. "She's an executive for a cosmetic firm." That was one way of putting it – well, it took brains and personality to sell; Mimi said so herself. All those postcards she had saved, even if Aunt Gen did think it was silly, written on trains, in cheap hotels, waiting in small-town Beauty Shoppes whose harassed owners might or might not buy, pencil propped against the sample case. "She's getting married again, though. To her boss."

"My mother went away when I was a little kid," Mary Jean said, measuring with her hand from the floor. She looked intently into the mirror. "I'm going to be a photographer's model. You'd make a cute sub-deb model yourself, that little round face and dimples. Ever think about it?"

"They say it's hard work."

"All work is terrible. The pay's good, though."

The thought of being a model and making wads of money lasted all the way down the two flights of stairs, into the dining room at the end of the first-floor hall. There awe overtook her. The room was long, and lit by candles as well as an overhead chandelier with dangling prisms, and it was full of talking girls. The second-year students had changed to Scarlett O'Hara type dresses, only mostly ballet length, and the new ones stood around singly or clinging to their roommates, trying to look aloof but only looking alone. Mrs. Abbott swam, whale-smooth, through all this femininity, still in her black but with rhinestone glitter added and new make-up. "Let's see, you will be at Miss Bannister's table the first six weeks. I know you'll see that your delightful little roommate meets all the girls," she told Mary Jean, smiling sweetly. Mary Jean smirked back. Joyce felt about five years old, likely to wet her pants or start sucking her thumb any minute.

"Go screw yourself," Mary Jean muttered after Mrs. Abbott's broad retreating back. "Don't look that way, honey. She makes me sick, too."

"Which one's Miss Bannister?"

"Dean of Women. That's a silly name for it. What is there to be dean of in this nunnery?" Mary Jean steered her around clusters of talking girls. There were six or seven long tables, each set for twelve, and they were something: damask shiny with ironing, hanging in folds to the floor; candles burning with straight flames; silver bowls with pink roses in them. She gave a worried look at the line of flat silver alongside her plate and stood behind her chair, like the others.

Miss Edith Bannister, Dean of Women, was at the head of the table. The only dean she had known was Ma Henneberry, unmarried, at Community High, who lectured the girls about purity and was built on the lines of Uncle Will's morris chair. This one was like tubular steel. Slender, erect, rather pale, all in beige, with one big splashy ring. She turned her head and looked the length of the table.

Something stirred in Joyce. She looks like Mimi. No, she doesn't either. Maybe if Mimi wore her hair like that, plain. Still, there's something. The old longing rose in her. She was caught and held by smooth-lidded eyes, neither gray nor brown but something be- tween. Miss Bannister smiled a little, turning her hand so that the light winked on her ring.

Somebody rattled off a blessing, and chairs scraped on the par- quet. Joyce sat down, copying the others. A dark-brown hand reached over her shoulder and set down a glass of tomato juice, and suddenly she was hungry.

Miss Bannister was listening to one of the girls, her head bent. She didn't exactly look like Mimi, but still – Joyce reached for her glass without looking, and tipped it over. The girl next to her squawked and jumped up, shaking out her flounces. Joyce got mixed up in a flurry of apologies and pushed Mimi out of her mind, the first time since the news of her engagement to Irv Kaufman had come to the farm.

Chapter Two

The shrilling of an alarm clock broke through the humming of insects in the roadside grass. Joyce pried her eyes open, then shut them again and was immediately back on the farm, standing beside the RFD box at the end of the lane. Gray velvety dust rose up from between the clover and dandelion stems and powdered her ankles, smudging the white socks and dulling the patent-leather slippers she had sneaked out of her closet while Aunt Gen was busy in the kitchen.

Heat waves shimmered over the cornfields, distorting Uncle Will's stocky figure atop the tractor. The soy beans were too dry for the time of year, and the big elephant-ear leaves on the catalpa trees hung down dry and lifeless. Sweat ran down Joyce's face. She wiped it away with her starched sleeve.

She was so hot her tongue stuck to the roof of her mouth, and she'd torn her skirt rolling under the barbwire fence. Aunt Gen would be awful mad at her for putting on her Sunday dress. Her lips would get thin and straight, and a double crease would come between her eyes. Joyce could hear Aunt Gen's voice already, sharp with exasperation. "Do you think I haven't got anything to do but wash and iron?" She kicked at a pebble. Seemed as if nothing she did was right; either she forgot to shut the bathroom door – "a big girl like you!" – or she didn't wipe the dishes dry, or something. Now she'd ripped a big three-cornered tear in her brand-new dress, after Aunt Gen sat up late to finish it in time for Children's Day.

Mimi wouldn't care, though. Mimi would hug her tight, smelling of tobacco and perfume and Doublemint gum (Aunt Gen smelled like white soap and cookies baking). Mimi would say, "Hi there, baby, how's everything?" and everything would be fine. Joyce stretched on tiptoe to see over the rise in the road. The sound of a car coming nearer filled the whole air.

If was the mailman's car, with packages and rolled newspapers piled on the back seat and Mimi sitting erect and taut beside Mr. Kellar. Joyce ran out on the road, and now she was barefoot and the gravel stones were burning her summer-tough soles. "Stop, stop!" But the car kept coming on, heading straight at her, then it was on top of her and she couldn't run. Her feet were stuck to the ground. She opened her mouth to yell for help, but no sound came out.

"I've been a hell of a mother," Dean Bannister said. She sat on a drugstore stool with a coke straw in her hand; there was lipstick on the flattened end. "Things are going to be different from now on. Look, baby, this is Irv; he's a model." But it was Mr. Kellar in the snapshot, with a douche bag in one hand and a Sears Roebuck catalog in the other. "I saw it in *Harper's Bazaar* and made it myself," he said. "How do you like it?"

"Made it myself," Mary Jean Kennedy said. She gave Joyce a tentative poke. "Hey, you haven't heard a word I said. Get up or you'll miss breakfast."

Joyce pried her eyelids open. Sunshine flooded in at the uncurtained window and lay over the heaps of clothes on the floor. "Gosh, it's hot."

"That's one thing about pajamas, they soak up the drips." Mary Jean slept raw. Now she stood on one foot, pulling on a pair of black and chartreuse pedal-pushers. Her skin was clear cream, her breasts full and heavy with dark-ringed nipples.

Mine are prettier, Joyce thought, but hers are more – voluptuous. "Can you wear that to class?"

"First day, nobody does any work." Mary Jean buttoned her waistband. "You circulate around and get your books, meet the teachers and so on. What a bunch of squares!"

"All women?"

"You could call it that. Matson in science is supposed to be a man, but personally I think he's a fairy. The gym teacher's a dyke." Mary Jean pulled a chartreuse middy over her head, knotted a black chiffon scarf around the collar. "They had a young prof here once," she said, "but he got two girls in trouble at the same time and the board fired him. I think prob'ly they knocked him down and took it away from him," she added thoughtfully. "This is no place for anybody with normal glands."

Breakfast was fruit and coffee, hot rolls and bacon and hominy grits. Joyce had read about hominy grits but she had never really believed in them before. They tasted like chicken feed, cooked. The meal was served by two young Negro women. One was slim and had sad eyes; the other was cheerful and motherly-looking, with a roll of stomach under her starched apron. The girls ignored them. Joyce felt she ought to say good morning, or make some sign of recognition. At home she had been on the debating team with Betty Montgomery, the only colored girl in school, and they were good friends. Also Uncle Will always opened his *Chicago Tribune*, when it arrived a day late by RFD, to see how the Supreme Court was making out with the integration question. But she wanted to be like the others, so she made no sign.

After breakfast a small, bright-eyed freshman with her hair skinned back in a ponytail offered to walk to the registrar's office with her. Her name was Bitsy Harrison and she was the third generation of her family to be educated at Henderson Hicks.

Anyway, she knew her way around. The red brick buildings all looked alike to Joyce and she wondered how she would ever find her way from one to the other in time for classes. It was worse than the first day of high school in Ferndell when the big yellow bus rolled off down the street and left the country kids standing on the corner beside the big many-windowed building. For weeks, then, she had a recurrent nightmare of being lost in the strange winding halls and blundering into strange classrooms. Now she stubbed her toe on the brick sidewalks, which went up and down hill following the terrain, and was glad to be following Bitsy. The very way Bitsy's heels hit the walk was sharp and independent-sounding.

"It's old-fashioned," Bitsy said with affection in her voice. "Hasn't changed much since my gramma was a girl. They had coal stoves in the dorm then. Imagine."

The buildings were comfortably familiar inside – long halls with white fountains (like bathroom fixtures) and finger-marked cream plaster walls. Classrooms with armed chairs, one in the back row for a left-handed pupil; *Webster's Unabridged* on a stand near the window; flattop desk on a little raised platform; pictures, Washington looking uneasy in his false teeth, some Roman orator in a toga. Smell of chalk and sweeping compound, mingled with Evening in Paris and Ecstasy. She signed registration cards and received an armful of books in a room like the one where she had taken her IQ test at Community, trembling with nervousness for fear of being classified for all time with the dumb pupils. Here there were no tests except being white and able to pay, but the old insecurity made her knees wobble as she waited in line.

The curriculum had been planned, or had grown, to develop attractive wives in the junior executive, ten-thousand-dollar bracket. Joyce signed up for Art Appreciation, Elementary Spanish, and Design, then added up her credits and elected Hygiene rather than swimming or corrective gym. The hygiene teacher, who was athletic coach too, was a thin, flat woman in very long, narrow shoes that turned up at the toes. She had no figure, but her hair, surprisingly, was worn long and bundled up in a bird's nest under a net.

"That's to show she's female," Bitsy explained. "You'd never guess it otherwise." The teacher slapped an assignment on the board in an Egyptian scrawl and thumped off down the hall beside her student secretary, a giggling little girl in a pinafore.

Mary Jean was lying on the bed eating a Hershey bar when Joyce got back to the dorm. She looked over the schedule cards. "You sure aren't going to strain your brain."

Joyce didn't answer. She thought about Aunt Gen leaning over the dining table on her last night at home, dish towel in hand, the light shining on her glasses and wrapped-around braids. Aunt Gen had an idea she ought to be taking some solid subjects.

"Seems like she'd get more at the State U," Aunt Gen said, looking worried.

Mimi, chain-smoking and endlessly walking from window to window, said, "Oh for God's sake, Gen! I know I've been a terrible mother, but honest, it's been all I could do to make both ends meet."

Uncle Will said with dignity, "We ain't complaining. We both think the world of Joy."

Mimi lit another cigarette, dropping her half-smoked stub in a saucer since there were no ashtrays at the farm. "Then you better be glad she has this chance. Girls from some of the finest families in the country go to Henderson Hicks."

She wasn't sure what Mimi expected her to get out of being here, but it wasn't history or Latin.

The girls from the finest families stood around her in the lounge, waiting for the lunch gong. Their clothes were casual to the point of sloppiness, they wore baby-pink lipstick and flat sandals, their faces were as composed as if charm depended upon impassivity. Joyce began to worry about her clothes, which had already taken a lot more time and attention than her courses. She and Mimi had picked them out with help from *Charm* and the *Ladies Home Journal*, and doubtful consultations with *Vogue*. Even her shorty pajamas had come from Ferndell's one specialty shop instead of Penney's or the mail order. Now she wondered. Too fussy? Too kiddish?

A small brunette said, "Ah'm just crazy about that skirt," and Joyce glowed. It was important to be accepted.

Lunch was like dinner the night before, beautifully served but not quite enough of it. There were bits of fat pork in the string beans and a side dish of some slippery green vegetable that was new to her. Okra, Mary Jean said. She didn't care much for it. But the dining room was attractive by daylight, too, and afterwards they went up to the lounge. It didn't seem quite fitting to sit on the floor in pedal-pushers, the way Mary Jean was doing, and she was relieved when a maid came to the door and said softly, "Telephone, Miss Kennedy."

"That was Bill," Mary Jean said when she came back. Her eyes were bright. "You want to go on a square date tonight? Blanket party?"

"Sure, I'd love to."

"I don't know this boy," Mary Jean said carefully, "He's a freshman. Pledge, you know. Bill has to look after him. He might have pimples or be feeble-minded for all I know."

"Well, he's taking a chance on me too."

"True."

"Freshman where?"

"Caton College. Relief station for lonesome women, you know. Bill's a senior this year, the dirty bird." Her voice deepened possessively. "The bum."

"You like him, don't you?"

"He has his good points."

The heat didn't lift. They spent the rest of the afternoon unpacking and putting away their clothes. That is, Joyce unpacked. Mary Jean put a few dresses on hangers and then stretched out on her bed, an arm over her eyes. "I'm going to catch me a little shut-eye. No tellin' when we'll get in tonight." The hall echoed with voices; footsteps clattered in and out of the bathroom; down the corridor someone was practicing "Minuet in G" on the violin, the first few bars over and over again. Mary Jean slept, snoring a little.

Even after the sun went down there was no breeze, only a sort of breathless hush. Either this climate is terrible or I'm tired out, Joyce thought, peeling off her damp clothes after dinner. She went into the washroom and waited her turn for a shower stall. The room was full of girls washing their hair and scrubbing each other's backs and all talking at the same time.

"Never saw so many happy drunks in my life," Sue-Ellen Levey shrieked. "So I told my mother I was staying all night with her, and she told her mother she was staying with me, and we went up to these kids' cabin," the redhead said. Her towels were purple, like her shorts. She paused to glare at Joyce, and Joyce felt good about having a date and said, "Well, excuse me for breathing," and set her soap and toothbrush down on the edge of the basin.

"That's Charlene Wilkens," Mary Jean identified the redhead from her description. "She's one of these professional honeychiles, the kind that make a hit with college men up north." She pulled on pink shorts, a striped shirt. "She had a thing for a married man who worked in a fillin' station last year. I wouldn't go out with a married man, not even if I lived to be a dried-up old maid." Mary Jean completed her outfit with embroidered cloth flats. Joyce asked, "Don't you ever wear pants?"

"What for?"

She wondered what you did on a blanket party, but was ashamed to ask. She put on shorts too and a sleeveless blouse and touched her lips with Cerise Poppy from Mimi's new line, but left her face shiny like Mary Jean's. "We look all right together."

"Except we can't wear each other's clothes. I'm too tall."

"No, I'm too short."

"Have it your own way."

"Don't we have to get permission to go out, or something?"

"We're supposed to sign the book in the hall. But if we don't sign out, then we don't have to sign in, see? Besides, Bannister hasn't been around all day."

It sounded reasonable, but it felt illicit and dangerous crossing the leaf-rustling area in the dark. Under the railroad arch a yellow convertible waited. The two boys leaning against the car were not quite men yet, but you could tell they thought of themselves as men and pretty sharp, too. Bill was stocky and fair, with sprinkled freckles and a flattop. Tony, the freshman, was dark and skinny. His Adam's apple stuck out and the rest of him hadn't quit caught up to his hands and feet, but just the same, he was a College Man, and not too bad-looking, Joyce thought. She sat down beside him and pulled her shorts down, exactly like a Victorian belle adjusting her hoops – and for the same reason, to give her hands something to do. She didn't know how to start a conversation, but at least she was conscious that there was nothing wrong with the way she looked.

The way Bill drove, they couldn't have talked anyhow. Wind whooshed past, singing in their ears and carrying the smell of exhaust fumes, mown grass and blacktop hot from the sun. People on street corners looked after the bright car, admiring or resentful.

Tony dropped his hand to Joyce's knee. She ignored it. There is nothing you can do about a hand on your knee, it's not high enough to call for moral indignation and it's hard to act reluctant without seeming prissy. She sat unmoving, careful to make no sign of re-sponding. After all, she reminded herself, I just met this character about fifteen minutes ago.

The countryside was strange to her. At home you rode through flat country, with little clumps of trees along the riverbanks and gently rolling fields. This was up-and-down country, and after they turned off the highway onto a gravel road there were tangled stretches of wood-land, thick with underbrush right up to the barbwire fences. These woods looked as though they might harbor snakes and vultures.

Tony yelled, "Hard on the tires," as they bounced, and Bill shrugged.

"Those woods look as if wolves lived in them," Joyce said, trying to put the ominous in words.

Tony wasn't interested in scenery. He squeezed her leg. "The wolves are all in the car," he said. His fingers were thin and hot.

The lake lay flat under an orange moon and the sandy beach stretched on and on, unbroken. Farther down the beach some picnickers had made a bonfire; their grotesque shadows moved between the leaping flames and the sky. Bill said, "Get busy, you females."

Joyce caught the army blanket and the carton of beer. It made a heavy load. The sand slewed under her open sandals. She slid against Tony and he caught her and held her, too tightly, so that she dropped the blanket. Bill walked back under the edge of the wooden pavilion where the slot machines and pop vendors were locked up for the night. "All clear," he said. He dropped the other blanket and reached out his hand. "Opener." Mary Jean slapped it into his palm. He opened beer cans and handed them around. "God, that's good and cold," he said proudly.

Joyce didn't like the bitter medicinal taste of beer much, but the sweat-beaded can felt good against her cheek. She held it there and let the others reach for seconds. Tony spread a blanket on the sand and squatted down on his heels. She could see his throat wiggle up and down as he gulped. The boys had shucked off their slacks and were in swimming trunks, narrow strips of dark-colored stuff against skin that looked white in the moonlight. Bill was blocky and solid – the kind of man who grows a potbelly in the middle thirties – but Tony's ribs stuck out. He hasn't really got his growth yet, Joyce thought. Everybody knows girls are older than boys the same age. The thought made her feel protective and maternal.

Bill tossed away his third beer can. Tony's plunked on the ground beside it. "You're a quiet gal."

"You're supposed to get men to talk about themselves. It says so in the book."

He punched another can of beer. Looks like all you do at a blanket party is sit around and guzzle, she thought, smothering a yawn. She lay back on the blanket and stretched out to look for stars, but the night was overcast. Summer nights on the farm, if you slept out in the back yard you could see millions of stars, from low-swinging planets to tiny pinpricks. And in the winter if you got up early enough there was Venus hanging in the frosty air – so clear, so bright.

Tony flopped down beside her. He pulled up her knit shirt a little and laid his head against her bare midriff. His hair had just been cut, the stiff bristles prickled her skin. "You're a cute little kid."

"That brightens up my whole evening."

"Let's not talk. Waste of time." He reached up and touched her shoulder, then moved his fingers down a little. A winey heat ran down her arm and melted into the warm spot where his hand rested. His palm was calloused – tennis, maybe, or a summer job. It tightened against her, then moved again and reached into the front of her shirt. He lifted one breast in his hand, and she felt the bud of it harden and rise. "Nice," Tony said. "I bet you're nice all over."

She looked nervously at the others. They had covered themselves with half of their blanket, which was moving convulsively. Crazy kids, in this weather. She tried to sit up, but Tony pushed her back. "Don't be scared. I'm not fixing to hurt you. Just wanna feel."

"You tickle."

"Like to be tickled?"

He rolled against her. His elbow dug her in the side, his hand was at her waist. "This damn thing's too tight. The elastic."

"Please don't."

"Minute."

His hand was hot under her waistband. Answering heat grew in her. The hand moved. She moved closer. She couldn't help it; she was so scared she couldn't breathe, yet she had to get closer, she had to know. She laid her hand against his and pressed. Fingers dug in. "Ouch," she said.

"Hurt?"

"I like it."

His belt buckle cut into her as he rolled over. Below she could feel the little bulge she always tried not to stare at, yet couldn't help being conscious of when boys where in shorts or basketball trunks. He picked up her hand and moved it. Large and solid, embarrassing and menacing yet mystic and exciting.

"I got something for you," Tony whispered.

Joyce stiffened. From somewhere in the past came the smell of freshly scythed grass. The boy in sixth grade, fingering his fly and looking at her out of the corners of his eyes. "Hey, Joyce, I got somep'n for you," with a mean little snicker. Miss Gordon had come around the corner of the schoolhouse then, while Joyce stood terrified, yet fascinated. Miss Gordon's heavy middle-aged face was a dull red and she grabbed the little boy by one arm and jerked him into the schoolhouse. Joyce couldn't even remember his name now, but she remembered Miss Gordon laying on with a leather strap while the kids looked through the schoolhouse window. Miss Gordon's eyes glittered like Mrs. Severtson's did when Uncle Will brought a cow over to be serviced by the Severtson bull. Excited, yet ashamed.

The same terror filled her now as when the bull bellowed – a crawling sensation along the back of the neck, a shrinking in the pit of the stomach. Night pressed down, a heavy sky, and this strange boy's hand was at the core of her body. She tried to sit up, but he was heavy on her. She gave him a shove and caught him off balance so that he went over backwards, looking stupid with surprise. "Hey, for God's sakes."

"I don't want to." Her voice was cold. She got to her feet, brushed the sand off her shorts, and pulled down her rumpled shirt. "I guess I'd better go home."

Tony lit a cigarette. The flame jiggled as if his hand were shaking. "Teaser," he said coldly.

Bill stuck his head out of the other blanket. How could he look and sound so ordinary, if he was doing what she thought? "You ever hear the story about the cat on the streetcar track?" he asked. "Damn cat went to sleep, and the streetcar comes along and cuts the end of its tail off. Cat whirls around, yowlin' and spittin', and the streetcar tears its head off." He rubbed his cheek against Mary Jean's shoulder. "Moral is, don't lose your head over a piece of tail."

"Very funny," Tony said. He unfolded his skinny height and walked away, his back poker-stiff. Joyce took a couple of uncertain steps toward the water's edge and stood there looking at the flat ripples, wishing she were back in her own room at the farm, with Aunt Gen putting away the supper dishes and Uncle Will watching "What's My Line" on the television. Anywhere but here.

Tony sat on the extreme edge of the back seat all the way home. Like I had leprosy or something, Joyce thought, hurt and angry. What made it worse was that he wasn't a bad-looking boy, really; it would have been fun to go out with him again, if he didn't have to be such a wolf. She sneaked a glance at him. He gave her a dirty look and turned his face away. His adolescent male pride, still shaky, had been rebuffed. She sighed.

In the front seat Bill and Mary Jean sat glued together, hot and silent.

Back at school, Tony sat unmoving and wordless while Joyce opened the door for herself and climbed out. She decided not to say good night; it would be too embarrassing if he didn't answer. She stood in a little clump of trees while Bill and Mary Jean kissed as if they never expected to see each other again. The car rolled away, was lost in the late-night traffic.

The girls found the front door unlocked. They tiptoed into the front hall and up the stairs. Already, after the evening's letdown, the dorm was beginning to look like home. The tan-and-brown diamond pattern of the hall carpet seemed dear and familiar.

"How to win enemies and antagonize people," Mary Jean said, pulling off her shirt and shorts. She shook the sand out of her shoes onto the floor and tumbled into bed without bothering to wash or brush her teeth. A sour smell of beer hung around her, and a ripe sweaty aura Joyce could only identify as female. A small purple bruise marred the ivory of one arm. "You made a real hit with Junior," she said, yawning.

"I don't like him."

"Nobody's asking you to marry the boy," Mary Jean said. "A good man is mighty hard to find."

She'll never ask me to double-date again, Joyce thought regretfully. My only friend in this place. "Are blanket parties always like that?" she asked.

"Depends." Mary Jean rolled over, kicking off her sheet. Moonlight made marble of her body. "Maybe you're frigid," she suggested, the sleepiness dissolving out of her voice.

"How do you tell?"

"I don't know." Mary Jean sat up. "I'm like my mother. That's all the old hens in my dad's congregations ever talk about – yak yak yak – 'You better keep an eye on that girl, Reverend, she's going to turn out just like her mother.'" Her voice was bitter. "I'd sooner be like her than them, the gossipy old bitches."

"Is your father a minister?"

"Sure. He's all right," Mary Jean said quickly. "My mother couldn't help it if she fell in love with somebody else, could she?"

"I don't think I know much about love," Joyce said sadly. She lay awake for a long time after Mary Jean had gone to sleep, listening to her roommate's light rhythmic snoring and watching the lights of passing cars move across the walls. I don't care if I am frigid, she thought. But when the A.T.&S.F. tooted across the corner of the campus and jerked her out of an uneasy half sleep, she was still remembering the pressure of Tony's hand and his insistent whisper in her ear.

Chapter Three

It's silly to feel guilty and apprehensive simply because you've been called out of class in the middle of the morning. It can happen to anyone, even A students or Council members; it doesn't mean anything is wrong. Joyce walked faster, trying to hush the clattering of her heels on the concrete floor because of the doors that stood open on both sides of the hallway.

She wouldn't have felt so alarmed in another building, she rationalized, some place where the hall wasn't so long and narrow and didn't echo so. Art Appreciation was being held in the basement of Old Main while painters were at work in the upstairs classroom. The science labs were down there, with their faint smells of chemical and preservative, and the ceramics room, which was always damp to the touch even in hot weather, and the coke and coffee machines at the west entrance were set out from the walls by a Rube Goldberg snarl of pipes and annulated cables.

She detoured around spread newspapers. The kids in Ceramics were bustling in and out of their workroom, laying their jars and candlesticks and stuff to dry where people had to walk. She brushed against something that looked like a chamber pot, only no handle. She hadn't elected Ceramics. Now she was sorry. *I could have made something for Mimi,* she thought, *a little ashtray or something. Mimi.* The name always brought excitement and loneliness. Ever since the news of her engagement had come to the farm, scrawled at the end of one of Mimi's short letters, she had been trying to deny a secret and unreasonable dream, the dream of her childhood, given substance and form. Even city apartments could have an extra bedroom, couldn't they? Now she sucked in her breath, standing at the outside door waiting for the excitement to go away. It was better not to plan, even a little bit. All the times you expected her and she had to see a new client or something, at the last minute – it was better not to look ahead, then you couldn't be disappointed.

Two weeks had made the campus browner and dryer. The brick sidewalks were as familiar to her feet now as Aunt Gen's kitchen floor and she made her way from one building to another without thinking about it; but she couldn't help noticing that the dropping leaves were dry and brown as wrapping paper. Back home, fall was a blaze of orange and red, with maple and elm and oak leaves whirling to the ground in every gust of wind.

Dean Bannister had a suite on the first floor of the dorm, at the head of the entrance stairs. Probably they had been planned by an earlier generation of deans to provide easy snooping, but Edith Bannister wasn't one to prowl around with flashlights after lights-out. In fact, she had abolished lights-out, only backing up the House Council ruling that everyone should be quiet after eleven. She kept her doors shut and let the student authorities take care of infringements. In her brief chapel talk, the first full day of school, she had said that she liked to treat people as adults. "I expect you to behave as young women of breeding and character," she had told them, standing erect, not leaning on the podium or fidgeting. One hundred young faces looked back at her, making no response at all.

The study door was shut now, black except for the typed namecard. Joyce wasn't sure whether to knock or not. She tapped lightly, swallowing hard, and a clear voice called, "Come in!" Her knees were jello. Her throat closed with dryness. She licked her lips and walked in.

Edith Bannister's study was done in Swedish Modern, like the dormitory bedrooms. A graduate of Henderson Hicks had gone to

Hollywood in 1938 and made good, partly in Grade B films and partly in the canopied Spanish bedroom of a Grade B producer. The furniture was her gesture of gratitude for having been educated. To the desk, chairs and thin sectional sofa in Miss Bannister's study, had been added some homemade book shelves and some monk's-cloth curtains. But the desk was clear of papers and decorated with un-teachery objects: a book of French verse with shaggy spaniel edg-es, open face down; a cut-crystal perfume bottle; a cigarette lighter striped in dull and bright silver; an African figurine of dark polished wood, with sagging breasts and bulging belly. Everything was neat, even the three cigarette butts, all the same length, in a glass ashtray. Miss Bannister herself sat beside the window, smoking, with her feet on the sill. Beautiful feet, slim and high-arched, in the kind of slip-pers that never get to the end-of-season sales. Mimi's shoes are too fancy, Joyce thought. Miss Bannister turned her head as Joyce came in, and again there was something too brief and illusive to be resem-blance, but something –

"You needn't have been in any hurry." She held out the telegram and Joyce took it, her first one, disappointed that it looked so trivial. She opened it, trying to be casual. In Aunt Gen's world a telegram meant catastrophe or death in the family. Miss Bannister, watching, crushed out her cigarette alongside the other three, swiveling in her chair to reach the ashtray. The tips were lightly tinged with pink. Lipstick, then, but so lightly applied it looked natural. "Nothing wrong, I hope."

Joyce looked up. "My mother wants me to come to Chicago for her wedding. Tomorrow, I guess."

The lighter snicked. "Will you fly?"

"Train, I guess." She was embarrassed. Mimi should have thought about flying, it was hick to go any other way. Images from movies and magazine ads flashed across her mind, chic young women stepping off the plane with smart luggage, lunch in the air served by a smiling stewardess. She felt called upon to say something, change the subject.

"I don't know the man she's marrying."

"Perhaps you'll like your stepfather very much," Edith Bannister said. "Can you remember your father?"

"He died when I was a baby," Joyce said. She had never in her life been able to face anyone when she said this, and now she fixed her gaze on her brown loafers, sunk in the pile of the textured rug. The old story, brought out to wrap around the truth because naked truth is indecent for public viewing, and when had she first known it was a story and how had she learned it? Nobody had ever told her. She felt ashamed inside, the way she had when Aunt Gen had caught her walking from the bathroom to her own room with nothing on. Cover yourself, Aunt Gen said, you're too big to run around like that. She must have been about ten or eleven. For a long time after that she was afraid to look at her bare body in the mirror, feeling that some parts of her must be dirty or evil.

The silence lasted. She looked at Edith Bannister. "You look like my mother," she blurted. That was all wrong. "Except you're better-looking." Apple-polisher, she accused herself, burning with shame. That it was true made it worse; disloyalty to Mimi.

"That's sweet of you," Miss Bannister murmured. You couldn't tell if she was amused, angry or uncaring, but anyway her words broke the silence and Joyce was able to move toward the door.

"Well, thanks."

"Let me know what time your train goes. I'll take you to the station." Miss Bannister put her hand on Joyce's shoulder. A small electric shock zinged down her arm. She stood outside the door, not sure how she got there or what to do next. Then she ran upstairs and into her own room, shutting the door on everything but her own jumbled thoughts and feelings.

Alone, it seemed reasonable enough to be going to Chicago for her own mother's wedding. Second wedding, she corrected herself. Although Ferndell was only about sixty miles from the city, her only trips there had been one each year with her high-school class. They had visited the Natural History Museum, the Planetarium, the Museum of Science and Industry – where everyone wanted to see the mummies and go down into the coal mine – and the International Amphitheater where the big livestock shows were held. She felt that the glamour of the big city didn't have anything to do with museums or prize steers, and although she was not sure just what to expect, it would be more exciting than tagging around with a bunch of kids.

The idea of really seeing Mimi was exciting, too. It was beginning to seem chic, having a mother young and attractive enough to get married. She sat on the edge of the bed and wove a daydream of herself marvelously well-dressed and about four inches taller, being escorted into a smart restaurant by an Ezio Pinza type of older man.

Mary Jean came in, slamming the door. She was a born slammer, except when the situation called for quietness, like dropping through the laundry window in the small hours; then she could be still as a mousing cat. "You sick?" Joyce asked. Mary Jean dropped down on the other bed, kicking off her shoes so she could think better. Her face took on the brooding look of a mother with young daughters to dress.

"Your gray suit would be all right if you had a couple good blouses to perk it up," she said. "We'll borrow some." She padded over to her closet and took down her new formal, never worn yet, aqua net over satin. "You could wear this if we shortened the hem a couple inches. I reckon it would do if someone took you dancing."

"I haven't any shoes to go with it."

"Buy some," Mary Jean said. "We'll get you organized tonight."

Getting organized took a lot of time. It involved going from room to room, borrowing whatever anybody had that looked as if it might be useful, and drinking coffee. Everybody wanted to hear about the wedding and she kept adding details to make it more interesting and to make it sound as if Mimi talked things over with her, like the mothers in magazine stories.

Bonnie said, "Look, you can take my nylon shorty pajamas. They haven't even been worn yet," and she was proud and pleased because she hadn't even known Bonnie liked her. They are really my friends, she thought, and a warm glow spread through her chest.

Mary Jean went out at ten. "Just down to the Honey Bee for a coke," she said, "be back in a couple minutes." She came back an hour and ten minutes later, breathing hard and with stars in her eyes. That meant she had met Bill someplace and they'd been parked in a side street or even at the edge of the campus, although that yellow car stuck out like a sore thumb. Tomorrow night they would drive out and park on some country road, and the excitement would build up again. So did she envy Mary Jean, or disapprove of her? She looked at her, wondering how a girl felt the first time. Would she be sorry and ashamed, until she got used to it? It's best to wait till you get married, she decided. Only, well, gosh –

Being married sounded terribly stuffy compared with being in love. After the honeymoon was over and you settled down, would it be dull? She lay awake for a long time after she had finally packed her suitcase and gone to bed, sticky with hand lotion and cold cream to make her beautiful for the trip. She couldn't decide what she believed. There was room even in Aunt Gen's moral code for smooching ("spooning" Aunt Gen called it), but going farther than that was more even than a question of morals, it involved sin. I don't believe in what Mary Jean does, she decided, though a lot of people do it.

She turned over, sticking her feet out from under the sheet. Uncle Will had always teased her about changing her mind so often, good-naturedly when she couldn't decide which piece of chicken she liked best, a little crossly when he had to wait in town while she picked out dress goods or a pair of shoes. He didn't know what she'd be up to next, he declared, out playing baseball in the back pasture with the boys one day and mooning around trying to write poetry the next. I wish I could be all one way, she thought; other people don't worry so about things, other people aren't so mixed up.

Whispering in a boy's arms, in the back of a parked car; pressing your body against his until you caught fire from each other, shivering when his hand slid under your skirt. Still, on the other hand, when you stood up in front of the minister to be married – she sighed, drifting off to sleep.

In the morning, though, the magic was back. She felt like someone else, just who was hard to decide, but not Joyce Cameron of Ferndell, Illinois. Certainly not a freshman at Louisa Henderson Hicks Junior College. She floated to breakfast on clouds of glamour and ate grits without even noticing them.

Time zipped by. She was ready to go, and then at the last minute the dorm felt like home and the girls were her family. She felt hot-eyed and teary, getting into Susy's best Dacron blouse and straightening her seams. She wasn't sure she wanted to leave.

Edith Bannister came down the stairs, swinging a key ring against her blue skirt. Joyce kissed Mary Jean, who blinked with surprise, and followed the dean to the school station wagon, which had peeling paint and one dented fender, but looked like Quality anyway. They drove through the streets of taverns and cheap stores, past the poor-looking people. "Terrible neighborhood," Miss Bannister said. "This was a fine residential district in its day; then the old families lost their money in the depression and those old houses went for almost nothing." She looked aloofly at Babe and Ernie's, from whose open door came a blare of rock and roll. Joyce nodded, noticing the granite cornices above the drugstore, the date 1867 cut over a doorway. But her attention was divided because Edith Bannister sat beside her. There was certainly something –

The ride was too short.

"Let me know when you'll be back," Miss Bannister said, and then she was gone, weaving expertly in and out of the morning traffic. Joyce stood looking after the station wagon until a Cadillac plastered with travel stickers cut in behind it.

The station was old, with rolls of dust under the benches and spittoons in the corners. The rest room doors were marked White and Colored, a thing she had read about but which she had never quite believed existed. She went out to wait beside the tracks.

The train came in puffing and snorting, and she climbed in and propped her suitcase on the overhead rack. The green upholstery pricked through her nylon slip and panty girdle, but there was a clean white doily across the back of the seat and she leaned her head back and was happy with a special kind of happiness that comes only on trains. Maybe a plane would have been better, she thought dreamily. Maybe next time I'll go on one. There's plenty of time. She crossed her knees and admired her pumps. I'm going to be as good-looking as Mimi, she thought. Everyone will think we're sisters.

She ignored the red clay fields sliding past and the cotton growing as it did in pictures in geography books, and the little unpainted farmhouses with wash-pots in the back yards and clothes flapping on the lines. Joyce was in a nightclub watching Mimi dancing with a Man of Distinction (something like Clifton Webb, only without the mustache) and herself talking to somebody like Mary Jean's Bill, only handsomer and with higher ideals.

At one – it's corny to eat early – she went into the diner. It was the first time she had ever seen the inside of a dining car, but it was all right, it looked like the ones in the movies. There was a fat steward with a huge roll of bills, and the waiters walked softly down the aisles balancing their trays. She unfolded the big linen napkin halfway and ordered chicken salad and coffee. The salad was mostly chopped celery and for a moment she hungered for a good piece of White Rock or Wyandotte meat the way Aunt Gen fried it, crisp and brown on the outside and melting white inside. She picked up her fork, smiling.

A cute kid, the salesman at the next table thought. Bet she's never gone anywhere alone before. He thought about his daughter, who was an honor student and would probably be valedictorian of her high-school class next June. He thought about the week ahead, hopping from one middle-sized town to another, registering in a series of all-alike hotel rooms, trying to sell carbon paper and stenographic notebooks to a series of bored purchasing agents. A hell of a life for a family man.

Joyce gave him a grateful look. Everybody knows salesmen are very sophisticated about women; their life is one round of beautiful pickups and wild parties. His attentive look made her feel beautiful, too. She broke her cardboard toast carefully and drank her cooling coffee.

Chapter Four

Union Station was a television spectacular or a wide-screen color film, stupendous, colossal, magnificent, all the superlatives that screamed across the pages of newspapers. Joyce came up from the echoing underground passage, pushed from behind by a young man with a sharp, angry profile, hindered from the front by an arthritic old woman who clung to the handrail with gnarled fingers. The whole thing hit her in the face: light, color, the intricate crisscross of people coming and going.

This is a crazy place, she thought. How would she find Mimi in this mob? Oh God, if she didn't come! All she had was a ten, a one and some small change, and anyway, where would you find a place to stay in a town this big? She realized suddenly that she didn't even know Mimi's address since she'd taken the apartment; it hadn't bothered her before, because Mimi had never really had an address before, she left her out-of-season clothes with friends while she moved from town to town, cheap hotel to cheap hotel. Now she realized that a human being could be swallowed up in a city and never heard from again.

The depot at Henderson had been dusty and almost empty. The one at Ferndell, which hardly anybody used because only one train a day stopped there and bus service was handier, was a single room with three scarred benches and a rusty pot-bellied stove. This was an arena with ceilings so high they looked unreal. Little stores surrounded it, with gifty-looking stuff in their showcases. There were places to eat. There was even a barber shop and a man being shaved in it.

Out in the middle of the room, if a place that big could be said to have a middle, was a hollow-square counter with candy and oranges pyramided on it, looking bright and healthy. Behind it was a stocky middle-aged woman in a white uniform. And there was the magazine rack where they were supposed to meet, with stacks of pocket books and neat tiers of magazines. But no Mimi.

Joyce stood still, her mouth a little open. Sweat trickled down her back under the Dacron blouse. It was as if all the times they'd been ready for Sunday, the cooky crock full of raisin brownies and clean sheets on the spare-room bed, and then the party-line phone rang and it was Mimi to say she couldn't come. Only that was simple disappointment and this was under-laid with panic.

A billowing dark woman, suckling her baby on one of the benches, pushed the little face away from her breast and smiled at Joyce. She smiled back, half grateful for the little gesture and half shocked to see someone so uncovered in a public place. A drop of milk hung on the nipple, dropped, and rolled down that mountainous front. There was comfort in the sight of the mother and baby, as much at home as in their own kitchen. Joyce took a deep breath.

And there was Mimi! She should have remembered that Mimi was always late and always in a hurry, unlike Aunt Gen, who made a religion of being on time. Her ankles tipped a little on high heels, her fur neckpiece was slung in the Chicago manner over a dressy suit, she wore a cocky little red hat. Joyce thought, It's too fancy and she looks old. But that was silly. Because Mimi was only thirty-seven, only nineteen years older than she was, herself.

"Well!" Mimi said and they stood there looking self-conscious. They had never kissed except ritually at parting. There wasn't anything to say.

"You look wonderful," Joyce said. "Is that a new hairdo?" But it was too fussy, too many little blonde curls under the tipped brim.

Mimi smiled. "Thanks, baby. You look pretty nice yourself. Come on, we've got a taxi waiting."

There was a wind with a nip to it blowing off the lake, scuttling dust and paper scraps along the gutters. The El platforms and high buildings cut off the sun and darkened the street. The driver slammed the door shut.

"This is the theater district," Mimi said, and Joyce looked out eagerly. But there was nothing to see in the middle of the afternoon, the marquees were dark, the buildings looked like business offices, and the few people on the street were ordinary. She had thought of it as bright and glamorous, and she was disappointed.

The apartment building, on the near North Side, was made of stone blocks and had empty window boxes on the front railings. The meter said a little over two dollars, and Mimi gave the man three and waved away the change. She looked a little smug about it: this was not like the old days when she had to figure bus fares against the wear and tear on her shoes, and the expense account had to be padded a little to cover the single room with the part-cotton blanket and the last tenant's cigar smoke still in the air. Irv was paying for this. Would still be paying for it, if she was lucky, when the fine creases in her neck became real wrinkles. She mounted the steps leisurely, and Joyce trailed after her, feeling more and more like someone in a book.

The foyer floor was black-and-white marble in squares. There were carved tables with ugly Chinese vases on them, and small gilt-traced chairs not meant to hold anyone weighing more than ninety pounds, and the elevator swayed and shuddered upwards but had a Balkan general in full-dress uniform, with medals, to run it. Arrived, Mimi unlocked the hall door and snapped on the light so she could see everything at once. Joyce said, "Gosh!"

"Broadloom," Mimi said. "Wall to wall, sixteen bucks a square yard." The room was maybe twelve by eighteen, with two windows at the far end. Two chairs so modern you would probably have to back into them, and a black wire magazine rack but no magazines. There was a plump sofa in beige frieze. "I'm putting you out here, seeing it's only for one night," Mimi said nervously.

Joyce kept on looking at the abstract painting over the sofa, a swirl of bright colors. She certainly didn't intend to cry – nothing to cry about – but the reds and blues and yellows kept melting and running together. "One night?" she said in a small voice.

"I don't want to keep you out of school." Mimi kicked off her shoes the way she always did when she came in, then bent and lined them up, pinching the tops into shape. "I want you to meet Irv, though," she added apologetically. Joyce smiled brightly. "Sure." So what if she doesn't want me, so what if she hates having me here? I can take it.

She followed Mimi around admiring the apartment politely but feeling more and more like an unwelcome guest, someone who has to be entertained but who is really in the way. The bedroom was pastel, with twin beds covered in flounced chintz, everything neat, even the rows and rows of make-up jars and bottles on the long narrow glass shelf. That went back to when Mimi had worked in the beauty shop, giving manicures and facials, before she got her break and went on the road.

On the stand next to the farther bed, half an inch of cigar butt lay in the modern ashtray. Joyce walked to the window and looked out, unseeing. Will he be here tonight? Will I hear them, out there on that itchy-looking davenport? She was afraid to turn around and look at Mimi. But when she did, Mimi had put her suit on a padded hanger and was wrapping a flowered housecoat around herself. "This is the kitchen," she said, opening the other door.

The kitchen was too orderly to have been used much, and there wasn't much food in the cupboards. Plenty of liquor – gin, vermouth, rum, anisette, vodka, an assortment of new and partly filled bottles. It looked like an *Esquire* ad, but two things crossed Joyce's mind at the same moment – the price tags in the liquor store windows, and the stubborn expression on Aunt Gen's face when Uncle Will let the cider get hard. Mimi said guiltily, "Irv likes a drink after dinner. We eat out a lot, though." She slammed the door shut and found a jar partly full of instant coffee, and put on the water to boil. Joyce would have liked something to eat, but she didn't like to suggest it.

She unpacked her clothes and hung them in Mimi's closet, wondering what was in the other one but not quite daring to look even when Mimi was out of the room. They talked about school mostly. No, she wasn't homesick. (For what?) Sure, it was a beautiful place. She described Mary Jean, censoring the details and dwelling on how pretty and talented she was.

"She designs her own clothes," she bragged and brought out the aqua net to show off.

Mimi fingered the seams critically. "Nice. We'll make Irv take us out for dinner and have a night on the town. Won't that be fun? You can wear my satin ankle-straps with this; my feet are bigger than yours but it won't hurt if they're loose." She stood up briskly, and it occurred to Joyce that maybe she was embarrassed, too. It was even possible that she had been thinking about how it would be when they met, and whether this marriage was going to change anything between them. "I'll trim your hair," Mimi said. "You'd look nice with a feather cut."

That was more the way it had always been. At the farm, while Aunt Gen darned socks or put a hem in one of Joyce's dresses, Mimi had changed her nail polish or curled Joyce's hair or simply stalked around smoking and fidgeting. She couldn't sit still. It was like Sunday afternoon on the farm – but the thought of the farm suddenly made her feel lonesome and she tried to focus her attention on Mimi's sharp, thin scissors, going snip-snip around her ears.

Later, soaking in the perfumed bath with bubbles popping against her skin, she decided that beautiful described how she felt. Or anyway, good-looking. She hopped out and looked at herself in the long mirror, but it was the same body, young and flexible, narrow at the waist and sweetly sloping to the shoulders, the triangle of pubic hair darker and more curly than the hair on her head. Mimi came in to watch her dress. "Lean forward when you put your bra on," she said, "it gives you a figure," and she was right. The long-line strapless bra was too tight, even though the nylon and lace felt so soft; the little hooks cut into her skin, but it raised her small breasts above the top of Mary Jean's dress and gave her a definite cleavage. Voluptuous, she thought happily.

"You're getting a nice shape," Mimi said. Her voice sounded strained and tired. Joyce wrenched her gaze away from the mirror long enough to really look at her. Smeared with cold cream, her skin looked dull and rough, pitted a little on the cheeks and forehead, and her eyes were set in brown shadows. She made a grimace of smile as the doorbell rang. "Go and let him in, honey. I look like something the cat dragged in."

The fancy latch on the door resisted her first try. Then it opened, and he was there, the man Mimi had telephoned to come and amuse them, the man she was marrying tomorrow. Stepfather. Not exactly an Ezio Pinza or Clifton Webb type, shorter and stockier, with a small mustache and cheerful brown eyes. He looked like a man who would enjoy a good steak or a bonded whisky, or the feel of a fur. He hugged Joyce and then kissed her on the cheek, and his face smelled of expensive lotion but was already a little bit scratchy. "Some baby," he called to Mimi, and Mimi said something from the bedroom, but Joyce didn't catch it. She was a little disturbed by the kiss; it was not exactly like being kissed by boys.

Mimi came in, trailing white skirts. "Two girls at once," Irv said. "Look, you should have told me. I'd've dressed."

"It's all right," Mimi said, but Joyce felt a pang of disappointment. In the movies men wore dinner jackets. Mimi had put on a lot of pancake makeup and looked like herself again.

Irv put an arm around each of them. "Come on, females. Let's go and paint the town."

She got a little confused when she tried to remember, afterwards, the happenings of that evening. It was all kaleidoscoped without regard for time – the taxi ride down to the Loop and the crowds on the sidewalks, crummy neighborhoods squeezed up against glamorous ones. They went to a restaurant where the lights were dim and a man in an embroidered blouse went from table to table, making sad soft music on a violin. It made Joyce feel unhappy, but Irv sat studying the menu card.

"You ought to have a little beard," she told him, surprising herself, and he chuckled.

"I grew one, once, but my first wife made me shave it off."

Mimi frowned. "She had something there. How any woman can stand being scratched by whiskers!" Irv winked at Joyce, changing the subject. "The food is good here," he said.

It was, too. She had been hungry all day. She ate shrimps in a biting hot sauce and filet mignon with mushrooms, and a salad with bits of bread in it and plenty of garlic. Aunt Gen wouldn't cook with garlic, she said onion was common enough. Mimi dabbled, breaking little edges off her food with a fork and then not eating anything. "Oh, could I have baked Alaska?" Joyce asked, seeing it on the menu, and Irv said, "You can have anything you want, baby. Do they feed you bread and water at that school?"

"Hominy grits," she told him. He shook his head sadly.

The baked Alaska was a letdown. It was only sponge cake from a bakery, not very fresh, with ice cream and browned meringue on it. The meringue had scorched a little on its peaks and the ice cream tasted starchy. She ate it anyway, feeling bored and worldly, and drank black coffee and leaned back feeling lovely. The air the older girls at school had; it was all she could do not to smile idiotically over having achieved it. She composed her face to beautiful nonchalance.

Afterwards they went to a movie. This was a letdown; color and the wide screen had reached Ferndell and so had air conditioning, and she was sleepy after so much food. Still, the auditorium was bigger than any she had ever been in and there was a sprinkling of glamorous people in evening clothes. But so am I, she thought in some surprise, crossing her knees under the stiff folds of net and swinging one foot in Mimi's sandal, clasped around the ankle with a thin strap of rhinestones. She dozed a little, and jerked awake to look at Irv and Mimi. They were sitting side by side like an old married couple, not even holding hands. They're bored, she thought guiltily, they're doing all this for me and I ought to be grateful. I *am* grateful she assured herself, sitting up straight and focusing her eyes on the screen.

Pushing out through the lobby, which was gray with cigarette smoke and shrill with voices, she couldn't help yawning. "Sleepy?" Irv asked. "I was going to take you beautiful girls to a nightclub."

"Oh, all my life I've wanted to go to one," she told him, widening her eyes the way Holly Mae Robertson did. So he hailed another cab.

This was more like it. The room was pink and fuchsia, with black and silver zigzags across the walls, and the Negro musicians sat on a little silver platform. The drums were fuchsia and the leader was in white, with a pink cummerbund. Some of the men at the little tables were in evening clothes, and all the women were beautiful. Or at least glamorous, she amended it – some of them weren't so very young, maybe, but they all had beautiful complicated hairdos and lots of make-up, and the more wrinkled their necks were, the more bosom they showed.

Her eye was caught by two women at the next table, one fluttery in ruffles and the other solid in tweeds and flat heels. They were leaning across the table talking eagerly, letting their drinks get warm. Irv followed her look. "Those are Lesbians. You know, they go for women instead of men."

"Well, sure, I know that." But she looked with fascination at the two until they went out, arm-in-arm. I should think they'd try to keep people from knowing it. And anyway how could they – It must be something I don't know about, she thought, baffled, or else what do they get out of it? None of the biological facts she'd heard or read about seemed to fit in, and she decided to ask Mary Jean about it when she got back to school. Most likely a girl who knew as much about men as Mary Jean did would have the answer to this one, too.

Irv suggested having something to eat. "Or how about a drink?" Irv ordered Martinis for Mimi and himself. "How about you, lady? Are you old enough for a small drink?" Mimi gave him a warning look and said, "Sloe gin, weak." Joyce felt irritated because she was being treated like a child, then weepy because someone cared about her. She feels responsible for me, she thought.

The drink was pink and very cold; it tasted flat. "You don't feel it till later," Irv said.

She started to laugh, but her arms and legs felt as if they were falling off, and her head was queer. You can't get drunk on one drink, she assured herself, not remembering to count the excitement and the loss of sleep the night before, the smoke and noise and the impact of solid food on an empty stomach. She stared fixedly at the bass drum until feeling came back and her head cleared. "It's hot in here," she said, smiling at Irv.

A baggy-eyed comedian came on and told some jokes, mostly smutty and not too well timed, and then there was a hot number by the band, and then a ballerina came on. Very young, very light, she went through a *pas seul* to a tinkling music-box tune, and suddenly Joyce felt a tear slide down her nose. The woman at the next table was really crying, tears plowing through her makeup and smearing her lashes.

Nobody said anything, going home. Mimi leaned against Irv's shoulder, not amorously but sleepily. The shadows under her eyes had deepened and she had licked off most of her lipstick. Irv's eyes were as bright as ever and his full lips curved alertly. I wish I knew him better, Joyce thought; I bet he'd be fun to know, but I don't mean a thing to him. Her own indignation suddenly seemed comic to her and she snickered. What do you want him to do, throw his arms around you and holler, "My daughter!" He's taken you out and spent a lot of money on you; the least you can do is be grateful. Besides, he doesn't look like a fatherly type.

Mimi staggered a little, getting her long skirt out of the taxi. Irv steadied her. "Wake up, baby, we're home." He shook her gently, and she pulled herself together, a reflex of many a groggy morning on the road, and marched up the walk with her head high. Joyce noticed sleepily that Irv unlocked the door, taking the key from an expensive-looking pigskin holder. It's none of my business, she told the accusing shade of Aunt Gen. He pays the rent. They're getting married tomorrow. I wonder if he'll stay all night? She felt a queer embarrassment, and a tingling excitement she had never known before.

"I feel like hell," Mimi complained.

"Take a phenobarb," Irv advised her. He followed her into the bathroom, leaving Joyce perched uncertainly on one of the small straight chairs. She could hear the murmur of voices, the running of water, the slamming of a cabinet door. After what seemed like an endless time Irv came back. "Poor kid, she feels terrible. She'll be okay in the morning, though." They looked at each other uncertainly.

Joyce felt that she ought to say something, some kind of thanks for the evening. Mention the school fees, too. It's so good of you to spend all this money on me, I feel so grateful. The creaking of the bed in the next room distracted her from her dilemma. "Is she very sick?"

Irv shrugged. He looked embarrassed. "Aw, you know how it is. Lots of women feel pretty punk the first few weeks." He waited for her to answer. She didn't know what to say. "Well, hell," he said defensively, "she did it on purpose. You don't put anything over on that baby; she's been around." He glanced at his watch. "I was pretty burned," he said. "Me, getting hooked by the oldest racket in the world! Then I got to thinking, hell, a man gets up in the forties he sort of wants to settle down. Have a home and some kids." He looked at Joyce, who remained silent and blank with astonishment. "I'm marrying her," he said, sounding a little angry. "Christ, not every guy would be that decent about it."

Two tears trickled down Joyce's cheeks and fell. She felt, suddenly, tired and very sad. Irv patted her on the shoulder. "Don't feel like that, kid. I figured she told you. Happens all the time."

Now that she had started crying, she couldn't stop. She sniffled. Irv put his arms around her. His chest was nice and solid under her cheek. "I feel so terrible," she sobbed.

"That's excitement and sloe gin," Irv said. He sounded amused. "You'll feel all right in the morning."

She didn't want to feel all right, she wanted to go on crying because life was so sad and Mimi was in trouble with this man and she'd never had a mother and now Mimi was going to have a baby who would get loved and looked after. She thought, All I ever had was Aunt Gen scolding about every little thing. It felt good to cry. She snuggled up to Irv. "I like you," she said.

"You're a cute kid. Come on, give me a good-night kiss and then get the hell to bed. It's almost morning."

She put her streaky face up. They stood like that for a moment, without moving. Her eyes widened. The fatigue in her bones began to melt. His eyes were fixed on her. Something besides pity and amusement shone in them. She stretched, lifting her bosom. His arms tightened around her suddenly, hard with muscle. "God, it's been weeks –"

She lifted her mouth.

This bore no relation to the good-night kisses of high school boys. She was aware of deep danger, but suddenly she didn't want to break away. She wanted – she didn't know. She felt a queer prickling excitement compounded of curiosity and unaccustomed alcohol, fatigue, and the look behind the kindness in his eyes. She pressed against him. Like a pin stuck to a magnet, her body urged itself against his.

She felt alive and light. His arms tightened, and she took a deep breath. Her nipples rose and hardened, and there was a quivering tenderness down the inside of her legs. Sweat trickled down her back.

He laid his hand against the bosom of her dress, and waited. There was hunger in his face, and something like pity. She tore away the thin stuff, herself, and waited without moving while he undid the row of tiny hooks. In a dream, she saw that they had made little red marks on her flesh. He rubbed them away. His hands were brown and solid, with black hairs on the back. With her two hands she cupped her breasts, offering them to him like ripe fruit.

This is crazy, she thought. But she didn't care, it was a thing she had to do. She couldn't have stopped if she had wanted to.

Irv was pressing against her, his hands holding her down. "My shoes," she said. He bent and took the borrowed slippers off, setting them neatly side by side. She shut her eyes and waited, then opened them again to see him fumbling one-handedly with his clothes. Then he was on her, and she could hear his heart pounding fast and a little unevenly.

The last thought she had, as his left hand slipped beneath her head and his right hand began caressing her, was how silly he looked half-dressed that way. I'd like to see him with everything off, she thought. She lay shivering with excitement, while he shucked off what was left of Mary Jean's dress and turned back the crinoline.

Chapter Five

Sometimes words lie on the air of the room where they were spoken, and won't evaporate. They beat against the inner ear, pleading and accusing, shutting out all other sounds. You can go crazy, probably, if you listen to them long enough.

It was like that with Joyce on the day of Mimi's marriage. Now and then she couldn't help looking nervously around to see if anybody else was hearing them, too. Nobody seemed to notice – nobody was even aware that anything was bothering her – and while that was a relief it was also a worry. Maybe I'm delirious or something, she thought, standing up beside Mimi while the City Clerk's assistant read the marriage ceremony.

Over and over she heard Irv Kaufman's low voice, against the still air of late night. Traffic sounds coming up muted and diminished from the street below. The bed in the next room, squeaking under Mimi's drugged turning. That Mimi was so close made it seem worse, made it more of a betrayal than if she had been out of the house. "I'm sorry baby, but you asked for it." He really was sorry, it was in his regretful voice and his nice brown eyes. That's right, she thought wildly, I asked for it, but I didn't know what it was I wanted. Thought seemed to have no place in that surrender; thought had been suspended in favor of something older and more urgent.

"Lord, I've been so hard up it isn't even funny. Mimi hasn't been in the mood for quite a while, poor kid." Tucking in his shirttail, zipping up his trousers, straightening his tie, absent-mindedly but with precision. "I'm going to marry her," he said. "I'm not going to weasel out on it." He patted Joyce's shoulder as she sat hunched over on the davenport, holding the torn billow of net around her. "Try and forget it, will you kid?"

Nothing that he said made sense. After an endless time he went away and she locked the apartment door. Then she went back to the davenport and sat there for a while, trying to figure it out in her own mind. All she knew was she felt sick, and all her muscles ached. Later, turning from side to side on the scratchy upholstery – she was too tired to open it out or spread the clean sheets – and rolling over on her back again, trying to find a comfortable position and not make any noise, she was conscious only that her bones hurt. If I could only get some sleep, she thought.

It wasn't until morning that things began to come unscrambled. When Mimi came out of the bathroom, sallow-faced and shaking, and she went in to sit soaking in scented steamy water, the meaning of Irv's words got through to her. Sharp pity knifed through her and she forgot her fatigue and morning after dizziness. Poor Mimi, she did this, got herself into trouble so he would have to marry her. Uncle Will's worst, seldom-uttered curse flew into her mind and she told herself grimly, By Jesus H. Carrie Ann Christ, he'd better marry her. I'll kill him if he doesn't. If he had opened the apartment door at that moment she would have fallen on him tooth and fist. The moment of pure compassion passed, and she was back in a hurricane of remembered words again.

There was one other thing, for what comfort it might be worth. Partly, it made up for all the hateful rest. She remembered it in the course of brushing her teeth, and her anger softened. While she had been standing at the door, wishing to God he would go home so she could cry, he said softly, "I'm sorry, kid. It was the first time for you, wasn't it? I'm sorry as all hell. I made up my mind a long time ago I'd never start a girl." So it was true, they could tell if you'd done it before or not. Or had she done something that gave it away, moaned or moved when the quick brief pain came?

Still, he was sorry. He said so, and she believed him. It didn't make sense, but she felt a little better because of it.

The mushy books never said anything about the way it made you feel, the first time. There was a lot of stuff about the wedding night – they took for granted you were getting married, you wouldn't be having anything to do with it otherwise – about undressing and whether to turn the light off or not, and a lot about mutual consideration and getting adjusted to each other, all in such polite language that if you didn't already know what it was about, you'd never guess. She had always wondered who read that stuff, and now she wondered whether they were surprised when they found out what it was really like.

They didn't mention the dull knife stabbing where you were tender, how sore and achey you were the next day, pains across your lower back and down the insides of your legs. Of course, lying awake on a folded-up davenport isn't exactly restful either, she admitted. Maybe it was different in a double bed, in the arms of someone you loved. They never mentioned the way your eyes ached, and how sick you felt when you saw the little purple bruises on your thighs.

Maybe Aunt Gen was right. Right to turn her face away when the neighbor women started any discussion of mating or birth, and change the subject at the first pause. Right to shut the east windows when a wind from the barnyard brought in the lowing of a cow in heat. Right to drop her household magazine in the woodbox when it carried a story about a bad girl. Joyce looked out of the train window, but she could see Aunt Gen's round face set in forbidding lines, hear the little edge to her voice when she greeted a younger neighbor whose first child had been born too soon. That edge was there when she spoke to Mimi, on Mimi's visits to the farm; Joyce wasn't sure when she had grown into an understanding of it, had first known what it was that lay between the sisters after so many years. It made her feel both resentful and ashamed, when Mimi came into the kitchen and her older sister turned from the stove to look her over – her curled hair, reddened lips, high heels.

Now she thought she knew what Aunt Gen had known all along, the dirtiness and meanness of men and women and what lay between them. She shivered.

She tried to keep in mind that this was Mimi's wedding day. Keep it light, make a real production of it, make Mimi as happy as a bride in her situation can be, because she must have had some worried moments herself.

A crazy mixed-up day. Dragging herself out of bed at seven, after five hours of no sleep. Locking herself in the bathroom and scrubbing as if hot water and French soap could wash away the touch of a man's hot hands, the pressure of a man's body. Refusing breakfast because of so much food last night, then feeling remote and hollow with only coffee inside. Getting dressed for the wedding, which Aunt Gen would have said was no wedding at all. Mimi had brought the matter up, while they were breakfasting on black coffee; maybe Aunt Gen's rockbound ideas of right and wrong had been chewing at her.

After all, she'd been brought up by Aunt Gen, with fifteen years between them and Gen taking the place of a mother the best she could. She said she guessed it would be legal, all right, according to the laws of Cook County and the State of Illinois. "Irv hasn't been inside of a synagogue since he made *bar mitzvah* and I'm not anything, so I guess we won't have any fights over religion, anyhow. Neither of us has any." Joyce had smiled back, stirring the coffee around and around in her cup and trying not to listen to the voices.

She dreaded seeing him. The thought of seeing him made her feel a little faint, unable to breathe. All the time she was putting on the gray suit and borrowed pink blouse and her good hat – too loose now, because of the feather cut – her hands were shaking. Then the buzzer sounded and he was there, still bright-eyed and alert. It didn't tire a man out, then, the way some of the girls said it did.

He wore a diplomat's hat, a small white flower in his buttonhole. He had brought identical corsages for them and she pinned on her own while he fastened Mimi's and then kissed Mimi. Whatever she said to him, she guessed it sounded all right.

Seeing him lighted a hard bright flame of anger in her, warming her so that she could leave the apartment with the two of them and walk up the steps of the big echoing courthouse and even smile when Irv introduced her to the young salesman who was his best man. She stood close to Mimi, angry, while the man behind the wicket window read the service, which sounded churchey, even in this building and with these people.

Forget it, he says. Like hell I'll forget it. Who does he think he is? She stood stiffly while the clerk mumbled words that should have been poetry. Mimi's hand shook when she signed the certificate. Joyce's didn't. She fixed her mind on the dusty spitty smell that was like the courthouse at Ferndell, and the one brown petal in her corsage of small pink roses and blue lacy stuff. Everything looked very clear and bright.

Things aren't so bad when you are actually living through them. It's looking ahead, dreading them. And then looking back, figuring out all the implications and possible outcomes. She was all right in the restaurant where they went for creamed chicken and salad in aspic; in fact, the food tasted good after no breakfast. Around three o'clock they wound up at the railroad station, the best man still tagging along, and she shook hands with everybody and kissed the air beside Mimi's cheek so as not to smear her make-up. Mimi cried a little and the two men bought her copies of *Life* and *Collier's* to read on the train. She guessed they looked like a nice family party.

It wasn't until the train pulled out of the station and was clear of the rows of tracks and the overhead red and green lights, back porches of tenement houses sliding past, that her busyness began to wear off like Novocain from a sore tooth. Then the words began uncurling out of the air again.

I'm sorry, baby, but you asked for it.

You wanted it didn't you?

Mimi's a smart kid. She knew what she was doing.

That meant she hadn't taken any precautions, hadn't used any-thing. Joyce's former vagueness about these matters had been cleared up by living with Mary Jean. Mary Jean was loaded with informa-tion, and she had equipment which, she said, you could get in any drugstore – it was better if you had it prescribed by a doctor, though. There were things you used to keep from getting in trouble when you were with a man.

But Mimi knew about such things. She'd slept with men, differ-ent men, all these years. Now how did I know that? Joyce puzzled. Nobody had ever said a word about it, and if Aunt Gen had any suspi-cions she wouldn't have mentioned them to anyone, not even Uncle Will. Aunt Gen thought even married sex was a little dirty.

She did that with him, so she'd get in trouble. So he'd have to marry her. Realization jumped at her. What had happened the night before was not only whispers in the air, it took on the solid form of catastrophic fact. Mimi is pregnant, she told herself.

And so am I.

Why not? I did it too, she reasoned. The weight of Irv's body against hers, pushing her back against the scratchy cloth; excitement and hunger rising in her body like bubbles in a fountain. He didn't take any precautions; I would have known. She sat up straight, look-ing out of the window and seeing nothing.

Until now it had been a thing terrible in itself, but over and done with. I'll never see him again, she had told herself in the depot. Now she saw that it was not over at all, because she was in trouble. I'll faint and be sick in the mornings, she thought. Then what? What happens to girls when they have babies and aren't married? They go into some kind of a charitable institution, or die in childbirth like Tess of the D'Urbervilles. Her eyes filled with self-pitying tears. She held them wide open to keep them from running over.

Whatever happens, Mimi must not know.

Joyce rocked back and forth on the seat, her hands clenched, her eyes as bright and hard as glass marbles. I could kill myself, she thought. She suddenly felt intensely alive, her toes inside her pumps and her fingers against the clean seat cover full of awareness. She could cut her throat, but suppose the blood made her afraid and she changed her mind after it was too late? Or step in front of a car. Only she might be crippled for life, in horrible pain and without even the hope of death. She shivered, although the day was hot and the car stuffy. She could take a lot of sleeping pills and simply pass out. Never feel a thing.

But she didn't want to die. There simply wasn't any answer.

By the time they chugged to a stop at Henderson, she was incapable of thought. She was afraid to get up from her seat.

The school station wagon was waiting. Mimi must have phoned or something. Her first impulse was to go back inside the depot and hide. Then she saw who was at the wheel, calm hands folded on smooth lap. At the sight of Edith Bannister her knees crumpled. She had to lean against the wall of the station for a moment, careless of dust and crumbling paint. When her legs stopped wobbling she walked quickly to the car and got in, dragging her suitcase after her.

By the time you are thirty-six, if you have any sense at all and a reasonable experience of people, you know trouble when you see it. If you've been a dean of women for ten years you learn to sort out the different kinds before a sick, or crying, or sullen girl can get her mouth open. By the time she turned the ignition key, Edith Bannister knew that Joyce wasn't hungover or carsick, or coming down with anything. Traumatic experience, she thought in the jargon of Teachers' College. She drove quickly to campus.

Joyce stumbled up the stairs after her. Neither of them said a word. Edith Bannister shut the study door and turned the key. Sunshine steamed over the thinly painted bookcase, the neat desk. She took off Joyce's hat and laid it beside the African figurine, and put a hand on her shoulder. The touch brought release. Joyce burst into tears and then, her face swollen and pale from lack of sleep, into words.

Chapter Six

The radium-dial clock on the bedside stand said eleven-twenty. Joyce rolled over, feeling the muscles in her legs crack, and squinted at its face until the numbers came into focus. Eleven-twenty, and the sounds that drifted into Edith Bannister's apartment were those of the dorm settling down for the night. Where had the afternoon and evening gone?

Footsteps tiptoed down the front stairs; that would be somebody sneaking out for a late date, leaving a roommate who would come down later to spring the Yale lock. Radio music trickled through a tissue-stuffed keyhole where some girl was getting at her books after loafing for two weeks, or hanging up nylons and slips illegally rinsed out in the bathroom. A drift of voices from the lounge suggested that the House Council, presided over by Bitsy, was still in session. Joyce lay listening, but not really caring.

She tried to account for the hours that had passed since the train pulled in at Henderson that morning. Let's see, she figured it got in at nine-something. That's fourteen hours. She remembered bawling like a baby – shame flickered through her at the memory of her collapse, and something like wonder at the memory of Edith Bannister's arms warm and comforting around her, the way a mother holds a crying child.

Then I took that little white pill, she reminded herself, but it didn't work for ages and I was lying here looking at the sun on the door wishing I could go to sleep. She shook her aching head.

The next thing was the afternoon light getting duller, the way it does around six, and Edith Bannister was standing beside the bed with some dishes on a tray. She didn't know whether she had eaten anything or not; she couldn't remember what was on the tray so perhaps she hadn't. She had no awareness of time's passing, either; it was like the time she was given ether when she had had her appendix out. I'm tired, she decided with some astonishment, really tired. She gave up thinking and lay unmoving for a while, looking vaguely at the dim square that was the curtained window.

The late-night freight clanked across the corner of the campus and the pigeons perched on Colonel Henderson's statue complained softly. Light cut across the trees and reached into a clump of bushes where the redheaded freshman snuggled against her date, a boy from Ace Hardware. They hushed their whispering and stood rigid for a moment, until the train passed and the shadows were deep again. "Do that again," the boy said; "Touch me like that again."

The rhythmic clanking on the rails roused Joyce. This time her head felt clearer. She lay unmoving, aware of the sore places, and thought back over the day with more coherence than she had been capable of before. The ride from Chicago, gathering tension and terror with each mile that passed. The dizziness. The wonderful, heavenly relief of spilling everything, no matter if they threw her out in disgrace or told everybody. Afterwards the air around her felt light and clear, the way it feels after a summer thunderstorm.

Later? Blurred by emotion and codeine, her memory refused to give up any definite picture of what had happened. I must have had a bath, she decided, because I can remember the warm water. Or was that some other time? No, because I was all sticky and sweaty from crying, and all. She sniffed cautiously, turning down the folded sheet. She smelled clean, and there was a nightgown of some thin crisp stuff, but she never wore anything but pajamas, so somebody must have helped her get to bed.

Once when she was in third or fourth grade she had had measles. She remembered a lot of things quite clearly from those days in bed,

isolated scenes that stood out with photographic sharpness: Aunt
Gen's round face looking sober, and Aunt Gen's hands, with the nails
unpolished and cut short and the skin a little rough from gardening
and housework. But what she liked to remember, nights when she
was falling asleep, was that Mimi had come and sat beside her bed.
She still didn't know who had called Mimi, or why – maybe she was
sicker than the grownups let on – but there was a magic moment
when she stood in the doorway and everything in the world was absolutely all right.

She felt that way now.

For a little while she floated contentedly between sleeping and
waking. Then the door opened – not the bedroom door but the one
beyond that led into the corridor – and there were two sets of steps.
The light tap-tap of high heels and the solid thud of a man's shoes
planted firmly. Edith Bannister said something, but the words blurred
and ran together. A deep voice answered. Joyce stiffened. Edith said,
"That's silly, Roger. I always like to talk to you. It happens I'm tired
tonight, though, so good night."

"Sometimes I think you're frigid."

"Think what you please. It would be a little spectacular, though,
if somebody came in and found you here. Or don't you think so?
After all, both of us are responsible for the manners and morals of all
these innocent teenagers."

"Oh, hell."

There was a small silence, about long enough for a ritual good-
night kiss. Then the outside door closed. Joyce heard Edith moving
around her study the way a woman does when she comes in at night,
taking off her hat, lighting a cigarette, dropping her earrings on the
desk.

The bedroom door opened. A blade of light flashed in. "Hi. How
do you feel?"

"My head feels funny."

"That's the codeine," Edith said. "Dr. Prince prescribed it for

Sally when she broke her leg last spring – lucky I had some left." She crossed the floor, laid a cool hand on Joyce's forehead. "You better stay in bed tomorrow." She switched on the bedside lamp.

Joyce shut her eyes again. She felt completely safe and cared for. She could feel her mouth curve in a relaxed smile.

"Look here, you're not still worrying, are you?"

Something dark and ominous stirred in the back of her mind. She opened her eyes and looked, but the dean's face was impassive. Only something looked out of her eyes, gray-hazel, like Mimi's. Compassion, or concern, or even affection. Joyce opened her mouth, but no words came out. Edith Bannister leaned over her. "Listen to me. No one gets a baby from the first time. The chances are very small, anyway; starting a baby isn't so easy as all that."

"Suppose it happened, though?"

"If it happened," Edith Bannister said in a light, crisp voice, "we would arrange a little operation and in a few days you would be all right again. It's very simple. But it isn't going to happen, so you may as well stop worrying and get some sleep."

She lay still and tried to believe this. Her mind had circled around the idea of pregnancy so long that she couldn't give it up now. Warm tears squeezed out from under her closed eyelids, making them sting. Edith said with quiet scorn, "Men. They never think about anything except themselves and their own needs. They're such fools. Forget it, Joyce. I tell you everything will be all right."

"Oh God, I hope so."

Edith turned back the top sheet, smoothing it. "You can stay all night if you want to," she said, "if you don't mind sharing the bed. I'm rather afraid to have you in your own room as long as you're in a confessing frame of mind, that sexy little slut you room with will have the whole story out of you and she'll spread it all over school in no time."

Remembering some of the case histories she had had from Mary Jean, Joyce was afraid this might be so. She didn't want to move, anyway; it was quiet here, the air was lightly scented and it felt good to lie still. She followed with her eyes the movements of this slender, quiet woman. Miss Bannister took her dress off and put it on a padded hanger with a precision that was like Mimi's. She tied a thin flowered robe around herself and went into the bathroom, and there were the sounds of water running into a basin, towel whispering across skin, cabinet doors clicking. She came back no less tidy, only with her hair flowing loose instead of knotted. She was the first person Joyce had ever seen with really long hair; some of the girls at school wore theirs loose on the shoulders, but the ends had been trimmed. It gave Miss Bannister an old-fashioned, feminine look.

She sat down on the edge of the bed and took off her slippers, then snapped off the light and got under the covers. Joyce was acutely conscious of her body, not touching, but close enough for her to feel its warmth. She shut her eyes, feeling truly secure and cared-for at least.

Edith Bannister stirred. "You'd better stay in bed tomorrow," she said calmly, "and it might be a good idea to sleep down here tomorrow night."

That was all right, too. Joyce fell asleep, feeling completely happy.

A confused and blurry day ensued, made up of alternate sleepings and wakings, and food on trays, but then she was too sleepy to eat. She went to sleep with bars of yellow sunshine lying across the floor, and woke to deepening shadows in the corners of the room. It was a sort of convalescence, she thought.

Now it was night, and Edith Bannister's warmth and delicate fragrance, familiar since yesterday, was in the bed beside her. She must have slept after she became aware of that, because when she opened her eyes again there was a late-night feeling in the air. She lay still, not quite sure where she was or what had happened to her. A spot of warmth – someone had rolled over against her and a hand lay on her breast. She realized that it was Edith Bannister lying against her, and that Edith was awake. Joyce moved closer, impelled by a loneliness she couldn't define.

Edith whispered, "Afraid?"

"No."

Joyce felt fingers stroking lightly, a warmth and comfort she had never dreamed of, and then a stirring, an awakening. All over her body sensations arose she had never known before. "Please," Edith Bannister said in a queer husky whisper. "Please."

Joyce wasn't sure what was happening or going to happen. Whatever it was, she liked it. This had no relation to being with a man, the touch and smell of a man. She nestled closer, feeling the fingers unbutton her thin, borrowed cotton nightgown. Electric shocks now, wherever there was contact. She whispered, "Oh, yes."

There was no fatigue or worry left. No yesterday or tomorrow and no world beyond these night-dark walls. Nothing but the stroking hand, and Edith's accelerated breathing at her ear, and the feeling that flooded through her.

Chapter Seven

Mary Jean had a theory about love which she expounded practically every time the subject came up, over cokes at the Honey Bee and tonight in Holly Robertson's room. Love, she said, is rugged enough even when everything is in favor of it. Even when all four parents are for it, Mary Jean declared, romance is certainly hell on the nervous system.

"When you have to sneak around and take it on the run," she said sadly, "you don't even have to diet to stay thin. Whether you do or don't," she added as a sop to convention.

Holly Mae picked up the cup Mary Jean had put on the bed. "Going somewhere, dear?"

"Late date." Mary Jean pulled on her tweed jacket, slanted a re-minding look at Joyce: the door. Joyce blushed. Last time she had forgotten it and Mary Jean had had to come in through a basement window, which involved dropping several feet onto a sorting table in the laundry. "I'm going, too," she said vaguely, taking one more cookie from the carton and sinking back with her spine against the leg of the bed.

If she'd had a boyfriend, she thought gloomily while Holly Mae refilled the percolator – if she hadn't made that Tony character so mad and he'd asked for another date, she could have talked about him the way Mary Jean did about Bill and the girls would have kidded her, offered good advice and asked prying questions to find out how far it had gone.

One disadvantage of this off-beat love, or whatever you wanted to call it – she guessed Mary Jean would have had a name for it but there were some things she couldn't tell even Mary Jean, not even in that hour after the lights were off, when confidences came naturally – one problem was that you had to keep it to yourself. You can admit being sexy or frustrated, but not abnormal. If love at its crazy best is a special kind of insanity that people hanker after instead of fleeing from it, at least being able to talk about it is a kind of therapy. She guessed that some of the girls got more real pleasure out of sharing their affairs than they did out of having them.

When you're a girl of eighteen, and suddenly all that matters much is a woman almost twice your age, the need to keep it extra-secret makes everything that much worse. For a while Joyce went through her days blind and deaf to everything but Edith Bannister, pretending not to pay any special attention to her – keeping her face composed when they met at the table or in the hall. It would have been even more difficult if she hadn't been feeling vague and exalted at the same time, like a person walking around with about two degrees of fever.

This love hasn't anything to do with movies and the sweet mush of popular songs, or even the poetry she used to copy at the library and carry around in the back of her chemistry book. Those were surface things. Two-dimensional, like pieces of paper.

She slept heavily at night, waking full of a queer excitement and not rested, rejecting sleep and needing more at the same time. She felt always a little hungry and thirsty. Yet it wasn't food she wanted. She ate what was set in front of her without paying any particular attention to it. She walked over to town with Mary Jean and Bonnie and Alberta, who had the same free periods she did, and in the slow interval between the last afternoon class and dinner they bought things to eat: Hershey bars and sacks of potato chips, sundaes with imitation whipped cream and maraschino cherries at the Bee. They were always stopping downtown for Cokes, though it cost a dime and tasted exactly like the six-cent coke in the vending machines on campus. Once she picked an empty sack off the floor of the room and asked, "Who dropped this?" and Mary Jean said, "Goofus, you just ate the peanuts." She rolled up the bit of paper and threw it away, but she couldn't remember eating any peanuts.

She must have taken showers and dressed, fixed her face, gone to class and recited when called on. She was always finding herself sitting in the library with a book open in front of her, and some of the print got through to whatever she did her thinking with in those days. But she was certainly not all there.

Mostly, she waited. It was appalling how much time you could spend just sitting around and waiting, and the way most days ended in blankness. Edith went out a great deal, evenings. She sponsored school activities and belonged to social and study clubs in town. She dated, too. She went out with a lawyer who was supposed to be looking for a second wife, an eligible bachelor who was on the governing board of the college, a wistful little man who wore the only male beret – red – in Henderson and was supposed to be a painter.

"How can you?" Joyce demanded. "How can you go out with men? Do you like to?"

"I like an evening out now and then," Edith said reasonably. She sat on the edge of her bed, smoking. She smoked a great deal in her own rooms, never in public.

"It doesn't seem honest."

"We can't be honest," Edith said simply. She dropped her cigarette into an ashtray. She sat with her hands in her lap, palms up – a characteristic pose. "We have to be careful."

Joyce touched her shoulder with the tip of an inquiring finger. The first tentative gesture towards what might be, this time, *the* time. "I don't care. I'd liked to tell everybody."

"I care," Edith said sharply. "I like my job, apart from having to earn a living. You don't know how they crucify people like us, tear us limb from limb and laugh when we suffer." Her normally cool voice was a little shrill; she shivered. "Everybody hates us."

"There can't be so many –"

Edith sighed. "You'd be surprised how many. All shapes and sizes." She moved her hand from under Joyce's and took another cigarette from the silver case with the initial G engraved on it. "If any of these brats found out – my God, how they'd love it. Your roommate would have a fine time with it, the little nympho." Her eyes narrowed.

Joyce had no answer for that, because it was true. Mary Jean knew more case histories than Kinsey. Accurate or not, she had a lively interest in everyone's sex life, and she used words Joyce had never heard anyone else use, not even migrant hired men. But still she liked Mary Jean. Even if they couldn't swap clothes, they had fallen into a comfortable roommate-best-friend relationship. She stood between two loyalties, feeling clumsy and childish and frustrated, wanting to cry.

Edith stood up, dropping her cigarette beside the other in the ashtray. She laid her cheek against Joyce's, their own special gesture of tenderness. "There isn't any future for us, Joy. You'll graduate, or maybe I'll get a better job. Or one of us will come to care for someone else."

"I don't care about the future," Joyce said painfully. "I'm thinking about now."

"A good idea," Edith said lightly. The wistful moment was gone. Her hand found Joyce's back and rubbed the tender spot between the shoulders. "I really place a great deal of confidence in you, darling."

"Well, you can. I'd sooner die than hurt you." That was mushy, that was like a Grade B movie, and she felt her face redden. But the hand kept rubbing her back, gently, relaxingly, like someone stroking a sleepy cat. She buried her face on Edith's shoulder. "Really touch me."

"Like this?"

"Oh, yes."

The times were too far apart and much too short. Like eating one salted peanut, Edith said smiling. Joyce didn't think that was funny.

Between meetings she burned with desire – yes, she really ached all over, it was like the romantic sentimental poetry you had always laughed at, in the old small-print books. You sat in Spanish class and listened to the teacher going through vocabulary lists and the rules governing use of the dative, and it was only noise that had no meaning to it although your mind kept nagging you that you ought to remember this for future examinations. Looking out of the window, all you could think about was the touch and the mounting thrill and, afterwards, when it had been extra good, the complete relaxation that was like being asleep, only better. Much better.

Late night. She crept downstairs after the building was asleep, after an endless time of waiting. Nobody ever goes to bed in this damn place, she thought, looking across the moonlit strip of floor to Mary Jean's empty and unmade bed, listening to the snickers and clinkings next door where Marnie and Jo had smuggled in a couple cans of beer with the help of Marnie's boyfriend. Two hours of rolling and turning, pulling the wadded and wrinkled sheet with her. Won't the fools ever turn off their light and shut up? The hands of the clock moved with irritating slowness, ten-forty when she looked and then, after ages of waiting, ten-forty-four. What if she's asleep when I get there, and the door is locked?

The night light at the end of the hall was a faint bluish glimmer. She looked around the half-open door, ready to scuttle into the bathroom if anybody was around. Anyone can be up to go to the bathroom. She tiptoed down the hall, scared of being caught but pushed by something more urgent than timidity. Nobody was in the first-floor hall. The round china knob of the study turned silently under her sweating hand. The door swung slowly open. Edith was waiting, not reading, not smoking, simply standing there ghost-pale in the moonlight, but warm and solid in the sudden, mutual and inevitable embrace. A quiescent volcano.

Edith's voice spoke an hour later, no longer cool, but rough and demanding. "Was it good? Did you feel it? Are you satisfied?"

"Oh, God."

Joyce lay on her back, arms and legs spread across the bed, her body wet with sweat. The curtains were closed and the moon had gone behind a cloud; the room was dark. I like the dark, she thought drowsily. She reached out an exploring hand, touched flesh still throbbing and pulsating.

"Yes. I got through to you that time, didn't I?" In a small voice, diminished by fatigue, Joyce answered, "I'm so happy."

"That's all I want. To make you happy."

"Where did you learn how?"

"I'm thirty-four. There have been others." An edge to the voice, cutting through the moment's contentment. "There will be others for you, too, before you're done."

Jealously stirred in her. She moved away a little. "There'll be more for you, too, I guess. Maybe there's somebody now."

"Don't talk like a fool." Edith turned on the lamp. She sat up in bed, clasping her hands around her knees. In the small light her skin was smooth and clear. Joyce laid her cheek against the smooth slope of thigh. "It's only that you mean so much to me."

Edith stroked the back of her neck, lightly and rhythmically. "You like to be rubbed? A little more and you'll be purring like a kitten." It was true, she was almost asleep. Her eyes dropped shut under the slow, hypnotic stroking. "A man won't do this for you," Edith said. Her voice was low and even again, as though having released her tensions she was once more in full control. "All men think about is their own pleasure. A man wants to relieve himself, like an animal. There's no tenderness in them. If they do anything for you first, it's only to get your worked up so that you'll be responsive and they'll have more fun. Ugh!" Her hand moved down Joyce's arm, inside the elbow. "A woman can do this for you because she knows what it means, she sees her own pleasure reflected in it. This is what matters. The rest is nothing but a trap nature has figured out to keep the human race going. What counts is here." She moved her hand again.

"There is where the thrill and the meaning are."

Joyce moved her head slowly. Heavy with sleep, drugged and groggy with needing sleep. "I know – now."

"Men don't know anything about women," Edith said in the same voice of quiet conviction. "How can they? Only a woman knows what it's like, the same as looking in a mirror or feeling in her own body."

"I want to do it for you, too. Make you happy."

"Next time you will. Lie still now, sleep a little."

This was the time of complete happiness. This is the best of all, Joyce thought, lying relaxed and half unconscious against the body she now knew like her own. She slept.

But at two o'clock in the morning, in the deep stillness that comes before daybreak, she had to go back to her own room. This was even more dangerous than the trip out, because anyone who bumped into her now would guess where she had been and why. "Some day we'll have a place where we can be alone," Edith said, dreaming. "A little shack on the coast of Maine with surf crashing on the rocks, or a country inn in France." You were not supposed to believe this, but it made a picture that dimmed the pang of parting somewhat. They clung together, rested, and feeling rose in Joyce again. "Go quickly," Edith said, opening the door a crack and peering out.

Joyce put on her housecoat, tying the belt tightly, pulled on the slippers she had bought down at the Henderson Variety because they had foam-rubber soles. Her breasts were tender; she felt them hopefully – they were getting bigger, weren't they? She tried to smile. The door shut.

The hall echoed with silence. Upstairs there were only the usual late-night noises, a creaking as someone turned over, a surprisingly deep snore, a mutter from Molly's and Charlene's room. Those two were supposed to be more or less queer about each other, but Joyce had never seen any signs of it. She looked at their door with some distaste. It's funny how different it seems when it happens to you, she thought.

She opened her own door very quietly. Mary Jean was in and asleep, rolled up into a bundle of sheet with one bare foot sticking out. Joyce eyed her, crawling into her own bed slowly, so the springs wouldn't creak. She was not sure how much Mary Jean knew, or suspected. She didn't know whether Mary Jean was talking about her to other people, considering all the gossip she'd repeated to Joyce, or whether the ethics of being a roommate made a difference there. Anyway, she reminded herself defensively, I can say as much about her as she can say about me.

That's different, though.

She sighed, pulling up a blanket and wishing again, as she had wished so often before, that she had someone to discuss things with. Then she shut her eyes and gave herself over to the pleasure of remembering.

There was only one drawback to this secret excitement and wonder. That was the letdown that came the next day. She woke in the morning cross from lack of sleep, headachey and irritable. Maybe this is bad for me or something, she worried, pulling off her pajamas and standing naked in front of the mirror, examining her reflection minutely. Maybe it can make me sick. Maybe it does some awful thing to you, she worried, throws your glands out of kilter.

She sat on the edge of the bed, too enervated to dress. When the door opened she jumped and began throwing on her clothes. Mary Jean was in a bad mood, too. Joyce wondered when she had come in. They went down to breakfast together, without talking. Bitsy joined them on the landing and Joyce looked at her with disfavor. You couldn't imagine Bitsy going all the way, with anybody. No, she would study hard and have dates with nice boys, and still be a virgin when she married – and she'll be happy too and have about four wonderful kids, Joyce told herself, and run the PTA.

Edith sat at the head of the table, pouring coffee. Never mind, she's worth it, Joyce thought. She avoided Edith's eyes because she was afraid to think what would show on her own face if that calm, grave look fell on her. For a moment she felt rich and comforted.

That was the day it rained and rained, a steady slow drizzle that got on everybody's nerves and soaked everybody's shoes and made people slow and sleepy or cranky according to their natures. Of course, it rained a lot in Illinois in October, too, but here there wasn't any glory of colored leaves or any deep-blue Indian-summer sky to make you feel good between times. Just a steady drip that went on and on.

That was the day Mimi's letter came, the first since that short catastrophic visit. Irv hadn't told her – good. She tore the stiff creamy envelope open and held the paper in her hand, feeling the raised letters of the engraving between thumb and finger, not quite realizing yet that it was from Mimi. Mimi was, she always said apologetically, no hand to write letters. Always, though, there had been the weekly postcard, two for a nickel off a wire rack in some crumby drugstore, with a bright-colored picture on the front and a couple of lines in Mimi's loose up-slanted scrawl.

Since she had come to college, though, Mimi hadn't written at all. Too busy – or too sick and worried, or too afraid she couldn't live up to this swell place where her daughter was now a pupil, chumming around with girls from the very best families. She knew what was what. Anyway, she had gone out and had some stationery engraved with her new married name and the address of the apartment, fragrant of money and culture. The message was the kind she used to put on the postcards. She was just fine. Let me know if you need anything. Irv sends his best regards. Joyce crumpled the page and threw it in the wastebasket, then fished it out and smoothed it the best she could. There was no need to spoil this beautiful paper that Mimi had bought for her benefit, just because she hated Mimi's husband.

Her mind turned to Edith Bannister. Edith was real and close at hand, and meaningful. The little pinch that used to come in her stomach at the thought of Mimi wasn't there.

That was also the day when Joyce definitely found out she was safe. In spite of Edith's reassurances and the charts in the little book, she hadn't felt too sure about it. A disturbing suspicion that she might be pregnant kept grinning out at her from the back of her mind. Somewhere around the middle of the morning, this drippy soggy day, a familiar stiffness inside her thighs and ache in her lower back signaled that everything inside was going along according to routine. I wasn't worried, she bragged to herself, not for a single minute.

Never again, though. You wouldn't catch me having anything to do with a man again. Ugly things, always using women for their own purposes.

She sat in her room, unstrung and relaxed all at the same time, listening to the plop of raindrops on the window. Temporary peace, between two tensions.

Chapter Eight

There are always ways and means. If you want something badly enough, it's almost always possible to figure out a scheme for getting it. And if you are a woman with looks and intelligence and that elusive thing the fashion magazines call charm, some man will frequently help you to it with a minimum of effort on your part.

Edith Bannister decided she needed a part-time secretary and set about getting one. She started by calling up the only member of the school's governing board who lived in Henderson, an eligible and cagey bachelor of fifty who liked women until their intentions began to get honorable, and suggested that he invite her out to lunch. "That is, unless you feel it's your duty to lunch here."

Wayne felt no such obligation, and said he would like to take her out to lunch – as soon as she could be ready, in fact. His pleasant voice came out of the receiver tiny but clear. "I don't know what you're fishing for, Ede, but you'll probably get it. You almost always do."

"I enjoy your company," she told him demurely. She cradled the phone and turned to her closet, humming under her breath.

The authorization for a part-time secretary came through the next day, typed by Wayne's sixty-dollar girl. One dollar an hour, minimum for employed women, for services not to exceed five hours a week. Joyce read it, leaning against Edith's shoulder. "Evenings," Edith pointed out. "I hope you can type."

"Well, I had a year in high. I'm slow, though."

"You can type. Come down after dinner tonight, unless you have a date."

"You know I don't have dates."

"I've told you about that," Edith said sharply. "If you don't go out with a boy now and then, someone's going to get suspicious."

"I hate boys. Always trying to get their hands on you."

"I have a little trouble along those lines myself," Edith said with a faint smile. "It won't hurt you to let some adolescent wolf make a pass at you once in a while. It wouldn't even hurt you to act a little bit responsive. My God, I go out with men all the time. I make a point of it. You have to think how things look."

"I don't care."

"I mean it. Do you want some brat starting a rumor?"

"I think you worry about it too much."

Edith sat down. "Look, I was about your age the first time it happened to me. Maybe a little younger – I was still in high school." She shook her head, looking back, wonder in her face. "It's a pattern that repeats. Gwenda did everything for me – the way I'd like to do everything for you. We were together as often as we could manage. I had the flu that winter, and she came into the house and took care of me. My parents didn't think anything about it – why should they? She was a teacher. It was a real thing we had, not anything promiscuous or cheap."

"I know."

"It would have been all right if I'd kept my mouth shut," Edith said. "Happiness is like trouble, though, it's easier to bear if you can share it. I had to tell someone.... The girl told," she added after a momentary silence.

"What happened?"

"Well, that was during the depression, when there were a hundred teachers for every job. They called a special meeting of the school board."

"Fired her?"

"They let her resign. I was expelled from school. Luckily my father had a little money left, and enough pull to keep it out of the papers. I passed my College Boards that summer. But Gwenda – she killed herself the next winter. She'd tried to go on relief. It was a horrible mess."

She was living it over again, and there was nothing to say.

"She was a little thing, like you. Only dark. Olive skin and brown eyes. I loved her, Joy."

"I know you did." Go ahead, turn the knife.

"So that's the way it was. There have been others, but never one that was cheap or trivial. Don't think about it, darling, learn to take it the way it comes."

So then there was contact again, and the wave of feeling that washed away thought. I'll never want anyone else, Joyce promised herself, shutting her eyes so that sight couldn't break in on rapture. I'll never want anything but this.

If anyone had any mean little doubts about the secretary plan, no snickers reached her. Twice a week, after dinners that went on forever and were full of talk without meaning, she sat at Edith's desk and took dictation in a kind of lecture-room shorthand evolved by herself, and then sat figuring out her notes and turning them into letters. She developed a professional pride in the results, which had sentences and paragraphs and read like real letters typed by genuine secretaries. She even began learning to smoke, partly for the pleasure of sharing Edith's cigarettes and partly because it was such an adult thing to do. She didn't care for the taste much, or for the way shreds of tobacco stuck to her teeth, but she stayed with it and practiced illegally in her own room when she had a chance.

There was a special excitement in sitting in front of the typewriter, clicking out letters about supplies and credit transfers, erasing carefully when she made a mistake because her mind would rush ahead into the good part of the evening. There was even a special pleasure in putting off the time, after Edith came in from her D.A.R. meeting or Glee Club rehearsal. The longer you waited the better it would be, like getting good and hungry before a meal.

"Leave the light on. I like to look at you."

"I like to look at you, too."

Not always sure which of them was talking, was moaning at the instant of fulfillment, because it was happening to both of them at the same time.

"Let me stay with you this once. I want to sleep with you."

"Will you be sure to hear the alarm if I set it for five?"

But it was Edith who woke at the first click and pushed the little knob down. Joyce slept heavily, like a child. Even after she was awake she hated to get up, but lay looking at Edith. Part of the thrill was the contrast between the cool and composed daytime Edith and this woman who lay naked and curled up against the pillow, her long hair tangled, still smelling faintly of sweat and excitement. Joyce touched her lightly, in wonder, before she crawled out. She picked up her pajamas and duster from the floor beside the bed and got into them, yawning with sleep. The trip upstairs was more dangerous than usual because this time a film of light was spreading over the windows – it was not quite day, but almost, and someone might be up or awake. But there was nobody in the hall.

Mary Jean was awake. The little reading-lamp that clamped over the head of her bed was on, and she was sitting up in the round pool of light, waiting. Joyce jumped at the sight of her, then stiffened her shoulders and shut her mouth tight. Deny everything. Been to the bathroom. Heard noises down the hall. Couldn't sleep and decided to walk around a while.

Then she saw that Mary Jean's eyes were swollen almost shut and her face was red and puffy from crying, and her head hung forward as if there were no bones in her neck.

"For heaven's sake, are you sick?"

Mary Jean tried to smile. It was a ghastly grimace, and a new flood of tears washed it off her face. "I'm all right," she said. Her voice cracked under the strain of trying to be calm. "I guess this is it. I guess it's the real thing, all right. You'll have to throw me out in the snow with a bundle in my arms."

"What are you talking about?"

"Oh God, you fool, I'm in trouble. That's a goofy thing to call it, isn't it? That's what the old ladies back home call it, and they're so right." Mary Jean shoved back the covers and sat up in bed, rocking. Most of the time she slept naked, but tonight she had gone to bed in a slip, as though to hide her betrayed and betraying body even from herself. "I'll have to get rid of it, or something, but oh God, I'm scared. People die from it sometimes."

"Maybe there is something you can take," Joyce suggested. She sat down on her own bed. Beneath her real concern for Mary Jean's predicament was relief that she wasn't caught, that it was somebody else's trouble and not hers. It made her feel ashamed. "Ergot," she remembered. "There was a girl in high school and she always –"

"That's an old wive's tale. You can't take anything. I mean, you can but it won't do any good. And it won't do any good to run up and down stairs, or get chilled, or sit in a tub of hot water." Mary Jean's voice wobbled. "It's an operation, and they don't give you any anesthetic for it. People get blood poison from it sometimes."

Joyce shivered. She said, "Maybe you're just late. Lots of people are late sometimes. Maybe you've got a little cold or something."

"Look, I'm the original clockwork kid." Mary Jean's face puckered. "I told him and told him. He wouldn't wait. I kept telling him, and he wouldn't listen to me."

Men, Joyce thought with a cold anger rising in her. She felt a new affection for Mary Jean. She would have liked to pat her head or put an arm around her, but was afraid of being sentimental. She felt so alive and secure herself that she was ashamed. "Please don't make so much noise," she begged. "Somebody'll hear you."

"This will kill my dad," Mary Jean sobbed. "He's a preacher, did I ever tell you that? Baptist preacher. Not like the ones in the movies; he's the kindest man that ever lived. Only he always worried about me too, I guess." She was really bawling now. She fumbled for a tissue, didn't find one, and wiped her nose on the sheet. "All the damn housekeepers. All the goddamn women all the time hollering about my mother. Ever since I was knee-high they've been waiting for me to get in trouble," she said bitterly. "My dad wants to think things like this only happen to girls from down by the railroad tracks," she said. "It'll kill him if he ever finds it out."

"Well, my goodness, you don't have to let him find out anything about it."

"You've got to help me. I'm afraid to stay by myself after – when it gets bad. People die sometimes."

They looked at each other. "There must be plenty of doctors that do it," Joyce said. "It happens to a lot of people."

"Sure it does. Only you never think you're going to be the one. You think about it sometimes when you're, you know, all excited – what will I do if I get caught? And you think, well, if anything happens I can have an operation. But you don't expect it to really happen." Mary Jean wiped her eyes, sniffling. "I'm sorry I'm so chicken."

"Does Bill know?"

"Sure. Oh, sure, I couldn't wait to tell him. I thought maybe he'd even marry me. I wouldn't mind being married."

"And?"

"He swore at me," Mary Jean said. "I think he can get me some money for the operation, though. His folks have plenty."

"How much will it cost?"

"I think it's around two or three hundred dollars. It's against the law, that's why they charge so much. If the doctor gets caught doing it they put him in jail. That's why the good ones won't."

"There must be some good ones who need the money, though." Joyce hoped she sounded calm and reasonable. She didn't feel that way. "Look, tomorrow we'll go and look for a doctor. Don't they give you a rabbit test or something first?"

"Not in this hick town we won't. They'd call the college first thing."

"Okay, we'll got to St. Louis."

"We can ask Abbott for permission to go shopping. She's going to be a problem," Mary Jean said, "she's such a snooper and she has a dirty mind."

"You won't have to tell the doctor your right name."

"You won't tell anybody, will you? I mean, not anybody at all."

"Of course not. You'll be okay."

Mary Jean shut her eyes and slid down against the pillow. "My head hurts. I wish I could go to sleep and never wake up."

Joyce would have liked to sleep for a week, herself. "Don't worry," she said, "you'll get along all right." I hope to God I'm right, she thought.

Chapter Nine

"Maybe this time we'll hit the jackpot," Joyce said. There was no assurance in her voice, and her face was tired. She stood back and looked at the building. Grimy brick crisscrossed by a black webbing of fire escapes, its uncurtained windows lettered in black and gold: Painless Dentist, Furs Re-styled, Attorney at Law, The Clarion Press. "It doesn't look very sanitary," she said doubtfully.

"You sure this is the right address?"

"Says Fourteen Twenty-four." Joyce looked at the slip of paper she had carried all afternoon, rumpled now and smudgy from being clutched in a sweaty hand. "My feet hurt," she complained.

"You ain't just beatin' your gums, grandma." Mary Jean eased one heel out of her black suede pump, and stood lopsided for temporary relief. A red blister showed through sheer nylon. "Next time I'll wear flats."

"There better not be any next time."

They stood eyeing each other. "We sure haven't made any headway so far. We might as well go in."

"Do we have time before the train's due to leave?"

"Unless he has a million other people waiting. We can't go back till we find somebody," Mary Jean said fretfully. "We can't ask for another Saturday leave without making Abbott suspicious."

"This is a crazy way to look for a doctor. Like looking for a needle in a haystack."

"Do you know any better way?"

"We couldn't exactly call up the AMA and ask for the name and address of a good abortionist," Joyce admitted. They climbed the stairs quickly, both afraid of losing their nerve. Joyce's chest hurt, and she was having trouble breathing. Feels like somebody's sitting on my stomach, she thought crossly. Nerves, just plain old nerves. He can't do any worse than say no, the way the others did. Only if he looks at us like that fat one –

Heck, he doesn't even know who we are. She held her purse more tightly. She and Mary Jean had removed every scrap of identification from their bags before they left school that morning, feeling, in spite of their anxiety, like characters in an Agatha Christie novel. Family snapshots, identification cards, the Social Security card she'd kept as a proud souvenir of the summer she detasseled corn. Mary Jean had even bought a wedding ring in Woolworth's and put it on. "So he'll tell me the truth. If they think you're single they might not want to help you." This reasoning seemed a little lopsided but Joyce got it, finally: if you weren't married, people were likely to think it served you right. Maybe one doctor could do the diagnosis and another one the operation, she suggested. Mary Jean looked dubious.

This waiting room wasn't as slick and clinical-looking as the others they had tried. It was as dingy as the outside of the building. The others had been brightly lighted, two by tubular fluorescent fixtures, the third by an abundance of little modern lamps. Two had amateur paintings on the walls – one was a seascape with sailboats, the other an abstract that reminded Joyce sickeningly of Mimi's apartment. "Do all doctors paint in their spare time?" she asked, and Mary Jean said lifelessly that she didn't think doctors ever had any spare time and probably the pictures were gifts from grateful patients.

"Or maybe their wives do it, waiting up nights for them," Joyce suggested, but there was no answering smile.

The patients in the other places had looked bright and prosperous too. Young mothers with healthy-looking little children, there for shots or a routine checkup. A couple of middle-aged men, and young wives in smocks. You couldn't imagine any of these folks ever being scared, or having anything to hide. Nor could you imagine any of the doctors, two of them youngish and partly bald, the third middle-aged and tonsured like a monk, doing anything illicit.

That was the trouble, they were all too respectable. The first two young men had sized the situation up before Mary Jean could make any disastrous confessions and had said they didn't have time to take any new patients, they were awfully busy right now. The third said he was full just now, but why don't you come back this evening, Mrs. Uh, and bring your husband. He was nice about it, but firm. Still, it was his office nurse who had stopped them on the way out and given them this man's address.

This room – well, you could imagine the people collected here being involved in almost any kind of furtive circumstances. Shot by gangsters, or infected with the kind of diseases they told you about in the back of those street-guide books. Or getting rid of babies.

She sat down on an old wicker couch covered in faded cretonne and picked up an old *Saturday Evening Post* from the pile on the table. Then she realized that she was still hanging on to her list, copied that morning from the Red Book in the depot phone booth. She folded it and slipped it into the pocket of her suit jacket, and looked at her watch. Forty minutes till train time, and we haven't bought a thing to take back. Even if Abbott doesn't get suspicious, Edith is going to ask questions. She shied away from that thought and looked at Mary Jean, who was sitting absolutely still on a straight chair with dusty rungs.

The doctor came to the door. This one was an old man, not just on the other side of middle age, but really old, maybe seventy-five. He had no hair at all except a few oily wisps combed over the bare top of his head. He was thin, and dressed not in a professional white jacket but in old wash pants and a short-sleeved shirt with a bar of rust across one shoulder, as if it had been dried over a radiator. He walked slowly, stooping. He had a neck in folds like a turtle's and his eyes were hooded like a turtle's too – or like a cobra's, she told herself in unreasoning terror. There was something really reptilian about him and also something dingy, not quite clean, like the room. He beckoned to one of the waiting women, and she got up heavily and followed him into the inner office.

Mary Jean leaned over. Her cheeks were sallow. "Let's go, kid. I can't –"

The others watched them leave, incurious, wrapped up in their own troubles. Their heels were loud on the wooden stairs. Out in the street, electric signs were coming on and after-work crowds thickening. Mary Jean puffed for breath, leaning against the outside wall of the building. "I'm sorry, Joyce. I simply couldn't stand it. He looked like, I don't know –"

"An old snapping turtle. Or an alligator, or crocodile, whichever one it is eats people."

"I can't ever remember either."

They made the train by the skin of their teeth. The conductor had to wait while they dug up the return half of their tickets. It was a commuters' train, filling up quickly at this hour. Joyce was glad they didn't have to stand up, she didn't think she could have managed it. She looked at Mary Jean, sitting lax and still beside her. "Are you all right?"

"Tired, is all. It's funny; I've been thinking, in the books they always get faint or something. I feel perfectly all right only I'm three weeks late, that's all."

"Maybe they don't put that in the books because it isn't polite or something."

"Right this minute what bothers me is my feet are killing me."

"We've wasted a whole day," Joyce said sadly.

"I couldn't let that man do it. Do you reckon they're all like that?"

"I wouldn't trust him to give a sick dog a dose of salts," Joyce said scornfully. It was Uncle Will's expression. "We'll have to think up a better way. We could ask around all day and not hit on the right person."

"What we need is to ask somebody who's full of sin and wicked-ness," Mary Jean said in a frayed voice. She smiled to show she was joking, but it wasn't much of a smile. "We don't know the right kind of people. I know a lot of girls who've done their share of sleeping around and admit it. I even know a couple I think have had opera-tions – but you can't ask."

"They won't tell, you mean."

"I can't wait much longer." The train jerked to a stop. Mary Jean grabbed the edge of the seat with both hands to steady herself. "The longer you wait the more dangerous it is. Besides, I'll go crazy if something doesn't happen pretty soon."

"We're doing the best we can." That sounded sharp, and she didn't mean it to. I'm tired, Joyce excused herself. Tired and worried. It's no use to take it out on the poor kid, though, she has enough already. "We're going to be way late for dinner; you can go right to bed. Me too. I'm pooped."

"Oh, you don't have to be literary tonight?"

"That sounds like a dirty crack."

"Sorry, I guess I'm kind of jumpy."

"Sure."

"I can't wait much longer," Mary Jean said again. "People can tell by the way your eyes look, or something. Besides, it's not safe after three months." She was close to hysteria; it showed in the way she clenched her hands and in the muscle that jerked beneath her ear. "We've got to do something right away."

"Have you ever thought about going ahead and having it?"

"Very funny. I can see myself getting kicked out. It's only three and a half months till this semester's over. I can see Pop's face when I tell him. And the deacon's. He'd never get another church."

"Well, girls do sometimes."

"Yeah. Maybe I could get into some kind of a shelter for immoral girls, or whatever they call it." Mary Jean smiled thinly. "I think they teach you how to do housework. That's a bright future. Anyhow, I think it's a sin to bring a child into the world when you can't even take care of it or anything. An orphan in an orphan asylum, without anybody to even love it."

"I wish you wouldn't talk as if it were a baby already. It's only a little clump of cells."

Mary Jean swallowed. "That's what I keep telling myself. Let's not talk about it any more."

"Okay. You brought it up, I didn't."

They got off the train in Henderson. Same old depot, mellowed by twilight; same old troubles, Joyce thought drearily. Good Lord, were all women's troubles on account of men? They went into the waiting room, for no good reason except both of them were reluctant to go back to school. Nobody was there except an old colored man who was pushing a cloud of dust ahead of a broom, looking as if his feet hurt. Well, Joyce thought, he's not the only one. At that moment she was not as worried about Mary Jean as she thought she should be, because what she wanted more than anything in the world was to take her shoes off and go to bed.

"Let's go downtown and have a drink."

"Okay, let's."

They walked through the streets quickly, not stopping to look at any window displays – typical small-town, stodgy streets that got shabbier as they neared the college. It was silly, Joyce felt, to have such a high-class or anyway high-priced school on the edge of an area like this, but times changed and you couldn't always predict which neighborhoods were going downhill. They walked past the Honey Bee quickly, looking the other way in case some of the girls were inside, and stopped in front of the Bobcat's Den, its neon sign alight, a curvaceous nude with red flashing nipples. Mary Jean looked up at her. "Keep 'em covered, kid. You're likely to get in trouble that way."

"In here?"

"All right."

It was dark inside and nearly empty; it smelled clean, but faintly sour. Colored bubbles of light chased each other around the rim of the giant juke box, which was mercifully silent, and the mirror behind the bar caught and reflected what light there was. Glasses and bottles arranged in artistic stacks and pyramids glittered in the dusk. The faces of the three men sitting perched at the bar were in shadow. "Martini," Mary Jean said. Joyce nodded. She had never been in a bar before – Aunt Gen, who still deplored the passing of Prohibition, called them saloons, and back in Ferndell no nice girl went into one. She looked around curiously, forgetting herself and her tired feet and her worries for a while.

One of the men laid a bill on the bar and stood up to wait for his change. "Hi," he said, nodding to the girls. Mary Jean glanced up. "Hi, Scotty. Working or loafing?"

"Some of both, I guess. What are you beautiful dolls doing out on the town, all dolled up like Mrs. Rockefeller's plush horse? The duchess know you're out?"

"We're like you, we like a break in the monotomy once in a while. How about another Martini, Joyce?"

The drink still stung Joyce's throat. She was terribly thirsty; she would have liked another, but Scotty's eyes were fixed on her inquisitively. She shook her head. "No. You've had enough."

"All right, meanie. If you're in a mood for work," Mary Jean said to Scotty, "why don't you take us back to the salt mine? We're too pooped to walk."

"Take your time. I'll be ready when you are."

Joyce fished the olive out of her glass and chewed it up, dipped a paper napkin into her water glass, and wiped her sticky fingers. She was hungry, too – they hadn't bothered about lunch. The drink and the short rest had perked Mary Jean up; she looked less pallid and she walked out to the taxi almost briskly. Scotty had vanished into the men's room, but they climbed into the back seat and sat there waiting.

Scotty piled in and slammed the door shut. "You kids out lookin' for new hats?"

"Looking for a doctor," Mary Jean said, sounding quite calm and even a little pleased with herself. Joyce thought: Oh dear, she never should have taken that drink.

Scotty shifted gears. "Bellyache?"

"You can call it that."

"I always figured some of you kids knew your way around," Scotty said. "Can't all be lessies in a place like that, the way I got it figgered. Some of 'em's bound to been caught and broke in before they cooped 'um up. Have any luck?"

"Nope."

"Well, hell, you don't have to go outa town for that. Doc Prince right here on Elm Street, he's turned many a one loose in his time. One hundred bucks, and he's as careful as any of 'em. My wife's kid sister, she got fixed up a couple times already."

"That's the one in the Medical Arts Building?"

"Sure." Scotty grazed through an amber light. "You tell him Stella Chivari sent you. He'll give you a shot, too, if it gets hurtin' too bad. Some won't. My wife, she went there with Stell once and she says it's bad, all right, but no worse than having a kid." Scotty swiveled around to look at them. "I guess the dames figure it's worth it, or they wouldn't have it done. When they get in that kind of a fix they can't be bothered by a little pain, right?"

"Right."

"Don't seem fair," Scotty said. "Does it? Us guys get off easy. Hell, I had the clap a couple times when I was in the army, but that ain't nothin'. That's kid stuff. I guess the way it works out for the girls is, they had their fun and now they can take their medicine. Right?"

"Men have fun, too," Joyce said angrily.

"Sure, that's so. Doc give my old woman some fixings to keep her from gettin' caught. Cost seven-fifty, but that's better than havin' your insides scraped ever so often."

"I guess you're right," Mary Jean said.

"Well, it looks like this is it. That's one buck even for the both of you. Hope you make out all right."

"Oh sure, I'm not worried."

And that's a big fat lie, Joyce reflected. She said in a small, angry voice, "He'll tell."

"I don't think so." Mary Jean's voice shook. "You have to take some chances, don't you? Scotty knows plenty about what goes on in this crumby town."

"I bet plenty goes on."

"I bet plenty goes on in this building," Mary Jean said, giving her a sidewise glance.

The campus looked like a movie setting for a girl's school, ivied brick buildings set among spreading trees, the dryness of the grass and sparseness of the leaves veiled by night. Lights came on in windows. Sweatered girls by twos and threes walked down the paths, talking. A pang struck Joyce. If this could only be the way it looked, without dark things hidden underneath. She felt a sudden affection for the place and her classmates, and a deep sadness, as though this day's doings had set her apart from it. She took Mary Jean's elbow as they went up the dormitory steps.

"Will you go to the doctor with me, kid?"

"Sure. Who else were you thinking of asking?"

Chapter Ten

Joyce learned a lot of things in the next week. One was that you can get away with almost anything as long as you keep cool. She had always supposed that someone would be suspicious if you did anything you weren't supposed to, either God, or somebody acting as God's deputy, like Aunt Gen or the teacher. Or maybe the neighbors, about whom Aunt Gen always worried. Now here she was walking around all loaded down with guilty secrets, her own and Edith Bannister's, and most of all Mary Jean's and nobody seemed to have any inkling that anything was wrong. She began to suspect teachers were not in a special class along with ministers and congressmen, but were merely human beings like everyone else and, like everyone else, primarily interested in themselves. It was disillusioning, but a relief.

Another surprising thing was the way time kept expanding and contracting. That was partly because she had mixed emotions on the subject. She wanted desperately to get through the next few weeks and come out on the other side, with all the worry and pain behind her and nothing to dread. But on the other hand, as the day of Mary Jean's appointment with Dr. Prince came closer she was more and more timid about actually going through with it. There were endless stretches when the clock hands didn't seem to move at all, and then she was counting days and the week had gone by and the time was now.

A week can be endless. Five days of going to classes and not hearing a word the teacher said, although she copied blackboard notes docilely with some idea that later she'd do some cramming. Two gym classes, with Miss "Butch" Ryan being sarcastic when she fumbled the ball and then walking down the hall with her afterwards, a bony arm slung across her shoulder and her dark eyes inquisitive and bright beneath that tumbled wad of hair. Any other time that would have bothered her, she would have tormented herself with questions and maybe skipped her gym periods. Now she ignored it.

A week was twenty-one meals in Commons, one Sunday chapel, to which she wore the little velvet calot Mimi had sent from Marshall Field's, and on which she received compliments. And then the week was gone and she wasn't ready to go ahead with the monstrous thing that had to be done to Mary Jean. But there was no choice.

Mrs. Abbott, who normally would have been around with aspirin and tender sympathy to hover over Mary Jean's touch of flu, was happily deflected by two freshmen with chicken pox. She moved into the infirmary and set about nursing them with so much zeal that they did their best to get well and out of there quickly. Now Edith Bannister was the chief hazard, not only because she had sharp eyes and a neat mind, but because Joyce wanted so badly to confide in somebody and she seemed to be the logical person. She didn't stop to ask herself why she should not trust Edith with Mary Jean's woes, but knew it wasn't possible. She tried avoiding her, which worked for two days. Then Edith stopped her in the hall on the way to Spanish class and asked outright, "Is something wrong? Have I done something to offend you?"

"Gosh, no."

"I'd appreciate it if you could get out a few letters this evening. They're piling up." Two students went by, carefully not turning to look back at them, but falling silent as they passed. Joyce took a deep breath. There was no way to get out of it. Besides, now that they were standing side by side on the path she could get a whiff of the light, delicate perfume Edith used, and for her it was evocative of the hours they had spent together. Nostalgia rose in her. She nodded.

She would have to avoid the subject of Mary Jean; if Edith asked, she would have to lie. She wasn't a very good liar – one look from Aunt Gen had been enough to get her stammering and tongue-tied when she was little – but she could give it a try. She would be braced against questioning.

࿊

She was surprised to discover how tired she was. The pencil-scribbled notes blurred before her eyes and her fingers kept hitting the wrong keys, so that after correction the pages looked as if they'd been through a meat grinder. Edith came in at twelve minutes after nine and looked at all the balled-up sheets in the basket. "This isn't important," she said, laying her hands on Joyce's shoulders. "You're too tired for work. For anything. Why don't you go to bed?"

It was all right, lying there between paper-smooth sheets and feeling capable hands turn back the covers under her chin. Like that first day when she had been so groggy and scared, only better, much better, because everything was all right now. She intended to stay awake and worry, but she was very tired; she slept.

She woke around one, feeling light and relaxed. This is best of all, she thought. Edith lay against her, unmoving but awake. Waiting, she thought, and felt a momentary irritation. Then need rose in both of them at once. This time the need was deeper and the pleasure more prolonged than it had ever been. Edith's voice was a thread of whispered emotion when she asked, "Was it good?" and Joyce answered, shaken, "Best yet." They lay side by side, their hands on each other's bodies, while the rapture ebbed away. There was no time or space or circumstance, only completion. They slept.

Once more it was nearly morning when she went back to her own room. Mary Jean was asleep, one hand under her blotched and swollen cheek. She had done so much crying that Joyce wondered where all the tears were coming from. She was sorry for the kid, but she was getting tired of having Mary Jean melt into tears every time she got off into a corner by herself. It couldn't be good for her, either. She got along all right in public; why couldn't she have a little self-control the rest of the time, too?

As she dozed off, she realized that Edith hadn't mentioned anything. Or else she knew all about it and wasn't asking, either to stay free of responsibility or out of a feeling of sympathy. It was smarter not to wonder which.

Mary Jean started out alone, the next afternoon, to keep her appointment with Dr. Prince. She got as far as the railroad arch, then came back and stood at the door of the room, looking like a new first-grader afraid of the other kids. "I can't do it."

"You have to."

"I'm afraid."

Oh, hell. A fine way to spend an afternoon, sitting around in waiting rooms like an expectant father. Joyce jerked on her jacket.

The nurse called Mary Jean into the inner office and she followed, quietly, looking all right except for the swollen eyelids. Joyce sat and looked at the only other waiting patient, a husky high-school girl with a bandaged ankle. After they had smiled at each other a couple of times she began to feel foolish. She got up and looked out the window. From up here she could see into the shopping district, the Square which would have been Main Street at home. Middle-aged women with paper shopping bags went into the dime store. The windows of the cut-rate drugstore were crowded with pyramids of adhesive tape and aspirin boxes on a One-Cent Sale. Red-edged posters advertised a grocery-store special. It seemed crazy that she was sitting here in a doctor's office, waiting for her best friend who was going to have an abortion.

Dr. Prince, when he came out, added to the feeling of unreality. He was a stout, middle-aged man in shiny glasses and one of those white tunic jackets, with his name embroidered on the pocket. He looked like the kind of man who drives a pretty good car, goes to church once in a while, and donates his services to the PTA tonsil-

and-adenoid checkup. He couldn't do a thing like that, she thought in a panic, he'll notify the college and we'll both be expelled. She looked at Mary Jean, who was expressionless. Mary Jean shook hands with the doctor and picked up her purse from the center table, and they walked out side by side.

"He won't do it, will he?"

"Of course he'll do it. Tonight. I can't eat any dinner," Mary Jean said. "We can't go back to the dorm for a couple days, though."

"So then what?"

"Scotty's sister has a cabin out on the lake shore," Mary Jean said wearily. "I don't think it can be much of a place, but anyway, we can be alone there. If you're with me in this."

Joyce waved an impatient hand.

"I sent myself a telegram from home yesterday," Mary Jean said a little smugly, "and asked Abbott to send me home for the weekend because Pop isn't feeling well. I'm supposed to bring along a friend."

"All right," Joyce said, feeling that she was committing herself definitely to something she would rather not do.

"Scotty's going to pick us up at nine."

"Well, aren't you the smart one?"

Two large tears rolled down Mary Jean's cheeks. "I hate myself," she said.

Joyce stopped to look into the window of the easy-payment jewelry store. Diamond engagement rings and watches against dark-blue velvet, with price tags attached. "How much is it going to cost?"

"Two hundred."

"Scotty said one."

"I guess they go by what they think you can pay. Anyway, Bill will give it to me. He promised he'd have it by tonight." Mary Jean's chin trembled. "He's mad at me."

"Well, my God!"

"I know. But this is sort of hard on him, though."

They stopped at the drugstore because Mary Jean had a list of things to get. Joyce read it, looking over her shoulder. They looked at each other. "It'll be all over it by this time tomorrow," Mary Jean said.

"Sure. That doctor looks all right, don't you think?"

"Oh, God Almighty," Mary Jean said prayerfully, "don't talk about it."

They elbowed their way through the crowds of women shopping for drug bargains. Inside, the walls were plastered with sale signs, and piles of merchandise blocked the aisles: flashlights, panda bears in plush, sacks of gumdrops, family-sized bottles of vitamin tablets. Mary Jean shoved her way to a counter where a salesgirl was wrapping hot-water bottles, and handed over her list. Joyce thought the salesgirl looked at her oddly. She should have worn the ring, she thought, but anybody would know what it's for anyhow. She moved away, backing into a wire rack where magazines were displayed. It went down with a clatter. She bent, red-faced, and picked up confession and detective magazines.

This is love, she told herself. You think it's going to be wonderful and this is what it turns into, this horrible sordid thing. She set the last copy of *Ranch Romances* in place and pushed her way to the door, where she could at least breathe fresh air. She was ashamed of Mary Jean. And ashamed of herself too, for getting into a spot like this and for being unkind and hardhearted. She took the bulky package, as if that would help make up for lack of charity. "What's in it that's so big?"

"Everything from a rubber sheet to a thermometer," Mary Jean said in a flat voice. "She suggested the thermometer. Joyce, she knew."

"Sure."

"If I get feverish, I reckon that's blood poisoning."

"You'll be all right. This happens to lots of girls. They get married afterward and have kids and everything."

"Do you think it'll be very bad?"

"I told you, I don't know anything about it."

"I heard about a girl who did it five times. Still, they do die sometimes."

Joyce didn't answer….

Mary Jean went out after they had stowed the big drugstore package in the back of the closet. Joyce didn't bother her with questions. She busied herself packing their suitcases, guessing at what they would need. For the first time she realized that they were actually going to do this crazy thing; there was no getting out of it. They were going off to some shack that belonged to a girl neither of them had ever seen, out in the country away from everybody, and she was going to get Mary Jean through an illegal operation. She had never taken care of a sick person, beyond bringing water and aspirin to Aunt Gen when she was laid up with the grippe. Her own appendectomy had been followed by a sedative-fogged convalescence in the hospital, and Aunt Gen had taken care of her through all the regular childhood diseases. Her hands shook so that she dropped the thermometer and it shattered, the mercury gathering into a little shiny globule that rolled away under the bed.

Mary Jean came in at a little before nine, after she'd started worrying. She had been drinking. At least, Joyce corrected herself, she'd had a drink. You could smell it on her, and she looked more cheerful, or maybe the word was desperate. She sat down on her bed, which Joyce had made up neatly as a farewell gesture, and reached into her pocket. "Ten twenties. Doesn't look like much, does it?"

"Where've you been all this time?"

"Talking to Bill. He feels terrible."

"He ought to."

"If I die, please tell him I don't hold it against him. It might make him feel better. He had tears in his eyes," Mary Jean said sadly.

"Sure, why not? He's afraid of getting blamed for it, if anybody finds out. I suppose you've been out smooching."

"Well, what have I got to lose? I can't get any more pregnant than I am." Mary Jean put her hands over her face, the bravado gone. "It might be the very last time."

Scotty's taxi was at the front door at nine. Edith came to the door with them. She looked closely at Joyce, but Joyce was too preoccupied to worry about the meaning of the look, whether it was reassuring or curious or only affectionate.

They got into the cab and Scotty shut the door, closing them away from the world of safe, normal people. "Here goes nothin'," he said, and Mary Jean laughed, but her fists were clenched. They went quickly through the nighttime streets, not talking or looking at each other.

Chapter Eleven

The waiting was worst. After Mary Jean went into the inner office, blank-faced, as if she were drugged, Joyce was alone in the doctor's reception room. There was a slight but sickening smell of antiseptic in the air, and the old-fashioned banjo clock on the south wall ticked loudly. She walked all around the room, looking intently at the snapshots of babies the doctor had probably delivered and that lithograph of the old family physician sitting beside a child's bed which must be sold by medical supply houses, since you never see it anywhere else. Her footsteps were hollow on the linoleum and she sat down again, embarrassed.

There wasn't a nurse here; Dr. Prince had assured the girls, before he took Mary Jean away, that nobody else would know about this. She guessed that should have convinced her that it wasn't too serious, but it only underlined the furtiveness of what they were doing.

There was a small radio on the end table. She snicked it on, keeping the volume down in case somebody else might be working late in the building. A song floated out, a mushy one with moon and June and love-above. She turned it off, then jerked the plug out of the wall socket.

There was a handful of bobby pins in her jacket pocket; she had taken them out of her hair on the way to an early class one day. So she set her feather cut, tiptoeing out to the hall to wet her comb in the drinking fountain. She was so nervous the pins kept slipping out of her hand and falling on the floor, where they apparently evaporated.

Finally she had a dozen or more little flat curls crisscrossed with wire. Then there wasn't anything else to do, so she took them all out and started again.

This was like waiting in a hospital while someone died. Maybe she will die, Joyce thought. Mary Jean's fears, which had been merely irritating up to this point, suddenly took life and substance. They *do* die sometimes, Joyce thought.

There was no sound from the inner room at all. She sat down in the corner beside the window and concentrated on hating men. If a man put his hand on me I'd kill him, she thought with vicious pleasure. She thought about her father, whom she'd never seen and didn't know anything about. Sometimes when she was younger she used to wonder about him – whether he was a neighbor boy or somebody's hired man or maybe a salesman, whether he died or went away, whether he ever even knew he had fathered a child. Then she quit wondering because there didn't seem to be much point in it; Aunt Gen wasn't giving out any information – had told the young-widow story about Mimi so often she almost believed it herself by this time. Now Joyce hated him, that unknown boy, along with the rest of his sex. He had got Mimi into trouble and left her to fight her way alone in a world that was hard on women, a world where men betrayed women's trust and deserted them.

She thought about the skinny black-haired boy on the beach, and his anger and hurt pride when she refused him. He wouldn't have cared if something like this happened to her; he might even have bragged about it. She knew how boys talked about girls when there weren't any older people around. Of course, she admitted, girls talk too, but that's different.

She remembered, against her will, Irv Kaufman. That was one thing she really wanted to forget. What it was like – and then the kindness and regret in his voice. If he had come into the room at that moment she would probably have killed him.

She hated Bill, too, with his freckles and grin and cocky walk.

Hating was good. It made her feel strong and warm. She smiled, not pleasantly. They'll never catch me that way.

Wonder how long it takes. They scrape you with a little knife, or something. What happens if she gets an infection or bleeds to death. What do they do then? Dump the body in an alley or out on a country road, so the cops can't find out who did it?

Oh, stop making up detective stories. She picked up a magazine and began to turn the pages.

Someone moaned. There was the current of a voice, low, but no words that she could make out. She sat still, waiting for some indication of what was going on in there, half expecting the doctor to appear at the door. But nothing happened.

It was over an hour before the door opened, and then it was Mary Jean who came out. She was dressed, and her hair was combed and her lips freshly reddened. That surprised Joyce, who somehow expected the suffering to show. Dr. Prince followed her. He had taken off his jacket, his shirt sleeves were rolled to the shoulder, and he looked tired and heavy-eyed.

"She'll be all right," he said to Joyce. "She's had a slug of penicillin to prevent infection. Get her right to bed and keep her there for a couple days. And look, there's a phone at that shack of Stell's. If she starts to hemorrhage, or if her temperature goes above one hundred, call me at home." He sounded conscientious, like a doctor talking to the mother of a child who'd had a tonsillectomy. She still found it hard to believe he had done this thing. Still, there was the two hundred dollars. "She's had food poisoning," he added with a small, dry smile.

Wonder how his wife feels about this. Does she know? Do they talk about it, go over the budget together and decide which bills to pay with the money?

"She'll start some time during the night," Dr. Prince finished.

"But I thought it was all over."

He didn't answer that. "Mind, call me if you run into any trouble."

She couldn't imagine being in any more trouble than they were in right then. She took Mary Jean's arm as they started downstairs, but Mary Jean pulled away. A small dim light burned in the deserted foyer. Mary Jean shoved the plate-glass door open, leaning against it as if it were heavy, and they came out into the chilly night air. Scotty was waiting at the wheel of his cab, cap pulled down over his eyes. He opened the door for them. "Everything okay?"

"Sure."

"Let's hit the road."

They drove out of town by the back road Bill had taken the night of the blanket party. Memory made Joyce shiver, but if it had any association for Mary Jean she gave no sign. She sat very still, looking straight ahead. After two or three miles they left the gravel road and turned off on a narrow trail that wasn't really a road at all, just a place where cars had gone, long grass standing up between two wheel tracks. Mary Jean stirred and said, "Gonna be sick," and Scotty stopped the car at once, as though he had expected this, and helped her out. When she was through vomiting she stood for a moment leaning against a tree, wiping her mouth on her coat sleeve. "Hysterical," Scotty said helpfully. "It's the worry."

"Like to lie down," Mary Jean whispered. "My head feels funny."

The shack, Stella Chivari's shack, was set in a little clearing surrounded by second-growth timber and bushes. It was a little summer cottage, like people at home built along the riverbank for weekend fishing trips. A cane-seat rocker stood on the front stoop. Indoors, the circle of Scotty's flashlight traveled over a couple of wicker chairs with beat-up cretonne cushions, a davenport with one broken spring sticking up through the leatherette seat, a small stand that held a telephone and a kerosene lamp. Scotty scratched a match on the sole of his shoe, lifted the glass chimney, and a ring of soft yellow light sprang forth and widened. Joyce, standing beside him, picked up the phone and was reassured by the hum of the dial tone, promising contact with the outside world in case of any of the emergencies she vaguely pictured and acutely dreaded.

Behind a semi-partition was a sagging double bed freshly made up, an apple-crate cupboard with dishes and canned goods behind a cloth curtain, a three-burner kerosene stove on a small table. Scotty checked the supplies. "Pump out back. Rest of the conveniences, too. Stell, she keeps this place in pretty good shape." He grinned, eyes dark and gleaming under the cracked visor of his leather cap. "You might meet Stell's boss sometime. He helps run that female school of yours. Type his letters daytimes and sleep with him nights, that's what I call earnin' it the hard way."

Mary Jean sat down on the bed and put her head down between her knees. "I'll see you later," she said, muffled. Scotty nodded. "Sure, that's all right."

"Fifty bucks," Mary Jean said when the door closed behind him. "For that he could say thank you."

Joyce was surprised. She had been taking it for granted that Scotty was helping them out of the goodness of his heart, the way neighbors do when someone's in trouble. Grow up, she told herself severely. Nobody does anything for nothing. Except me – I was born to be the fall guy. She helped Mary Jean pull off her clothes and get into bed. Mary Jean's forehead was cold but her face was beaded with sweat and the back of her blouse, between the shoulders, was soaked through and stuck to her skin. She lay flat in the middle of the sway-back bed with her eyes shut. Joyce said, "Was it very bad?"

"I don't want to talk about it."

That was a switch, anyhow. "Is it all right if I go out and look the place over?"

"Go ahead."

She forgot the flashlight, but moon silver lay over the path and the tangle of weeds and bushes in the back yard. There was an old-fashioned backhouse with a crescent cut in the door, such as some of the farmers around home still used. The pump was at the corner of the house, set in a cement slab. From here she couldn't see the lake, but the air felt fresh and cool on her cheeks. Crows stirred in the treetops, cawing sleepily. She thought it would be fun to come out here in the daytime, or with a bunch of girls for a weekend. The time of slumber parties and Scout camp lay a long way behind her, a lost land of innocence. She went back into the house.

Mary Jean was lying still, staring at the ceiling. She said dully, "It'll start some time in the night. He gave me some pills to take if it gets too bad."

"It'll be all right."

"If it gets too bad, you call the doctor. I don't want to die."

"Look, quit worrying."

Mary Jean's face didn't change, but tears spilled over her eyelids and ran slowly down her cheeks. "I've killed my baby," she whispered.

"It was only a clump of cells like in the biology book."

"Yeah, I know. Don't pay any attention to me."

Joyce lay on the davenport, her legs pulled up because it was even too short for her five-two, and her body curled around to avoid the broken spring. Her back and legs ached with fatigue and tension, and her eyes hurt. I have to stay awake, she admonished herself, staring at the lamp's flame, which she had turned down to a thread. The chimney was already getting smoky, and the furniture made giant shadows on the walls. I have to keep awake. Suppose it doesn't work? She shut her eyes for a second, to rest them.

It was almost morning when she woke, to the sound of somebody groaning. She sat up, trying to figure out where she was and what was happening. "What's the matter?"

Mary Jean's upper lip was pulled back so that her teeth showed. Her pajamas were soaked through with sweat. In the yellowish light from the lamp the circles under her eyes were black. "I think I'm going to die," she said. She pulled her knees up convulsively.

Joyce turned the lamp up, so that a streamer of soot blackened the chimney. This wasn't something you saw in a movie or read about in a book; this was really happening right here and now. Her hands shook. Men, she thought. I wouldn't let a man touch me, not if I lived a million years. Aloud she said, "Don't be scared, I won't let anything happen to you."

Chapter Twelve

Mary Jean was being unreasonable. She should have been jumping up and down and yelling with joy because she was out of trouble, not lying in bed like a doll with all the stuffing out of it, bawling, shaking her head and refusing to answer when you asked her what was the matter, refusing to eat after you'd stood over the damn smoky oilstove for an hour trying to fix up something appetizing.

"Do you hurt anywhere?"

"I'm all right." Mary Jean lay on her back, crying without sound or change of expression. The tears ran down her cheeks and trickled coldly into her ears and the edge of her hair. "Let me alone," she said in a weak voice.

Joyce sighed. "Look, you couldn't have had it."

"I know it."

They had been over and over this. Joyce looked around the cabin to see what still needed doing. She had already swept the floor, driving clouds of dust ahead of the broom, and washed the breakfast dishes.

It was a fine crisp day; goldenrod mixed with the weeds in the backyard and there was a sprinkling of brown-eyed Susan along the barbwire fence that bounded it. Oak leaves were sailing down silently in the windless air. Joyce threw her shoulders back and took a deep breath. It was quiet out here, like on the farm. The first quiet place she'd been in for quite a while The solitude rested her, but also made her feel uneasy. She wasn't sure whether she liked it or not. She stood for a moment in the sunshine, planning her day.

Almost eleven. She was hungry already. Be some point to cooking if Mary Jean would eat instead of turning her face away as if the thought of food repelled her. It might be fun to cook if you had somebody to cook *for*. I wish I had a man and a bunch of kids, she thought; they'd come in from work and school all hungry and tired out and I'd have supper on the stove. The wish, primitive and unexpected, rose to the surface of her mind from some place where it had been simmering. She quickened her steps as if she might walk away from it.

For the last two days she hadn't thought about anything much except Mary Jean and her danger; when she stopped working with her hands for a moment the sickening fear of exposure rose in her, so she kept busy. All through the first day, when Mary Jean lay half asleep under the mingled influence of pain and aspirin, moaning now and then, tossing when a cramp struck, she had been obsessed with the dread that something might still go wrong. She stayed by the bedside, not knowing what to do and yet afraid to turn her back. Then, when the pains let up and they were sure the operation had been successful, she was too weak with relief to look farther than the next chore.

It was surprising how much work there was, keeping house in a place like this. Simply fixing meals took a lot of planning, in a place without electricity or running water.

It was the first time she had ever taken the responsibility for running a house. She wondered how Aunt Gen did it, even with electrical appliances. Aunt Gen had time for PTA and church doings too, she reminded herself, pushing back her hair and leaving a sooty smudge on her forehead.

She opened the cans of food and dumped them into sauce pans, lit the round burner of the kerosene range, and stood back as the flame flared orange and angry almost to the ceiling. There was always this nervous moment before it settled down to a clear, hot blue circle. She burned her finger on the edge of the pan and said, "Oh, damn!" in a heartfelt way. Mary Jean stirred but didn't say anything. She ignored her tray when it was fixed, simply lay there with tears running down her face and making little damp blisters on the pillowcase.

I'm going to call the doctor, Joyce decided. It can't be good for her, all this bawling, and it sure isn't helping me any.

She took her plate out to the front porch, which was just a square of boards measuring about five feet each way, and sat down with her back against the house wall and her legs stretched out in front of her. Food tasted finer out here in the fresh air – delicious canned beans, wonderful Vienna sausage. She wiped up the juice with a piece of bread and peeled back the foil from a Hershey.

Chewing, she tried to sort out her thoughts. What was happening back at the college? Was there really such a place? Could you drive a few miles down the road, steer through a shopping center, and actually be there? Open a door without anyone stopping you, walk up stairs that were familiar to the feet, go into your own room and find your stuff there? She doubted it. Maybe it was only a movie she'd seen and remembered, solid brick buildings set among trees and a stone library with ivy growing up around the windowsills and long tables with drop-lamps above them. The gym, floor marked off in black lines and circles for basketball, high, wire-screened windows, skeletal rows of bleachers. At this moment girls she knew were taking notes on the Renaissance, practicing "Panis Angelicus" in the auditorium for next Sunday's chapel.

It seemed unlikely.

Edith Bannister seemed unreal too. She had expected the thought of Edith, when she finally got around to it, to be sharp with hurt. She had not, in fact, supposed that she could possibly be away from Edith three days without missing her acutely. She had been too busy and worried to have time for loneliness, up to now, but she hadn't doubted that it was lying in wait for her as soon she had a chance to pay some attention to it. Now she thought about Edith, and there was no reality in it. All she got was a flat two-dimensional picture.

She shut her eyes and tried to remember Edith's voice, the deepened and roughened timbre of it in their moments of closeness. All she got was the sleepy cawing of crows in the tops of the oak trees, resting through the hot part of the day before they fanned out over the countryside in search of their evening meal. She tried to conjure up the remembered pressure of Edith's body against hers and the soft firmness of her flesh under searching hands. But it wasn't real. It was a story she'd read someplace. What was real was this sunshine on the back of her neck and the splintery roughness of boards under her palm.

But I love her, she thought. She opened her eyes on stalky weeds and almost bare trees. A sparrow hopped up to the edge of the porch and stood looking at her, its head cocked. She threw out the crumbs of her meal, but the gesture alarmed the bird and it flew off. She got up a little stiffly and went into the house, picking up Mary Jean's untouched dishes. Mary Jean was lying with her face to the wall; Joyce couldn't tell whether she was crying or sleeping.

She called the doctor's house number. He wasn't there. A calm, satisfied voice – a wifely voice – said that he was at the hospital and did she care to leave a message? She hadn't counted on this. Half a dozen times in the last two days she had lifted the receiver and listened to the humming, comforted that if things really went badly wrong there was help for her. Now she felt cheated. She left her name, hesitating, tried to frame a message that would mean something to him and nobody else, and gave it up. She felt that he had to come; she couldn't stand any more of this. She could have cried like Mary Jean, she was so tired, but it would have been too silly.

She jerked the sheets straight, and said "We're going back pretty soon, you know. You better straighten up and start thinking up a good story for Abbott."

Mary Jean said, "Oh, to hell with Abbott."

Joyce put the dishes in the pan with a lot of unnecessary rattling and took them out to wash under the pump – sanitary or not, it was easier that way. She couldn't help thinking that she could have gone through Mary Jean's operation, if she had to, with a lot less fuss.

When the doctor did come he wasn't alone, and that surprised her too. A young man was driving the car, a boy really, not much older than she was. At the sight of him she felt self-conscious and somehow ashamed, perhaps because her slacks were wrinkled and her blouse dirty and she hadn't set her hair. He didn't seem to be aware of her embarrassment. He slid out from under the wheel and stood looking around. "My nephew," Dr. Prince said proudly. "He'll have the practice when I'm too old to work, likely. No –" as she moved towards the house – "you young people stay out here and get acquainted. I'll call you if I need you."

So she was alone with a strange boy and the whole outdoors, and nothing to say. She looked at him. He was slim and flat-hipped, naked from the waist up, as if he'd been showering or taking a nap when his uncle called him; the hair on his chest was curly yellowish-red, but his head bristled with bright red that would have curled if the barber hadn't practically scalped him. He had freckles and narrow gray-green eyes. She didn't know whether she liked his looks or not. "My name's John," he said. "You live out here?"

"Oh no." She was startled; did she look like the kind of a person who would live in a place like this?

"What's the matter with your sister, or whoever she is?" Not very interested; making conversation.

She blurted, "She had an operation. You know – an operation."

He stared at her. Color rose in her face. She backed away. "You got Uncle Doc out here to clean up after some quack?"

"Well, he did it."

His jaw dropped. She had often read about jaws dropping, but she hadn't supposed it ever really happened. "You're lying," he said.

"Why would I lie?"

"He wouldn't do a thing like that. He's a doctor."

Anger burned in her. He was all the safe, respectable, moral people from whom she was alienated by this week's happenings; he was on the other side – the enemy, out to hurt her. All right, she would hurt him first. "He does it all the time," she said coldly. "The girl that owns this place, she's had two operations from him. Even the cab drivers know about it. How do you think Mary Jean found out?" For a moment there was silence. She gave him a cold, triumphant smile. They stood looking at each other. "Lots of doctors do it," she said in a thin voice. She turned and walked to the porch, leaving him alone.

Dr. Prince came out, pulling off a rubber glove. "She's all right," he said cheerily. "This depression is perfectly normal. Glands. She'll be all right when she gets up and around."

"When?"

"Tomorrow." He lowered his voice. "I don't have to remind you to keep still about this, do I? It wouldn't be so good for any of us if anybody found out." He glanced past her to the boy standing motionless under the trees.

For a moment she was sorry she had betrayed him. Then she hardened her heart. "I won't tell," she said, looking him in the face. After he went out she pulled down the dusty paper shade that covered the front window.

That was a crumby thing to do, she scolded herself. She leaned her head against the door frame, feeling tired past words. I hate him. I don't even know what his name is. John what? Who does he think he is? She went into the back room and stood by the bed. "You can stop crying now and get up," she said firmly. "We've had about enough of this foolishness." She sounded like Aunt Gen.

Mary Jean's eyes widened with surprise. "All right," she said. She pushed back the blanket.

Chapter Thirteen

Winter came overnight, not with stinging snow and heaped drifts as in Illinois, but with heavy fog and a day-after-day drizzle that made everything soggy to the touch. The smart faille raincoat Mimi sent to Joyce was about as effective as tissue paper against this soft, permeating wetness. Joyce tried it on in front of the mirror and was delighted with the lines, but she came back to her room after walking across the campus in it and threw it across a chair in disgust, the lining clammily damp and dark streaks showing along all the seams.

Her feet were never dry. Mary Jean's suede pumps, shoved back under the bed and forgotten, were spotted with mildew when the maid finally swept them out. The countryside was a monotony of gray and tan. Dispositions dragged and drooped, roommates who had been happily wearing each other's clothes all fall almost came to blows over a pair of nylons, and Edith Bannister got five applications for change of residence in one afternoon. Everyone was too bored and dejected to study, except for a few conscientious A pupils like Bitsy, and grades would have gone down like lead sinkers if the teachers hadn't been informed about curve grading and the social promotion.

"This would be a good place to wear a fur coat if you had one," Joyce said.

"The sunny South," Mary Jean said. Her voice was dull. Joyce gave her a worried and warning look. She seemed all right, and said she felt fine, and Dr. Prince had given her a general going-over two weeks after the operation and found her condition good. But the sparkle was gone. She spent a good deal of time in bed, not reading or anything but lying there looking vacant. Joyce felt uneasily that even when she was doing something, like eating, or writing themes, she wasn't quite all there. The oval of her face had sharpened and she looked older.

As far as anyone could tell, though, they had gotten away with it. Joyce could hardly believe it, even now. Sooner or later, she figured, someone would ask an innocent sounding question or let some remark slip to show that everyone knew they hadn't spent those three days in North Carolina, that everyone knew what had really happened. She still watched faces sharply and listened for undercurrents of intonation that would betray knowledge. She stayed close to Mary Jean, as much as she was able, ready to cover up for her. Now she was beginning to relax in the hope that they were safe. It was over. She looked at Mary Jean, standing between Ann and Claudia, and rubbed a hand across her forehead in bewildered relief. "Come on, let's go. It isn't going to get any dryer."

"I hate this place," Mary Jean said.

Joyce wondered if she hated it too. There were times when she would have given anything to be somewhere else – anywhere else. Other times, she would have liked to go back to that first hot day in September and start over. Or even be back in high school, back on the farm. A picture of Aunt Gen's kitchen flickered through her mind. You came in from the school bus around this time of day, just dusk, and the house would smell of good cooking. Neighbors might make their cakes and cookies from packaged mixes, but Aunt Gen kept her recipes written down by hand and pasted in old school notebooks. My Best Cookies, Mrs. Sullens' Potato Salad, Grandma Bates' Gingerbread. That was how the kitchen smelled.

There would be a length of dress goods spread out on the dining-room table, and Aunt Gen might be sitting at the rolltop desk in the kitchen, bringing the farm accounts up to date. Uncle Will said you had to be a doggone cross between Burbank and Einstein to make a living farming these days. For just a moment Joyce was violently homesick, so that her arms and legs ached and her vision fogged.

You can't go home again; Wolfe knew what he was talking about. You can't be a kid jogging over gravel roads in a school bus. She sighed, feeling heavy with age.

"Matter with you, Smilin' Sam?" Mary Jean said.

"Tired." Joyce looked at her sharply, now the other two were walking ahead on the narrow path. "You feel all right?"

"Oh, honestly! I told you a million times, I'm fine."

"You don't have to bite my head off."

Mary Jean shut up.

Joyce scuffed her loafers on the door mat of the dorm, noticing that water actually oozed out of the them. A yellow smear of mud. Even the earth down here didn't look like real dirt. It was an ugly yellow hardpan when dry and a churned-up sticky mess when wet. You couldn't imagine planting in it, though of course people did. "I hate it too," Joyce said sadly.

"What else is new?"

"You sure you're not running any fever?"

Mary Jean scowled. "Anybody'd think I was married to you, the way you nag."

"I'm only asking for your own sake," Joyce said stiffly.

She was tired. Nobody had ever told her that fright and suspense had a physical aftermath – fatigue, this ache in the back and arms, this fuzzy feeling in the head. She was glad to flop down on her own bed, unmade as usual.

Mary Jean sat down on the desk chair and stared into the middle distance. "Bill called," she said tightly. "I don't think I want any dinner."

"You going out with him?"

"I'm scared, I don't think I could stand it," Mary Jean said. "Going through all that again." Two tears rolled down her face. "I think about it all the time; I wake up in the middle of the night and think about it."

"Well, for heaven's sake! Quit, why don't you?"

"I'm his girl," Mary Jean said. "He's the first fellow I ever – well, he is. All the way, anyhow." She frowned at Joyce, daring her to contradict that. "I did a lot of dating in high, but I never – Bill was the first one."

"I don't see what that has to do with it."

"You can't break up just like that. Not if you've really had anything together."

"That's crazy."

"You don't know." The voice of experience, full of scorn for the uninitiate. Joyce bit back her answer. "Anyhow," Mary Jean said dully, "that's the kind of a girl I am. Like my mother. If it wasn't Bill it would be somebody else."

Joyce struggled on, though there didn't seem to be any special point to it. "You're not going to marry the guy, are you? Well then, you'll have to bust up some day."

"Not till he wants to."

"Then you'll be the one that gets hurt."

"I reckon so. Look here," Mary Jean said, pulling at the edge of the dresser scarf, "do you believe in sin? That God punishes people, and so on?"

"I don't know."

"Oh, well." She let it go. "You think an operation like that could do something to a person's insides, or something? I always figured I was real normal. Only that's a thing you wouldn't know anything about, come to think of it."

This was it. She had known Mary Jean knew. Probably a lot of people knew. But knowing was one thing. Hearing her say it out loud was something else. Lesbian. Abnormal. Perverted. Words people didn't say, no matter how aware they may be of them, hung on the air. Joyce stood exposed and shamed, her secrets dragged out of their dark corner and held up to crude daylight. She grabbed at a defense. "That sounds like a dirty crack," she said hoarsely.

"You're damn right it does. No female fairy can tell me anything about love."

"You don't know anything about it," Joyce said hotly.

"Sure I know. I was adolescent once." Mary Jean's voice sounded tired and a little disgusted. "I went through all that when I was about fourteen, for about three weeks. Bro-ther! I thought I was the most romantic thing since Sappho."

Joyce didn't know who Sappho was, but this had an irritatingly familiar ring to it. The voice of convention Edith was always talking about, the pack baying after those who were different. "You've got a dirty mind," she said.

"I've got eyes," Mary Jean said. She picked up a pencil and rolled it over and over on the desk, under her flattened palm. "What do you get out of it, for God's sake? That's what I'd like to know. There can't be any real kick to it, no more than you can get for yourself if it comes to that. That stuff is just the preliminary bout, that's to wake you up and get you hot for the main act. The big thing." She grinned unwillingly. "That was real corny, I didn't mean it the way it sounded. It's true though, you don't get the real big thrill till you've had the whole works."

I've had it, Joyce thought of saying, and believe me it wasn't anything to brag about. She looked at the floor. "It must be wonderful," she said.

"I'll tell you something else, too, you'll never get from a Lesbian. The more you do it with a man, the better it gets."

"Yeah," Joyce said, "it must be delightful. As Abbott would say. Counting the days on your fingers and marking the calendar and wondering if you'll get caught this time or maybe not till next month. You don't know how I envy you."

Mary Jean took a deep breath. Let it out again slowly, like a mother praying for patience with a troublesome child. "You're a mean little bitch," she said evenly. "I've been trying to kid myself maybe you weren't really perverted, maybe you're just going through a phase. Retarded development. Maybe something happened to make you scared of men, I told myself. Maybe you'd outgrow it. Of course," she said thoughtfully, "I still can't see why you picked Bannister, of all people. I can't feature her getting hot for anybody, male or female or half-and-half. She's so goddamn self-centered."

"You take that back."

"What for? It's true."

"I happen to love her."

"Oh, sweet Jesus." Joyce wasn't sure whether Mary Jean was swearing or praying, or some of both. Or whether she was laughing or getting ready to cry, if it came to that. Her shoulders shook and her voice was blurry. "What gives you the idea that you know anything about love? Why don't you grow up?"

"I'd rather be that way than go around having abortions," Joyce said. "It may not be normal, but then maybe you think murdering babies is a nice thing to do."

"I wondered when that was coming. That's the one I've been waiting for."

"Now you don't have to wonder any more."

Mary Jean smiled. It was a thin smile rimmed with malice. Joyce refused to see the hurt under it. "You can move out of here any time you feel like it – I had the room first, you know. It'll be kind of a relief, not having you sneak in here in the middle of the night stinking like that woman's perfume."

"It's no worse than you sneaking in stinking like some college boy's cheap liquor."

"I never did like queers much."

"That's gratitude," Joyce said. Her voice was trembling. She stopped and swallowed. "After all I did for you when you were sick. After all the big fat lies I had to tell, covering up for you."

"I'm sorry I've been so much trouble to you," Mary Jean said formally. She didn't sound sorry. "You can tell on me any time you want. Of course you're pretty involved, yourself." She got up, stretching, walked to the dressing table and switched on the side lights. "I can always tell on you, too," she said, taking a bobby pin out of her hair and running the comb carefully through its feathered edges. "It might be fun to bring some charges against your two-faced friend while I'm at it, too. What have I got to lose?"

Joyce was cold. "Don't be silly," she said quickly. "Why would I tell on you?"

Mary Jean crossed to the closet. Even in anger Joyce noticed how graceful she was, what pretty legs she had. Mary Jean took her plaid jacket off the hanger. "You never can tell what perverts are likely to do." She shoved her arms into the sleeves, humming a little.

"Where are you going?"

"Out," Mary Jean said. "I'm going to go out and get drunk. A girl has to have some little pleasures in life."

She didn't slam the door. She shut it quietly.

Joyce sat there. No noise distracted her; everyone else had gone down to dinner and the halls were mealtime-quiet. I've lost my best friend, she thought. She would have liked to cry, but she had forgotten how.

Edith, she thought. But it was only a word, no reality in it. In the two weeks since they had been back, she had seen Edith only in public for brief, unsatisfactory moments. Edith had been away for several days at a convention of college and university deans, and they had exchanged whispers in corners and looks in the dining room – that was all. The secretary fiction had been laid aside for a while through the pressure of events, with no need for any scheming on her part. She had been too worried and tired to care much, but now she turned for reassurance to the thought of remembered tenderness.

Edith, she whispered. But it didn't mean much, it didn't stir her to desire or bring any consolation.

Mary Jean's voice echoed in the room. What do you know about love?

Mimi, she thought. All her childhood long, when Aunt Gen spanked her or Uncle Will scolded, when her report card was poor or she squabbled with a friend, she had consoled herself with the idea that Mimi loved her, anyway. Some day Mimi would send for her and they would never be separated any more. Now it didn't work. The magic gone. The picture that rose to her mind was of a monstrous and repulsive swelling, a disfigurement of that slender, tense body. I hope I don't have to see her until after the baby's born, she thought, but the baby didn't seem real and it was true, though she hated to admit it even to herself, that she dreaded seeing Mimi ever again. The thought of Mimi brought with it a sense of outrage connected with Irv Kaufman.

After a while she got up, pulled off her clothes and got into bed. She turned the light off, but in the dark a vague unease overcame her and she turned it on again. It was really raining now, beating against the shut window and streaming down the panes. She wondered where Mary Jean was, if she was warm and dry in the back of Bill's car or sitting in a tavern or maybe in some rented room somewhere, and if she would get home without catching cold. She was angry at Mary Jean, but worrying about her had become habit and she couldn't throw it off. She lay awake for a long time with the light on, ready to jump up and fetch dry towels and aspirin if they should be needed, but Mary Jean didn't come home. Finally she fell asleep, to wake now and then and wish heavily that she didn't have to get up in the morning.

Chapter Fourteen

Mary Jean showed up at breakfast the next morning. She wore the same clothes she had on when she left, so she evidently hadn't got back in time to change. There was a slight stale odor of alcohol hanging around her and a spot near the hem of her skirt, as if a stain had been imperfectly sponged off. But she looked neat, the hems of her stockings were straight and her face freshly, if generously, made up. Only the purple smudges under her eyes and the slight trembling of her hands when she lifted her coffee cup, the small rattling it made against the saucer, betrayed the fact that she had been out all night. Joyce was impressed once more by the fact that it's possible to get away with a great deal as long as you remain calm about it.

She was ready to be polite if Mary Jean spoke to her. To forgive her, even, and let things go on the way they were before the quarrel. She felt magnanimous. But Mary Jean, sitting down at the far end of the table, didn't look her way or offer any greeting. She sat stiff and straight, breaking up her food with the fork but not eating anything, drinking cup after cup of black coffee as if she were famished with thirst. When the meal was over she got up without a word to anyone and walked out. Joyce had brought her books downstairs, and there was no way she could follow Mary Jean up to the room without seeming to be apologetic. She went off slowly, feeling that everything was a mixed-up mess and she'd like to go back to bed and sleep for a week.

She got through an hour of Art Appreciation blankly, forgetting to hand in the report she had toiled over all one afternoon, and

138 | *Whisper Their Love*

then wandered over to the gym and changed into her blue romper for folk dancing. Miss Ryan came over and leaned against her while her section was waiting on the bottom row of the bleachers. Leaned against her, breathing close to her ear. Joyce saw the exchange of glances between some of the other girls, the quick look her way, the tactful glancing away, the knowing expressions they exchanged with each other. It didn't matter – much. She was aware of a vague relief as Miss Ryan moved away, cracking out in a sergeant's voice at the group already on the floor. Her head ached and she felt drowsy and confused.

I'll forgive and forget even if it kills me, she promised the vague sense of guilt that had attached itself to her.

When she got back to the dorm, dragging her feet, it was evident that she wasn't going to be given a chance to forgive anybody. The room was in much the same state of confusion as when she first saw it. Everything Mary Jean owned, and a few things she had borrowed and forgotten to give back, had been dragged out of the closet, dresser, and desk. Clothes and books lay around on the beds and both chairs and all over the floor, dresses with their belts trailing and the hangers sticking up under the shoulder seams, mismated shoes, her plaid housecoat. The beds were littered with the cosmetics May Jean was always buying and not using, and the prescriptions she was always getting filled and not taking. There wasn't a bare inch of floor space: pastel tissues, wads of nylon stockings, candy wrappers, pages of lecture notes, clutter. Joyce stood in the doorway a moment, spellbound at the confusion. Then she realized that Mary Jean would be coming back any minute for another load, and the thought of bumping into her wasn't pleasant, in spite of all the noble resolutions. Joyce threw down her books, sorted out the ones she would need after lunch, and fled. I'll cope with it some time but right now, she told herself, I've had about all that I can take.

Groups of girls were in the before-meal huddle all over the downstairs hall and the lounge and the stairs. They chirped and chattered like birds, a pretty girlish sound if you weren't feeling sick. Mary Jean was nowhere in sight, but Edith Bannister detached herself from a waiting group and walked over to Joyce, a thing she very seldom did. "I've got to talk to you," she said in a low voice.

"It's lunch time."

"This won't wait."

Joyce followed her into the study, head down, like any girl about to be scolded by the teacher. Whatever it was, it wasn't going to be good. She stood and waited.

Edith shut the study door and turned the latch. She put a finger under Joyce's chin and lightly, delicately turned her face up. The two pairs of eyes met. Joyce began to tremble. This is it, she thought. This is where I spill the whole thing. Sadness grew in her because she had gone through all that mess for no purpose, wasted so much danger and terror. She moved her shoulders a little, but the intent look in Edith's eyes held her.

"What's the matter between you and Mary Jean Kennedy?"

The question fell so far to the side of the real issue that Joyce's eyes widened in surprise. I don't really care any more, she told herself – and knew she was lying. She felt her way carefully. "She wants to be out all the time," she said. "Nights. She runs around all the time."

"That doesn't concern you. Unless you're jealous. Are you jealous? Are you starting to care for her?"

"Gosh, no."

Edith dropped her hand to Joyce's shoulder. "You must see that this puts me in a spot," she said reasonably. "As a dean, I'm supposed to keep an eye on my students. Their morals are my affair. Of course, as a reasonable adult I believe that the sex life of any person is his own affair." She smiled, ruefully. "If your little chum wants to howl on every back fence from here to St. Louis, it's nothing to me – as long as she's discreet about it. This is off the record, of course."

"Sure."

She stroked Joyce's shoulder, narrow rosy nails against the dark sweater. "If you get involved, then I *am* concerned. You know why."

"Please don't worry about it."

"When you went to Charlotte together, when her father was supposed to be sick." Edith hesitated. She's afraid to ask, Joyce thought, and pushed the thought out of her mind because she couldn't imagine Edith being afraid of anything. "Anyone else, in my place, would have called up her father or something. I didn't. I knew there was something, but I trusted you. Where did you really go?"

She doesn't know at all, Joyce realized, or she's playing dumb – but that's not likely. Even now she couldn't betray Mary Jean; it would have been the denial of her own qualms and protective efforts. There are a few things you can't do. "We went to Charlotte," she said stubbornly.

"You didn't go somewhere to be together?"

"No."

"Then you were with men. If you can call those pimple-faced boys of hers men."

Joyce jerked away. "Look, you've got it all wrong," she said angrily. It was the first time she had ever opposed Edith or denied her anything. She stopped, because what could she say without either telling the disastrous truth, or making up some long story nobody would believe anyway?

Edith's eyes widened. "It's all right. I trust you."

Joyce began talking rapidly to cover up her anxiety and to comfort Edith, because Edith looked on the verge of weeping and it was embarrassing to see anyone so self-possessed cry. "We had a fight because she kept coming in late and waking me up. She got mad and moved out. She's messy, too." It seemed like a good idea to pile up all the evidence she could against Mary Jean, to distract attention from her real crime. "She never picks anything up."

"You're not so tidy yourself," Edith said. Her lips were warm against Joyce's hair. The lunch buzzer sounded. "Oh, damn. Look, darling, I'll come up to you late tonight. Mary Jean's going in with

Bitsy for a while; you know Bitsy's been alone since that girl from California flunked out." Her arms tightened. "Oh God, kiss me. Quick."

The kiss made up in intensity what it lacked in time. Joyce stood still for a moment, inside the door, before she felt her face compose itself. Thank God for smearproof lipstick, she thought; it would be too awful if anybody guessed. It was all she could do to keep from putting her hand to her mouth, or looking around to see if the others were watching her.

But I never cared. I honestly didn't, before. Then why now? She thought, laying her napkin across her knees, how awful it would be if anyone were to find out.

I wish she'd let me alone for a while, she thought suddenly. I wish I could go back and start over, I don't know if I'd do it all over again or not.

She thought about it, chewing and swallowing, but it wasn't a yes-and-no matter and she couldn't make up her mind. She gave it up.

Chapter Fifteen

Joyce made a point of staying away from the room all afternoon. She was dreading the prospect of another fight with Mary Jean, and also she was pretty sure there would be something popping if they bumped into each other now, tired and hurt as they both were.

But there was more than that. She had this silly feeling her home was being broken up, the only home she had. It didn't make sense, but there it was.

The stay in Stella Chivari's shack had been a turning point in her feeling about the school. She didn't know why it should work that way, but there it was. After all her feeling of remoteness and unreality, when she got back the place had enfolded her with a dear familiarity. She hadn't known it was possible to put down roots so quickly in a place where she hadn't felt quite at ease. Now she was almost afraid to find everything different. It was like the breakup of a family. Not because she was so crazy about Mary Jean, she reasoned, but because things have changed. She told herself that it would be heavenly to have things neat and quiet, not to have anybody sneaking in at two, three o'clock in the morning; she told herself Mary Jean ought to be ashamed of herself. But all the time she had the sick letdown feeling that follows a family quarrel.

So she stayed downstairs after classes, and when dinner had dragged to its routine tapioca-custard close she wandered around for a while, picking up copies of fashion magazines off the window seats at the end of the hall, glancing at the preposterous exaggerated styles without interest and laying them down again. A couple of young men wandered in and sat down on the window seat, obviously waiting for their dates, and their appraising looks made her uneasy. She knew that her sweater and skirt were all right, and she had gone to have her hair done a few days before, but she felt as if her clothes were all twisted and lopsided and she needed a bath. She looked into the lounge, but some kind of a committee meeting was going on in there, so she started out again. Just then a small red-haired freshman whizzed around the corner and yelled, "Hey, Cameron, you got company. Front door."

She hadn't expected ever to see John again. She hadn't expected anybody, but him least of all. He stood at the head of the stairs, looking even more like a faun – she wasn't sure what a faun was but she knew that was what he looked like – in pressed slacks and a loud sport shirt. His hair was even redder than she remembered it. "Hi," he said grinning. "Look, I have to talk to you."

"I'm busy."

"You don't understand, I *have* to talk to you. Where would you like to go?"

"I don't care where *you* go," she said impatiently. "I have studying to do." She waited.

He laid one hand on the newel post. "You're the most unreasonable person I ever knew," he said in exasperation. "Look, I told you this was important. Don't you think I know what's important and what isn't? Don't you have any sense at all?"

She looked at him. He wasn't kidding. He was pale, and his freckles stood out. She disliked him intensely. Still, there was that empty hollow room waiting upstairs. Mary Jean would be running around with armfuls of stuff, Bitsy helping her, most likely, looking moral and righteous. She cleared her throat. "All right. Not very long though." They stepped outdoors.

It was dark under the trees. Even now, with most of the leaves fallen, their interlacing branches made a shade. "I thought maybe we could walk out in the country a ways, or are you like all these people – lost the use of your legs?"

"I don't care."

They walked side by side, not touching or speaking. The blocks past the campus were built up in small houses and here and there an old farmhouse cut up into apartments, the garage fixed up from a shed or barn. The voices of children playing out in the chilly dusk mingled with the evening television programs. Out here the street lights were only at the intersections, and the middle of each block held a deep well of shadow. "Street's kind of rough," the boy apologized.

"That's all right."

He looked straight ahead, his profile sober. "Look," he said, "you were right."

"Right?"

"What you said about my uncle. I asked him." In the dim light she saw his mouth tighten. The muscle in his cheek twitched. It hadn't been an easy asking. "He tried to weasel out of it, but it didn't do any good. I guess everybody knows – I wouldn't be surprised if Aunt Peg knows even."

"I shouldn't have said it."

"No, that's okay. It was true. Look," John said, "all my life I've wanted to be a doctor, see? I guess all kids have a favorite aunt or uncle when they're little, somebody who seems like some kind of hero to them. Specially if they don't have folks of their own, like me." He looked at her, and she nodded.

"Me either," she said.

"Well, that's the way it was," he said. "It hasn't got anything to do with being a doctor, though. Not any more. Even if he is a fake, I'd rather be a really good doctor than have a million dollars."

Shame washed over her.

He went on doggedly talking, as if he'd been planning this out sentence by sentence and didn't mean to skip any of it, as if he didn't dare stop until he got it all said. "When I was in Korea I was jealous of the medics the whole time. Everybody else was tearing guys apart, and here they were patching 'em back up. There're only two kinds of people," he said as gravely as if nobody before him had ever had the same idea. "A good doctor, a good *person* even, ought to help life along, not destroy it. That's why I can't forgive my uncle."

"I don't see anything so terrible about it," Joyce said stubbornly. "A lot of people do it."

"A lot of people steal."

"I suppose you think people ought to go around having babies all over the place."

"That's a damn silly quibble. There're ways to keep it from happening." She had no answer for this, because she'd thought it, herself, a hundred times during those first nights of panic. Said it, too. All this mess and suffering because somebody was too lazy to stop at a drugstore. She scowled at him. "I don't think so much of these girls who're always jumping into bed with somebody," he said. "They get sort of messy and sloppy."

"I suppose you think there's something the matter with sex."

"I guess it's here to stay," John said, "right along with baldness and the common cold. It's a question of emotional maturity, that's all."

They were on the edge of real country now, the last block of little window-lighted houses behind them. Tall weeds grew along the edges of the highway, dry and rattling in the cold wind. A single late cricket chirped. It was an unbearably lonely sound.

"I'm going to be a doctor," John said again. "I've read a lot about this stuff, see? Besides, anybody ought to know – it's crazy that what you don't know won't hurt you. Just the opposite." He was better-looking when he smiled; sadness didn't go well with his face. Still, she had a feeling that he'd often been unhappy. "Here's a nice soft culvert we can sit on," he said amiably, "and I'll brief you on what every young girl should know."

"You're crazy."

But she sat down on the culvert, which was cold. Her calves

ached as they hadn't since her Girl Scout days.

Little kids, John said, folding his hands around his knees, got curious about their own bodies as soon as they had sense enough to know anything at all. They had a hell of a fine time experimenting around, until some dumb grownup got them full of batty ideas about this is wrong and that's wrong. Matters of manners, not morals, really, but try and get parents to see it. Then, the way the psycho men had it figured out, they grew into a parent-fixation stage where little boys were in love with their mothers and hated their fathers, and vice versa. Freud started that idea, he said, and bright people now weren't shocked by it any more. "Of course, you realize this is just the synopsis."

Joyce reflected that she wouldn't know. Still, there had been a time when she tagged Uncle Will all over the place, and looked to him for babying when Aunt Gen scolded her. Well, but then Aunt Gen – Oh, no. No, not a mother's place. Or had Aunt Gen really been her mother, for all she'd been born out of Mimi's body?

Around junior high, John went on, ignoring her abstraction, kids got into a sort of homo stage. Girls fell in love with their women teachers mostly, and fellows went around together and maybe did a little experimenting. Perfectly normal, even if the newspapers did make a scandal out of it every once in a while. "Most kids grow out of it. Thing about all these middle-aged queers you see around, they never grew up past the age of fourteen. The gifted ones develop lopsided, smart as hell about painting or music or something, but they're like dumb kids in other ways." He pulled a stem of seeded grass, wiped the dust off absent-mindedly on his pantleg and starting chewing it. "Course, there are a lot of things to keep people from growing up. You can't really blame 'em." He spat green juice.

Don't be touchy, Joyce admonished herself. This kid doesn't even know you. He doesn't mean anything in your life. He couldn't possibly know. She turned her face away from him, but his voice pierced through her thoughts. "Then they get all wound up in the opposite sex, and then they grow up – if they're lucky – and learn to put the whole thing in its right perspective." He got up and stretched. "Now you know all the facts of life," he said, looking embarrassed at having talked so much.

"I suppose you're an expert," she said.

He shook his head. "I didn't mean to give you a lecture. All I was going to do was tell you you're right about Uncle Doc. I'm sorry I called you a liar."

There was no reason to feel so hateful about him. Only she didn't like anything about this fellow, his looks or his clothes or his cocky know-it-all talk. Who does he think he is, going around lecturing people about their emotional maturity? As if anybody cared what he thought.

Still, he wouldn't have had to apologize. "You wouldn't have had to apologize," she told him.

He looked surprised. "Well, but you had it coming. I was pretty nasty to you." He sauntered away a few steps. "I have a feeling," he said, "I'm going to tell you a lot of things. God knows you're not the kind of girl I ever saw myself falling for. I always pictured myself with a kind of motherly, big-boned type – looking for a mom, I guess. It makes me mad as hell, but I can't stop thinking about you. I'll tell you all about it, the next time I take you out."

"I wouldn't go anywhere with you if you were the last man on earth."

"You wouldn't get a chance to," he said smugly. "The competition would be terrible."

"Oh!" She began walking back toward town, away from him. Her heel caught in a rough piece of pavement, and she felt herself falling. He grabbed her by the elbow. "Watch where you're going, stupid." She glared, but he held her arm tightly. "I'm going along, you might as well wait for me," he said pleasantly. "I might even take you out and buy you a Coke, if you ask pretty."

"I suppose you think I'm a case of retarded development."

He raised one eyebrow. It gave him a look of insatiable curiosity. "I'm not your parish priest," he said, "but if you care to tell me what's eating you it might be good practice. I intend to spend the rest of my life with you that way: you tell me your troubles, I tell you my troubles."

"Oh, you have troubles too? Just like ordinary people?"

"Well, I wasn't as polite to Uncle Doc as I might have been," he said. He fell into step with her, the two of them walking in an easy rhythm. "I've been going around here feeling as moral as hell because I told the old boy off. It was horsey of me. Some day I'm going back and tell him so."

"You moved out?"

"Sure. When I go on a bust I go full length, as the fellow told the photographer. Going back to school in January anyhow; I just dropped out for a semester because I was short of money." He shook his head. "I'm in a real nice rooming house, hot and cold running cockroaches."

"Now I know you're crazy."

"Don't change the subject," he said. "Give. What's the worm in your apple?"

"Nothing."

"You'll feel better after you tell." They were back among the little houses now. The volume of kids' shouting had diminished; upstairs windows blossomed with light. Bedtime. "Look, do you have to be in any special time?"

"No, I forgot to sign out."

"I bet. I'll buy you some coffee."

She made up her mind suddenly. Nothing else to do but study, and she was in no mood for that. "All right."

The place he took her to was one of those boxcars made over into a hamburger joint. Not much of a place for a first date; maybe he was really broke or maybe he didn't think she was worth impressing. She didn't want to be impressed by him, of course, but still –

Curiosity got the best of her resentment. She'd passed a lot of places like this but it was the first time she had been inside one. This one looked clean, though the air was smoky from the grill. The menu was written on a blackboard against the back wall. The man behind the counter, fat and mustached, said, "Hi, John."

"Hi. Two coffees."

"John what?"

"Jones. I know you don't believe it, but it's true. My middle name's Carstairs. That's what I'll call myself when I hire my second office nurse, J. Carstairs Jones."

"You don't look like a Carstairs."

"Thanks."

The coffee was hot, clear, and strong. John took a deep swig. "This the first affair you've had?" he asked.

"I don't know why you think such a thing. You've got a dirty mind."

"Uh-uh, there you go. Sex is dirty. Look, there's not much love in the world, let's not get snotty about it. Anything that has even a little tenderness and understanding in it – if you've got that you've got something, haven't you?"

"I don't know," Joyce said. She wondered how they had got to this point. "I don't know one single thing," she said.

"I should have said, is this the first affair you've had with a woman?" He set down his cup and grabbed her by the shoulder as she got up from her stool. "Don't blow your top, you're only mad because I'm right."

"How did you know?"

"Oh, honey," John Jones said tenderly, "you've got a face that wouldn't fool a week-old baby. If it really looked at you," he added quickly. "Most people don't." This was so in line with her own recent observations that she couldn't deny it. "You can't run away," he said.

"I'm not running away."

"Okay. Let's change the subject. How's your friend getting along, the one that had the operation?"

"Fine. We just had a big fight," Joyce said, noticing that her hand shook when she tried to stir her coffee. "That's why I came with you, I mean, that's why I don't much want to go back."

"Regular roommate fight, or is she the one? No, that's not so likely. Considering." She could see his mind working back to their first meeting. "It's reasonable she should pick a fight, you know too much about her. If she can work up a good peeve she won't have to feel so guilty. It figures. What did you do, get a run in her good stockings?"

"You think you're smart."

"Not so very," John Carstairs Jones said sadly. He shoved his cup across the counter and the fat waiter, who seemed to be cook and cashier too, filled it. "He's deaf," John said following her eyes. "Reads lips, though. Want another?"

"What time is it?"

"Twenty to twelve."

"Oh, good Lord." Edith, she thought. Edith would have come and gone, nobody in the room, no notation in the going-out book, no excuse for this kind of thing. She wouldn't bring it up before the House Council – how could she? – but she would certainly have plenty to say in private. "I've got to get back," she said frantically, buttoning up her jacket.

They didn't talk on the walk back, but he held her arm and it felt good, sort of cozy. Didn't make sense considering how insulting and snoopy the boy was.

He stood with her outside the door of the dorm, just off the side-walk where the light over the door casing was softened. "Thanks for walking with me," he said. "It's been on my mind ever since that day – I'm honestly sorry I popped off at you like that. Sorry if I made you mad out there tonight, too."

"It's all right. I wasn't very nice to you, either."

"That's okay."

"Well –" Now she was here, she was reluctant to go in. There didn't seem to be much of anything to hope for, inside.

"I'll call up first, the next time."

He planned a next time, then. She ought to get that straightened out right now. Tell him she didn't want to see him again. She licked her lips nervously. "All right."

She stood with a hand on the doorknob, watching him walk away. Maybe somebody would look out of the window and see her coming in at this hour. So what? She felt too lost and miserable to care. It would be my luck if the door was locked. But it wasn't, the knob turned smoothly under her hand and she was in, taking advantage of a precaution meant for someone else.

There was no line of light under Edith's door. She was asleep, or out. Or maybe upstairs, waiting. Anxious. Or angry. There was still that possibility to face, but Joyce felt too tired to care much. She walked up slowly, noticing in an abstracted way that her leg muscles were cramped and sore from so much walking. Sounds of slamming and clattering came from behind Bitsy's closed door. Joyce laughed. Bitsy studied by schedule and liked to be in bed by eleven. A fussbudget, a regular old maid about neatness and order. Living with Mary Jean was likely to be an eye-opener. She'd bet Mary Jean would learn to pick up after herself, or wish she had. Serve 'em both right.

There was no one in her room. Edith had given up, then, and gone to bed. She pushed the thought of tomorrow out of her mind. The room looked sort of nice; nice and bare. She tiptoed around picking up Mary Jean's leavings, used and wadded tissues, bobby pins, an old sock, a pried-off stamp, a dirty comb. She cleaned out the dresser drawers, then removed them one by one and shook them over the wastebasket to get the powder and dust out of the cracks. She made her own bed up with fresh sheets and stood back looking at the effect.

She wanted to go to bed for hours and hours, alone. In fact, the way she felt, she didn't ever want anyone to touch her again. I wish people would leave me *alone*, she thought fretfully. She felt the clean pillowcase cool against her cheek, and there was comfort in it.

I thought I loved her, she thought. I do love her. Or is it only because I needed to love somebody and she made the first move? That was an unhappy thought and she turned over, hoping that the position would make her sleepy.

Some time in the night she woke, thinking about John Carstairs Jones, and was unable to get back to sleep. He's unhappy, she thought. She hadn't noticed it while they were together, but his face was clear in her mind now and it was young, thin and strained. It must have been terrible for him to fight with his uncle, she thought, when he's always thought so much of him. She recalled the pride in the older man's voice, the one time she'd seen them together. It made her feel guilty. She tried to imagine how she'd feel if Aunt Gen turned out to be a – well, she didn't know, you couldn't imagine Aunt Gen doing anything that wasn't perfectly honest. Suddenly she saw Aunt Gen, too, standing beside the kitchen table in one of her big coverall aprons, her hair braided smoothly above her serious, suntanned face. Even through polished bifocals her eyes made you wish you didn't have anything on your conscience.

John Jones had the same trick of looking straight through you. I don't like him, she thought; he thinks he knows everything.

It took her quite a while to get back to sleep. Nothing was wrong, nothing at all. It must have been all that coffee so late at night.

Chapter Sixteen

"Really civilized people," Edith Bannister said. She leaned forward a little over the steering wheel. There was color in her smooth cheeks, and her voiced was pitched higher than Joyce had ever heard it before. She's excited about this, Joyce thought. Excited about getting out for an evening, like some farm woman who's been kept cooped up among the pigs and chickens since Lord knows when and is offered a trip to town. Can she be that bored with school?

Joyce wasn't bored with school. Since the three days away with Mary Jean, when she had been almost sure they would be found out and expelled, she was both happy and unhappy about college, but certainly not bored. I'd like to start over, she thought wistfully. Or maybe come back next year and get on the Student Council and take something besides snap courses. If I could start without Edith. Maybe she'll get a job somewhere else, she thought, but recognized it as wishful thinking.

She'd have liked to forget all that had happened in these three months and concentrate on just living for a while. She folded her hands on her lap and forced her attention back to what Edith was saying.

"She does everything. Ceramics, weaving, the modern dance. Not only talented but versatile. It's one of the few sensible marriages I've ever known," Edith said eagerly. "Both of them free to go their own way without any grudges or petty jealousies. Fritzi often has some man friend staying with him for a few weeks. He knows they're welcome.

"They've even talked about having a child, to make the picture complete. Still, they have perfect freedom now. And companionship. You can have a very fine companionship with a man as long as he doesn't get any silly ideas. You'll discover that for yourself when you have a chance to get acquainted with a more mature type of man." The traffic light flashed amber. She stopped the car with a lurch. "It's an ideal arrangement for both of them."

"I can see that."

"Are you tired, darling? You sound tired."

"I'm fine."

"Not shocked, are you?" The upward tilt of her mouth implied that the idea was pretty funny. *After all we've done, after all we've had together. Stuffy conventional people might be bothered by these things, but we* know. Joyce didn't admit that she was shocked, a little; she had supposed marriage was for the normally-sexed and that those outside the regular social-moral framework stayed single.

The light turned green. The line of city-bound cars moved slowly forward, many-colored and swimming nose to tail through the thickening dark. "I'm taking a chance introducing you to these people," Edith said. Her voice was edged with cold steel. "You could make a lot of trouble for me if you wanted to."

"You don't have to worry."

"You know everyone's against us. People hate us because we're free of their petty restrictions, because we dare to love honestly, without a lot of little social conventions to back us up. They discriminate against us socially, they deny us the right to earn a living, their damn preachers and social reformers would like to throw us all in jail. The only way you can survive is to have two lives, one for the stuffy narrow-minded people to know about and one with your own kind in the cracks and crevices of your days."

This was old stuff. She'd heard it a hundred times before, and the first few renditions had made quite an impression on her. Nobody loves us, everybody hates us. The only thing that could get Edith worked up, besides making love, was the idea that everybody had it in for sex deviates, including God. Joyce was beginning to wonder if people were that much interested.

What she did find fascinating just now was the idea that two of them so assorted as to sex would be married. Like this Fritzi and Anitra Schultz there were going to see, who were Edith's friends and had such a gosh-awful wonderful life together. She could see how Edith, fastidious, lonesome, and not interested in men, might end up as a Lesbian. Or someone like me, she thought wryly, that's had the pants scared off her. But for a man who was interested only in other men, and a woman attracted to other women – now there was something she wouldn't have thought possible. "I don't see what they get out of it," she said.

"Don't be dense," Edith said coldly. "Nobody questions them, don't you see? They're part of the conventional design, the pattern society wants to mold everybody into."

Yes, but then where's the wonderful honesty? She didn't ask it. The one thing she was sure of right now was that she'd better not ask any more questions. "Is this dress all right, or should I have worn something fancier?"

"You look very nice." The blue wool was a schoolgirl dress with a round white collar and little glittery buttons down the front. Mimi's feather haircut had grown out long enough to take a pincurl permanent. Edith approved of that, too. She supposed that was camouflage, too, looking feminine and being part of the social pattern. Keep people from finding out I'm not normal. It wasn't a happy thought.

Anitra Schultz was a painter, primarily, Edith explained. She worked in oil, water color and *gouache*. "She's had several one-man shows," Edith said proudly.

The Schultzes lived in one of those self-consciously informal suburban houses built by people living a little beyond their means. The lawn was manicured. An old-fashioned hitching-post painted shocking pink held a curly black iron sign, "The Bluff." Since the place was flat, she guessed it was meant to be cute. The drive was jammed with ordinary cars, convertibles, and those little English models that look as if you could tuck them under your arm while you went shopping. Edith parked in the street and Joyce got out of the car, smoothing her skirt, and looked around. The house door stood open and light streamed out. She felt like a child going to a birthday party. Edith took her hand as they went up the arty flagstone walk, and she was grateful for so much warmth.

Anitra Schultz looked like her house, sleek and expensive, but not quite real. She was tall and slender, with lacquered black hair drawn back in a bun on her neck and green eyes underlined with emerald mascara, fuchsia lips sharply painted on. Only her skin spoiled the picture; it was olive but rather oily and rough. She wore narrow velvet trousers and her feet were bare in flat black velvet slippers embroidered with gold thread and fake pearls. She laid her cheek close to Edith's and they saluted the air in a way that couldn't spoil makeup. "Darling, I'm so glad you could come. Is this your little girl you told us about? Charming. Fritzi darling, bring these nice people something to drink."

Fritzi looked rather like Mary Jean's Bill, stocky and fair, with a crewcut. Masculine type – nobody could call him sissy. He was carrying a tray of drinks, like a butler in the movies, and he gave Joyce a pleasant impersonal smile and Edith a curt nod. "Here, take what you like best. That's rum. That's Scotch and that's gin, with the peel in it." Joyce decided that she rather liked him, but didn't like his wife.

The drink she took felt nice and cold in her hand, smelled good, tasted bitter but slid down easily. It exploded in her stomach; she felt she must be breathing out smoke and flame. There didn't seem to be any place to set down the empty glass; she looked at Edith for a cue, but Edith was still talking to Anitra and she gave Joyce an absent-minded nod indicating: go on, don't be formal, have a good time and circulate. So she walked around, glass in hand, looking at the rooms which opened into one another and then, with rather less curiosity, at the people.

She guessed this was modern décor, or maybe moderne. She wasn't sure how to pronounce décor, but she was always running into it in magazines that told you how to paint your old walnut furniture bright green and make chic curtains out of Turkish towels. There were a lot of small tables covered with books and arty arrangements of flowers, weeds, leaves, and such things as gilded snap clothespins and little ceramic caterpillars. The davenport curved, but unevenly, and the coffee table was free-form. Some of the chairs were made of rawhide laced crisscross, like the paper-strip mats kids make in kindergarten, and some were wrought-iron with grape leaves and curlicues all over them. There was a grand piano which seemed to be the regular shape, but it was painted a deep pink. Someone had already set a drink on top of it and the glass had tipped over; a clear liquid was dribbling down onto the keys and splashing on the olive-green rug.

There were twenty or thirty people scattered around. It was hard to reach a closer estimate because the rooms were in series, with partial walls but no doors. A small, frilly, blonde girl sat on a cushion on the floor beside the piano, her knees drawn up in front of her so that the tops of her stockings showed and a stretch of bare leg. An older woman with gray hair and a gray suit buttoned primly around a matronly figure squatted beside her, talking. The girl looked sulky and bored. Some of the women wore full peasant skirts over crinolines, and jangling handmade jewelry. Some were in evening dresses cut right down to the nipples. Most of the men were less formal, they ran to tweed jackets and loud slacks, and there was one husky type who looked like Tarzan with a beard. She bet he hadn't ever wrestled with an ape. He wore Bermuda shorts and no shirt at all, just a fine mat of black hair on his chest that mingled with the fringes of his beard. But he looked different from these other characters, more like a real person.

Somebody handed her another drink. Her throat was still hot from the first one, but it looked too silly to walk around with a full glass in her hand so she sipped at it as she went from spot to spot, finding that the burn was less if she took it slowly. After a little while she thought about setting the tumblers behind one of the long hand-blocked curtains on a sill. There was a wad of chewed gum on the one she chose; she put a glass on each side of it, like a composition in balance.

The lights looked brighter and clearer than they had at first. A fat man rolled up with a platter of Technicolor appetizers, beaming at her. First thing she knew she was sitting on the floor like half a dozen of the others, legs doubled under her, wondering if she'd be too stiff to get up again when the time came. She smiled up at Tarzan, who came over to sit beside her. Nature Boy.

One thing about these people, whether they shared Edith's ideas about the way they were persecuted or not, it didn't show. They didn't seem to have any reticences among themselves. She had thought some of the girls at school were blabbermouths, but they were strong silent types compared with this roomful of party-goers. She looked around for Edith but she and Anitra were both out of sight. A month or so ago that would have been anguish. Now there were a lot of other people around, all talking, and tantalizing scraps floated her way; then Tarzan started telling her about himself and she forgot Edith altogether.

He was a psychologist, he said; a practicing psychologist, which wasn't as good as an analyst so he had an inferiority complex about it. She wondered why, if he admired analysts so much, he didn't have one go to work on him and find out why he was a homosexual. Maybe he knew too much about it or maybe he liked being the way he was. His name was Kenneth Tregillus – call him Kenny – but she went on thinking of him as Tarzan.

"You look like Tarzan," she told him, and he nodded and said, "Thanks. Any other time that would brighten up my whole day, but I'm low right now."

She asked why, trying to sound like a Dale Carnegie friend. The boy he'd been sharing an apartment with had gone off and got married, he said, he was really ambisexual, and a debutante type with a Vassar accent had hooked him. "Trouble is, I don't like fairy types. I don't mean you, old man," he apologized to the tall balding man with a touch of rouge on his cheekbones, who sat on his other side eating canapés and listening.

The rouged man smiled uneasily. "That's okay, Ken. You're a little too rugged anyhow."

"But why talk about him," Tarzan went on gloomily. "There are more interesting people around. Take Arline and Linda." He indicated two thin girls who sat with their arms around each other drinking something lurid-red out of the same glass. Joyce was more interested in the drink. "A Bloody Mary, tomato juice and vodka. Sickening, isn't it?" He explained that Linda had been married to Arline's brother for a couple of years and had a baby by him before she realized it was Arline she'd been attracted to all the time. Now the two girls lived together on Linda's alimony, which the baby's father paid to keep them from talking. He had married again, a nice little woman who took care of the child and never had a thought in her head. "Those two gals are nuts about each other," Tarzan said. "Either of them would break your neck if you looked at the other one. They're always fighting because somebody's made a pass, or they think somebody has. It's dangerous to say hello to them."

Joyce didn't see herself being tempted. The two looked like sisters, bony and tired, with blonde-brown, cheaply curled hair and long noses. Distaste stirred in her.

A group of three came in, two women almost middle-aged and a plump pink man who took their coats and handbags and stood in the middle of the floor smiling viciously while they rushed around greeting friends. They all lived together, Tarzan said. "He's more or less married to the short one. The girls share a bedroom and old Donno flops on the davenport." He sighed. "I don't know what he gets out of it; they won't even cook his meals. He's a nice fella too, I could go for him. I don't think he has any love life at all, though. Either his glands are inactive or he's been repressed – mother fixation, maybe."

Talk eddied around them, almost as visible as the smoke that hung in clouds and swirls on the air. Styles and decorating – Ted Somebody did the display windows for the city's most exclusive store, the one whose ads Joyce often read in the newspapers. Who went to the symphony last night? "I did," the fat Don said, "and I'm telling you the soprano sounded like a bitch in heat. Yowling to be let out of the cellar," he added, offering Joyce the sandwich he had just taken. He'd already had a bite out of it so she laid it gently on the nearest table. Fritzi came around, offering more drinks, and Joyce took one. This one made her feel a little funny and she told Tarzan so.

"Sick?"

"No, only the floor sort of goes up and down."

He said, "You've had enough." He took the glass out of her hand and drank the rest of it.

Arline took her face out of Linda's shoulder and wavered over to sit down beside Joyce. "You're cute," she said, owlishly, "who do you belong to?" Tarzan gave Joyce a reminding poke in the ribs. "'Cause look," Arline said, "you could come home with us and stay all night. We'd love to have you."

"Oh, I couldn't," Joyce said quickly.

Linda trailed over, smiling coldly. "You're making a fool of yourself as usual," she said to Arline. "I will not have it. I'll go home."

Tarzan patted her thin behind. "Sit down," he said hospitably. She sat cross-legged beside him, put her head on his bare shoulder and went to sleep.

Somebody had brought a violin, somebody a cello. A little night music, Joyce thought drowsily. There were small scraping and tuning noises. Joyce leaned against Tarzan's unoccupied side. He didn't seem to mind being a prop for two women, and it was rather like leaning against a tree, only with hair and skin instead of bark. All that liquor was beginning to do something funny to her sight and hearing. Everything looked a little fuzzy and sounds were intermittent, with gaps in between that she couldn't account for. The room and people were unreal, like those dream sequences in the movies where they dance among the drifting clouds and broken pillars. Don't think I would like this bunch much even if they were real people, she thought, shutting her eyes to rest them. Pretty soon she would wake up back in the dorm – ought to be studying for a Spanish test or something.

Somebody was breathing on her. She took her face away from Tarzan's fuzzy neck, where it seemed to have landed, and looked into Anitra's Egyptian eyes. She had forgotten all about Anitra. "Having fun?"

"I'm drinking too much," Joyce said. "Where's Edith?"

"Around." Anitra lowered herself to the floor with one fluid motion, like a dancer. That made four of them sitting in a row, like birds on a fence. "You look like a bal – ballet dancer," Joyce said with some difficulty.

Amitra smiled. "I've done that too." She leaned against Joyce's back. Her breasts were soft and firm at the same time – no bra, and she must be forty, Joyce marveled, aware of the warmth under the silk blouse. "You're a cunning little thing," Anitra said in a low voice. "How did Edith ever find you? She's always kept her work and her social life apart before. A model of discretion, Edith is."

"You know how those things happen." It didn't seem to mean anything but it sounded like an answer.

"She's a wonderful person. A little cold though, don't you think?"

"She hasn't been cold to me," Joyce said truthfully. The excitement, the husky whispers, the seeking and knowing hand. Maybe it was the drowsiness brought on by alcohol that made all those things seems so far away, like something read about but never experienced. The pressure of Anitra's body made her restless. She remembered for no special reason the cold night air and John Carstairs Jones's sober face. The room felt stuffy. "I ought to get up," she said.

"Look, the party's getting dull. Some of us are going to sneak out for a little while and go pub-crawling." But she's not English, Joyce thought, that's fake. "Like to come along?"

"Well, I don't know."

Edith materialized beside them. Through Joyce's alcoholic haze she looked quite a lot like Arline, the same tiny lines at the corners of the eyes and the same strained look around the mouth, but her pupils glittered instead of blurring.

"Oh, there you are, darling," Anitra said. "I was looking for you. Look, darling, do you want to go downtown for a while? Slumming, some of the gay places?"

Edith took both of Joyce's hands in hers, stooping to pull her upright. "How about it, Joy?"

"Of course she wants to come along," Anitra coaxed. "Don't you, doll?"

"Me too," Tarzan said. "Remember, I'm an orphan." He dislodged the sleeping Arline, who wobbled a little and then sat up, blinking. He scrambled to his feet like a good-natured bear.

"I'll go if you go," Joyce said to him. She felt fond of him, as if he were an old family friend.

Groggy as she was, two things were becoming clearer to her by the minute. One was that Edith had been drinking, which seemed out of character. The other was that Edith was jealous. She had brought Joyce here to be awed and impressed by Fritzi and Anitra, these free, charming people, and to admire Edith more because she knew them. Anitra wasn't supposed to be patting her and looking deep into her eyes. To complicate things further, Edith liked Anitra and probably wasn't getting anywhere with her. It was a touchy spot to be in.

She wanted to go home. She thought with deep alcoholic sadness that she had no home. No place on earth. She was sober enough to know that if she asked to leave, Edith would be coldly displeased. She blinked, seeing the two women still waiting for an answer. "If you want to."

"Wait right here. I'll get your coat."

There was no doubt about it, Edith wobbled a little when she walked.

The fat man came by with his tray and thrust it at her. "Caviar," he said, pointing. "Lines your stomach." She took one and bit into it. It tasted like BB shot in cold salty glue. Another illusion shot all to hell, she mused sadly. She laid what was left on top of the piano and turned an ashtray over it, mixing ashes with the caviar.

Now she was wedged into a car between Edith and Anitra, one pressed against her on each side. The white line down the middle of the road zigged and zagged. "Whoever's drinking driving," she said. "No, not what I mean." She giggled. She dropped her head on Edith's shoulder and shut her eyes because the wavery line made her feel giddy. Anitra's thin fingers closed around her knee, then pushed her skirt back a little. She smiled anxiously from one to the other. "Like you both," she mumbled, and went to sleep again.

Chapter Seventeen

The place, Club Marie, was a letdown. It looked like a dozen cheap joints she'd walked past, quickening her step and turning her face away from the smell of stale beer, the bursts of laughter, the seamy-faced little old man who always seemed to be sitting on the doorstep. Only this one was brightly lighted. There were thin fluorescent tubes in the ceiling, parallel rows of them picking out glitters on the bottles and showing up the spills and dirt on the bartender's apron and the gummy places on the tables. There were bars of colored light across the top and bottom of the jukebox, too, and little red bulbs in the wall beside each table.

Not the kind of place for a respectable girl at one in the morning. Likely she wasn't a respectable girl any more.

This place worked a change in Anitra's guests, somehow. In her house they had looked arty and exotic, if a little strained and tense. Here they looked wilted and second-hand, maybe because of the lighting. Only Tarzan was improved. He was still clothed only in skin and fuzz from the waist up, in spite of the chill night, and he looked unreasonably wholesome. She herself, reflected in the mirror that ran along two walls, was a nice little schoolgirl whose hair needed combing. There was Anitra, who had walked out on her own party and certainly had too much makeup on; Edith, refined but a little unsteady; Arline, and two young men she hadn't noticed at the house. She never did find out whether they too had deserted the party or had been picked up. They were both a little hollow-chested and pasty, and they sat together and held hands. Still, they didn't have any of the obvious marks of a queer, no hip-wiggle or visible makeup.

Besides Anitra's group, there were three young sailors at the bar, snickering and making audible comments about the newcomers. Out killing time, probably. But the others – Everyone needed a bath, or maybe it was the lavender-tinted lighting that turned all skins to dull clay and set shadows under the eyes and around the nostrils. At the next table sat a meager little man who might have been a bookkeeper or a bookie, the kind of man – except for some look of decay in his face – who takes his paycheck home unopened. He sat with his arm loosely around the shoulder of a young woman who, from her angular shape, was almost surely a man. High heels and pleated ruffles. Joyce poked Edith and made the least possible gesture, raising her eyebrows. Edith frowned. "Transvestite." It didn't mean anything, she had never heard the word before. "Man in a woman's clothes, or otherwise."

"Oh," Joyce said. She wondered if Anitra was, too, in a more expensive way. Probably not, though. Lots of women wore pants, which made it confusing.

At the table next to this scrambled couple sat two girls about whom there was no doubt. One was thin and flat, with a jutting jaw. The other had heavy lips and a sagging bust. Both had ducktail haircuts like some of the girls at school, but with no softening front waves or little tendril curls. Both wore regular men's overall jeans with fly fronts, heavy pullover sweaters, and one gold ring in the right ear. The heavy one winked at Joyce, who felt embarrassed but smiled back politely. The other followed her friend's look, and shrugged.

The waitress arrived, in flannel slacks. "Honey, what'll you have?"

"Beer, I guess." She hated beer but she was afraid to drink anything stronger after those highballs at the Bluff. The salty taste of the caviar was still in her mouth. The others were looking at her, waiting. "Beer," she said more loudly.

Arline patted her head. "You're smart, honey. I wish to God I could drink beer; these mixed drinks give me the awfullest head-ache."

"Where's Linda?"

"Sleepin' on Fritzi's bed, I reckon. She passed right out." Arline looked dejected. "Oh, well, more'n likely she needs the sleep. We never did get to bed at all last night. We were havin' a real good fight and I was scared she'd poke me in the ribs with a knife if I shut my little ol' eyes."

"Drunk and disorderly again?" Tarzan rumbled.

"Oh, she thought I was two-timin' her with some ol' married girl lives down the hall a ways. Silly baby, she knows I wouldn't look at nobody but her." She patted Joyce's knee. "Honey, anybody ever tell you you're right cute?"

A haggard, pretty girl in a cheap fur stole stood in the doorway, swaying a little on high, turned-over heels. The thin customer in jeans let out a yell of welcome and rushed over to hug her. "Honey baby! C'mon, let's go home!"

"I want a drink first," the fur-stole girl said. She sat down at the bar and crossed her thin legs, wrapping the fur around her throat with an elegant gesture. She leaned on one elbow and took a compact out of her imitation alligator bag. "Same as always, Herbie. I'm pooped."

"Big night?"

"So-so. You know how it is."

The heavy-set girl wandered around and stood by Anitra, who had gathered all her party's checks into a pile with a fine hospitable gesture. "You mind if I sit down with you folks for a while? My friend's late tonight."

"Not at all. What'll you have?"

"Just a beer, thanks."

Tarzan took his sandaled foot off the rungs of the empty chair and shoved it at her. "Your friend work nights too? Like that one?"

"Not that way. I'm cracked about germs." She scowled. She had a heavy face which, without make-up or curls, looked sullen but wholesome. "She's a waitress in an all-night café," she said defensively. "It may not pay much, but what she makes is her own and there's no pimp hangin' around the kitchen door when she gets done."

"True," Tarzan said politely.

"I forgot to tell you, my name's Bobbie."

"Do you work nights too?"

Bobbie looked up from her stein. A wisp of foam clung to her nose; she wiped it away with the back of her hand. "Not if I can help it, days or nights neither. Sometimes I clerk in a bookstore when they need somebody extra, like say Christmas. The boss knows me and he's a good guy. It ain't that I'm afraid of work, I was raised on a farm, only it's hard to find a job where they let you dress like you want to."

"Don't you ever wear regular clothes?" Edith asked. She smoothed her skirt with a slender hand. Joyce could imagine her thinking: After all, I'm not *masculine*. I'm *different*.

"Hell, no. What would I do that for?"

She was willing to talk about herself, as if they had all known each other a long time. Joyce forgot her giddy headache and listened with interest. She was nineteen, Bobbie said, and had lived on a farm in southeastern Missouri until her folks died, a couple of years ago. "I always liked to work in the fields, and fool around with animals and stuff. Pa always said I was the best hired man he had." She had never had a date when she was in school, never thought about boys much – she could pitch a ball farther than any boy she ever knew and lift a bale of hay as easy. "Boys never asked me to date, anyhow; guess they wanted somebody who could act cute and flirty."

An aunt here had got her a job as a checker in a grocery store, and that was where she met Karla. Pretty soon they were sharing a room, and Bobbie found out about this other kind of love. It made more sense than smirking at fellows. "She meant an awful lot to me. More than a fellow ever could, I'll tell you that. She liked me the way

I was, too." But Karla developed a cold that hung on, and when the store nurse sent her to get her chest X-rayed they found an advanced case of TB. She was in a sanitarium now, and Bobbie took a long bus ride to go and see her every once in a while. Francie didn't like it so much, she said, but she figured it was the least she could do. The poor kid had to lay there all day long and worry about herself, and if Francie was jealous, okay. She could get out any time she felt like.

It was while she was living with Karla that she decided to change over to men's clothes. She went to a man's barber shop and got her hair cut. "Real short, you know, he liked to scalp me. Now I like this here D.A. better, it's got more style. I always wanted to be a boy from the time I was little. Boys get all the breaks. Like home, Pa always had the say about everything. Ma never got to open her yap about anything. Work, work, work all the time. It's a man's world."

The market fired her for wearing jeans to work under the regular white apron, or maybe it was for trying to make a girl customer who looked lonesome. They never told you the real reason in those places, didn't have the guts to. "I didn't care, I was tired of the crumby job. Now I got so I feel funny with a dress on."

She had lived with five women in all, one at a time. "I wouldn't two-time nobody." The best break she got, she said, was with Janette. Jan was a TV actress but she didn't work at it much, the competition was terrible, she was kept by a rich old guy who set her up in a ritzy apartment and came to see her twice a week regular. Tuesdays and Fridays. "He couldn't do nothing, you know, he was too old, but he sure had some funny ideas. He used to switch Jan on the behind with a little switch he had, till she bled. She didn't care. Just so's he paid the rent and the grocery bills. You know, most hookers don't really like it; it's all business with them and that's why they go gay on the side. You gotta have somebody. That Janette, she was different, she liked men and women both. Take it any way she could get it, two or three times a day, and holler for more."

Two things she made up her mind about when she got started,

she said proudly, and she'd stuck with it too. "I won't have nothing to do with a girl that uses dope. Not even tea. They tell you tea won't form a habit, but I never saw nobody stop usin' it. First they do it for kicks, then they gotta have it to feel good, then first thing you know they switched to the strong stuff. You ever see a girl with a monkey on her back? They'll do anything to get a fix then, steal or even kill somebody. I don't trust *no* junkie." The second thing – she wouldn't have anything to do with a streetwalker. "Like that one over there." She nodded at the bar, where the girl with the stole was drinking her third straight brandy while her friend sat watching her, not drinking herself, just watching and looking impatient. "I don't mean if a girl lives with one guy, specially if he's educated and high class. They ain't so likely to get a disease that way. You get mixed up with some common hooker, first thing you know you got a dose of the clap or something. Or that syph, that's mean, that can eat your insides right out. I don't want none of that."

"You're a smart girl," Tarzan told her. "I'm a doctor and I know."

"Yeah? You're damn right I'm smart."

The two sailors at the bar looked at each other. Derision crossed their blurry adolescent faces. They stood up. "C'mon, let's go find us a place with some real women in it," one of them said. "There ought to be some real women in this town."

"Some big shots," Bobbie said.

Anitra asked, "Didn't you ever go to bed with a man?"

"Sure. I'll try anything once. Didn't mean a thing to me," Bobbie said proudly. "If you're a real butch you don't get hot for men. Only sometimes they're okay to have around for buddies, like doc here. I could go for him in a strictly platonic way. Not for lovin' though – uh-uh."

"You're so wise," Anitra said softly.

Bobbie smiled at her. The smile lightened her face, gave her a pleasant, almost motherly look. "You're cute," she said. "You got real style. What you doin' in a dump like this?"

"Just looking around."

"See anything you like?"

"Could be."

Bobbie nodded. "Say, come in the john a minute, will you? There's a question I wanta ask you."

They went out together, Anitra walking lightly in her pearl-sewn velvet slippers.

"That's going too far," Edith Bannister said coldly. "I don't care, some people have no discrimination at all. I really mean that. I wouldn't pick up a piece of trash like that for anything."

Tarzan scratched his fur chest. "Oh, I don't know. She's not so bad, if you like women."

Arline patted his shoulder. "That's right, honey. You gotta be broadminded."

The two pallid young men didn't say anything. They had pulled their straight chairs close together, and the tall one was stroking the other's leg.

After what seemed like a long time Anitra and Bobbie came out of the room marked *Ladies*. Anitra leaned over the table. A wisp of hair had come loose from her sleek bun and hung down on her neck. The effect was startlingly rowdy. "I'm going over to Bobbie's place for a little while," she said to everyone in general. "She wants to show me something."

"I bet she does," Edith said. "Will it be something you never saw before?"

Anitra ignored that with dignity. They went out together, pausing at the bar. "Look, Herbie," Bobbie said, "if Francie comes in, tell her I went around the corner for a cup of coffee, will you? Tell her I'll be right back and to wait for me."

"Okay."

Edith looked at her watch. "Well, I'm not like some of you lucky people. I have to work tomorrow. So we better push off. Can I give anybody a lift, or anything?"

"I have to go back to Anitra's place, honey, on account of Linda's still there."

"I don't ever want to go home," Tarzan said. "I feel crumby."

Joyce gave them all a farewell smile, unconsciously living up to Aunt Gen's ruling that there's no excuse for bad manners. It's hard not to observe these little rituals when you've been brought up right. Tarzan waved at her, then put his head down on the table. The others ignored their going.

The air smelled fine, even with exhaust fumes mixed in it. Edith took a good deep breath.

"Well, that was interesting, wasn't it?"

Her schoolteacher voice. Joyce concentrated on getting into the car and closing the door. The giddiness was gone now, but her head still ached. Be careful there, don't make her mad. "It was different," she admitted.

"Anitra's charming, don't you think? Of course she wasn't quite herself tonight; she does drink too much at times. I wouldn't let myself go to pieces the way she does, just for a cheap thrill."

Joyce sighed deeply. To hell with being tactful, to hell with making Edith or anybody else feel good; she was tired. The distaste that had been gathering in her all evening came to a head and broke, like a boil. "I think she's a fake. I think they're all fakes, but him, that doctor. He *knows* he's one. The rest of them make me feel as if I need a good hot bath and my mouth washed out with laundry soap."

"Oh, my dear." The car slid over into the four-lane highway, smooth, night-dark, uncluttered by much traffic.

"Well, I never saw so many crumby people in my life."

"That place was a little too much," Edith admitted. She turned her coat collar up around her neck. "That tawdry little thing at the bar. One felt she was crawling with germs."

She hadn't made herself clear, and it seemed important to explain. "It wasn't those," she said. "I thought they didn't know any better, they never had a chance to be any other way. It was the ones at the party. They didn't even seem to want to grow up." Yet it was the drinkers at Marie's Place, she realized, who had crystallized and shaped her dislike for their more ornate counterparts from the Bluff. "I know I'm not explaining this very well."

"You certainly aren't." Edith's tone was rimmed with frost. "You sound like a women's magazine. Part of the campaign against us. We certainly aren't anything like those poor creatures. We're –"

"Different."

A hurt silence.

In the small dim light from the dash she looked at Edith's profile. For the first time she looked tired and vulnerable, not young any more. Joyce laid a hand on her arm, lightly, not to disturb her driving. "Let's not quarrel with each other. Let's go home and get some sleep."

Edith sighed. "We might as well, if you're determined to be unreasonable."

I wish there were somebody I could talk to about this, Joyce thought. The image of a boy's face flew across her mind, high cheekbones and a mouth set in patient lines. She stirred on the seat, feeling cramped and chilled and lonelier than ever.

Chapter Eighteen

On the afternoon of December first she came out of the Ad. Building into the chilly dusk of five o'clock, to find John Carstairs Jones waiting beside the path as he had waited at the dormitory, a couple of weeks earlier. He stood there smiling a little, although every girl who came down the steps with an armful of books was giving him a good looking-over. She dropped her notebook. He stooped to pick it up. "You said you'd call up," she accused him.

"Well, if you insist I can go back downtown and find a pay booth. You're taking an awful chance, though," John said. "Those drugstore girls are mighty good-looking."

"I'm glad to see you, silly." And she was, unexpectedly; if he had called she'd have looked forward to the meeting with nothing but apprehension, but his sudden appearance gave her a good feeling of warmth.

"It must be true about absence making the heart grow. How about going downtown for dinner?"

"Then wait while I change my clothes."

She wished she had changed to a date dress, when they ended up at the Henderson Hotel instead of a drugstore counter or dog wagon. The hotel was nothing fancy, but it was the best the town had to offer, unless you were old and well-heeled and speedy enough for a membership in the Sportsman's Lodge. John said he wasn't any of those things, thank God, he'd rather be broke and have his own teeth even if hamburger was all they had to work on. He hung her jacket on the old-fashioned coatrack in a corner of the big, empty dining room and pulled out her chair with a flourish. "Onion soup's the thing to have. They make it like the French do and it smells so good."

Words crowded together in her mind. It didn't make sense, there was no reason why she should tell this boy anything, but that was the way it was. The soup came in big plates, with bread crusts in it and grated cheese odorous on top, but she couldn't eat until she got rid of the weight on her chest. She picked up her spoon and turned it over, looking at the silversmith's mark in order not to meet his eyes. "You apologized to me the other day," she said in a small high voice. "I have to apologize to you too. I guess you're right; I am a case of arrested development."

"Come on, tell."

"You'll hate me."

John said, "I couldn't hate you, not even if you murdered somebody."

"Edith Bannister. You know, the –"

He made a gesture of cutting off, the hand brought down sharp and level. "You don't have to say it," he said. He sounded weary. "Look, I might as well level with you. Uncle Doc told me." He grinned at her look of shocked surprise. "He'd guessed about her."

Bad as Mary Jean's knowing had been, this was worse. She couldn't look at him. She concentrated on the old-fashioned damask tablecloth, lilies and tulips alternating in the woven pattern. John began eating soup, as if to spare her feelings by looking elsewhere. "What difference does it make?" he asked.

"I don't know why I'm telling you all these horrible things. It's none of your business."

"We belong together," John said. He shook his head. "Lord knows I never planned it this way. I've got two more years of college to work through before I can even think about medical school."

"Love at first sight," she said scornfully. "Fate and all that stuff."

"I knew the first day, out in the woods. It didn't have anything to do with being mad at you. I was sure enough mad at you."

Tears rose to her eyes. "This makes me feel terrible."

John patted her hand. His touch was light but curiously alive. "Because you did it or because somebody knows about it? Look – just play like I'm the old family analyst. Give. You'll feel better."

"I don't know," Joyce said. She was ashamed, and yet it was easier to struggle for honesty with him sitting there. The confused thinking of the last few weeks, the need to be free of a relationship become distasteful, at grips with habit and the dread of loneliness, took on sharper outlines because he was listening. She shot a timid look at him. "It was wonderful at first. I couldn't keep my mind on anything else. Now I don't even like it. Yet I can't give it up." She blinked. "Sometimes I think I'm going crazy," she said.

"That's life," John said. "That's love. Falling in is fun, falling out's pure hell. Happens all the time." He finished his soup, tipping the plate. "It's that empty feeling that gets you."

"This is different."

"It's always different."

The waiter came and took away John's empty plate and, looking disappointed, her full one. He brought steak on thick hot platters and a whole armada of little vegetable dishes, which he grouped carefully in front of them. They sat silent, waiting for him to go away. Joyce could feel her accelerated heartbeat and the jerking of the pulse in her throat against the high collar of her wool sweater.

John leaned across the table and laid a hand on her arm. "Be honest with yourself, kid. If you're getting any real satisfaction out of it, then okay. I can wait for you to grow up. But if you're past it, then for God's sake put it behind you and move on. Only don't try to kid yourself."

"It's not just me. I couldn't let her down. Everybody's down on people like that anyway."

"Not half as much as they're down on normal people," John said. "That's a lot of hooey, that propaganda they give you, how persecuted they are. Most people simply feel sorry for queers. They're sort of handicapped, like somebody with an artificial leg." He pondered. "More. An artificial leg doesn't have to handicap a person."

"That's it. You're going to think I'm abnormal or something."

"Look," John said patiently, "you're nothing but a kid. You needed to feel safe and cared-for." He cut into his steak, releasing a little cloud of stream. "Hell, everybody's looking for that. I always figured on ending up with some deep-chested, motherly type myself – make up for not having a mother of my own when I was a little kid. Sure got things screwed up when you came along."

"I'm trying to tell you it was more than that."

"But that too. It's all mixed up together. I don't blame you," he said in an angry voice. "I blame her, though. God, she could have picked somebody her own size."

"She didn't mean to hurt me."

He swallowed hard. "I guess that's right. She's probably lonesome too. Lord, imagine being like that. Getting old like that. Like riding a merry-go-round, all the time getting off at the same place where you got on." He shook his head. "Gosh."

She said almost at random, "Aren't you ever shocked?"

"Only by fakes. You can't go around telling other people everything you know; it would be illegal. But listen, don't you ever let me catch you lying to yourself. Or to me, either."

"I'll probably never see you again."

He cut a strip of steak and chewed on it absently. "Don't talk foolishness," he said after he had swallowed.

The meat and the garnishing onions and mushrooms smelled good. She picked up her knife, then put it down.

"What's the matter?" John demanded.

"I'm sorry. You'll have to pay for it just the same."

"They'd be glad to have it in Korea."

"You weren't in Korea!"

He sighed. "Nineteen when I went in, twenty when they brought me out. Froze two toes off – real romantic."

She looked into her water glass. He went on eating, alternating meat and mushrooms with bits of vegetable. He wiped his mouth on the napkin and looked her way. "Feel better now?"

"About –"

"Telling me. It was a bright idea."

"Some." Tears hung on her eyelashes, but it was true, she did feel better. "Yes, I do. That's funny, isn't it?"

"Cathartic value of confession. Would you eat some dessert if I ordered it?"

"No."

"Suppose you broke it off, would she make any trouble for you?"

"How do you mean, trouble?"

"Have you expelled. Start a dirty rumor. Throw nitric acid in your eyes like that girl in the paper whose boyfriend jilted her. You said you did some typing evenings for her – do you need the money?"

She shook her head. "She fixed that up so we could get together. My mother sends me money all the time."

Yes, and that was a silly thing too. When she was a kid, she had supposed it was only money that kept Mimi from sending for her. Now a check came twice a month, with Mimi's married name printed on it, and she deposited it with the bursar and left it there. She didn't need money, except maybe thirty or forty cents for a soda or something. It didn't mean as much as the colored postcards used to. Must be close to a hundred dollars there, she thought, if I ever need it.

"How is your mother, anyhow?" As if he really cared, as if he wasn't just changing the subject to make her feel better.

"Fine. She's going to have a baby."

She couldn't tell if he was counting months or not. That was a woman's trick anyhow; men didn't care about stuff like that.

"That'll be nice, a little brother or sister for you."

Her eyes widened. Two tears, forgotten, rolled down her face and melted into the soft fabric of her sweater. Gosh, it will be, won't it? For the first time she thought about the baby as a live human being, soon to be born. Up to now it had been only a bulge, obscene, a reminder of Irv Kaufman and the dark urges of men. Now she visualized a chubby cherub like the one on Aunt Gen's kitchen calendar. I bet he'll be a good father, she thought to her own intense astonishment. The kind who spoils kids. A black dread dissolved and drifted away, leaving her mind clear.

"She'll be okay," John said, misinterpreting her silence. "Having a baby is safer than crossing the street these days."

"She's kind of old."

"You better break off with her," John advised, holding her coat for her. "If you want to. That's for you to decide."

She waited at the door while he paid the cashier. They went out into the chill air together. "I'm sorry for her."

"You're a good girl."

"Good girls don't –"

"Look, Joy." It was Aunt Gen's and Uncle Will's name for her; she was not sure she liked even Edith to use it as she sometimes did. Certainly not this boy. She shut her lips tightly. "This whole thing is part of growing up. Not wicked, not anything that's going to follow you all the rest of your life or make you different from what you are. You'll grow up and marry me yet."

"Never."

"Let me know when you change your mind. Will you?"

"You're the most conceited man I ever knew."

Nice romantic date, she thought, walking down the street soberly and silently beside him. Spilling everything and bawling like a slapped kid. She slanted a look up at him.

He met her eyes. "Look, I'm in the telephone book under Sawyer, Catherine Sawyer, that's my landlady. Call me up any evening after five. I work at the cannery till five."

She decided she never wanted to see him again. Now the first relief of telling was over, she was sorry. Talking about it hadn't settled one single thing. One thing though, he won't want to see me again either, after he's had time to think it over. That should have made her feel good, but it didn't.

Chapter Nineteen

December was really winter. The radiators in the dorm, mostly used as shelves until now, clanked and rattled and from time to time gave off puffs of heat. Not at night, though. Whoever drew up the budget had made up for all those sterling salad forks by cutting down on the coal bills. A new kind of pajama became a fad on the second floor; one-piece, like a long red union suit with drop seat and bone buttons. Thin girls looked good in them; plump ones bulged. Fluffy types sent home for long frilly flannel nightgowns such as their grandmothers had worn and their mothers had made fun of. Joyce, diving into one of these at midnight, wondered if Mary Jean still slept in her skin.

Everyone was wearing winter clothes in spite of the advertised Southern climate. Holly Robertson became famous on campus as the girl who had not one handmade cashmere sweater, but two, at sixty dollars apiece. It even snowed one afternoon, a frail sugary wisp of white that lay in the cracks of the brick sidewalks for a couple of hours before it melted.

Rehearsals for the Freshman play started and she was asked to be prop girl, an exciting job that involved borrowing furniture and evening clothes from town people. She would have liked to be asked to play the lead – all her life she'd cherished a daydream of being tall, dark and a terrific actress rather like Cornell. Unluckily it made her throat muscles freeze solid even to stand up in front of an English class and deliver a five-minute oral on "My Summer Vacation." So she had to be satisfied with attending practice and scrutinizing the girl who played Lady Beckley-Robinson, and thinking how much better she could have done it if she'd only been able to act.

It was fun to go around borrowing lamps and tables, with the understanding that the college truck would pick them up later, and to sit around backstage drawing diagrams of what went where. She was very professional about labeling her little pictures UR and CL. Also, she wallowed in the smell of theatrical makeup, stale smoke, and unswept dust that seems to haunt all places where plays are rehearsed.

School was home now. The cream-plaster walls and dark woodwork of her own room, like all the others and yet different because it was where she lived; the corridors echoing with voices, or still and hollow in the middle of the night; the classrooms, row upon row of one-arm chairs, with the teacher's desk on a little platform up front and the big Webster's on its lectern; the brick-framed windows looking out on a campus impressive with leaves and academic buildings. She was used to the dignified dining room and the smell of hot cocoa at seven-thirty on winter mornings.

She was beginning to like the liquid sound of Spanish words and sentences in her early section, and the awakening reality of the Art Appreciation course. She joined the class in folk dancing and found it fun. And now she began to notice girls she hadn't admired especially at first, serious ones like Bitsy and Kas and Margaret Sherwin who got As and were on committees for different things. The original impression of glamour had worn off, and they seemed more like girls she'd known back in Community High.

There were days when she felt she could be perfectly happy in this place, like a round peg fitting into a round hole, if God or Freud or Darwin or whoever it was hadn't invented sex. If the human race could reproduce by splitting in two, like an amoeba, people wouldn't have to go through a lot of emotional dither. Mary Jean was always claiming that women's troubles were all on account of men, and she was willing to believe it – with variations of course. There were no men involved in what was bothering Joyce, but she supposed even sexual abnormality might be an offshoot of the urge to reproduce.

Abnormality? Even Mary Jean, man-crazy, had thought she was Sappho for three weeks. She had looked up Sappho in the library and the stilted account she found there made sense to her, though it wouldn't have three months before. It did look more romantic after two or three thousand years, but she bet Sappho had had her problems too.

There was fussing and fretting going on in the back of her mind all the time now, even when she was wrapped up in the play or really interested in her lessons. It was like having a canker sore, it didn't hurt much unless you ate something salty, and yet you kept running your tongue around it all the time, conscious that it was there. She hadn't spent any time alone with Edith since the night of Anitra Schultz's party. Edith was plainly being patient and forbearing with her. The strategy was perfectly evident and she was afraid it might work, too. A glimpse of Edith across the dining room – the second six weeks were under way and the seating arrangements had all been shuffled – was enough to start confusion and uncertainty whirling in her mind. She didn't really know how she felt about going on, or breaking off, or anything.

What was evident was that something had to happen. She felt that her relationship with Edith had to stop. It was with her when she woke up at night and whenever she thought about home and Aunt Gen. But she couldn't come right out and tell Edith so; the thought filled her with terror.

I'd even be willing to die or get disabled, she thought dismally, if it would straighten this mess out. On the other hand, when she thought about being completely alone in a loveless world it was like being dragged out from under a soft, warm wool blanket to stand naked in a biting wind.

She gathered from reading the novels of Colette that something like this always happened to love. The first excitement wore off and one partner became bored and, later, antagonistic while the other went through hells of anguish. Maybe it happens to everybody, she thought, married or single. She bet Aunt Gen and Uncle Will hadn't had an exciting moment together for twenty years; they stayed together from habit and morality. They think they're happy, and maybe they are. Maybe that's happiness, not caring any more.

She felt tired, and thought with sad pleasure that she might have TB, something that would mean being sent away and having a long recovery. The old daydream came back: Mimi sent for her and they were a family together. But there were Irv and the apartment, scene of her surrender, and the baby to change the picture now, and she couldn't even imagine its being anything like the old daydreams. Mimi was gone, as much as if she'd died. In her place was a pregnant woman who sent bi-weekly checks and had no part in her daughter's life.

There were moments when she was so desperate for rescue that she kept making up a story about Aunt Gen getting sick and Uncle Will urging her to come back to the farm. For several days the sight of Aunt Gen's neat schoolteachery handwriting on the envelope of her twice-a-week letters started a train of thought that comforted her.

What surprised her was that she was homesick for Aunt Gen as she never had been for Mimi. That was a child's dream, not meant to come true. This was a longing for real and solid things that had been a part of her life since she could remember. She wanted to see the farm. Most of all she wanted to see Aunt Gen, her honest, middle-aged face – she was about the only person Joyce knew who didn't use lipstick – the suggestion of a double chin offset by her erect carriage, the smooth brown braids worn coronet style. Aunt Gen's homemade dresses hanging in a neat row in her closet, the polished low-heeled "comfort" shoes she wore, her bifocals, the lavender cologne she saved for Sundays and special events, all added up to some lost innocence she would have given anything to regain.

There were things you couldn't talk to Aunt Gen about, things she would never forgive if she knew about them. Relations between

184 | Whisper Their Love

men and women had to fall into a specified pattern. Nice girls didn't
let boys go too far with them, and even after marriage wives merely
submitted to the gross natures of their husbands. When Joyce tried
to imagine Aunt Gen in bed with Uncle Will, all she got was a picture
of smooth braids on the pillow and a sheet drawn up under the sleeping face. You couldn't believe –

She remembered suddenly, a Sunday afternoon when she was
about thirteen and had been asked to go the movies in Ferndell with
a bunch of neighborhood kids. Aunt Gen had said no, in her crisp
voice that left no room for argument. Sunday is the Lord's Day, she
said; time enough for the movies on week nights, and anyway it's
raining. Joyce had sulked a while, hanging around the kitchen. Then
Uncle Will came in, bringing a whiff of cold fresh air, and she ran to
put her arms around his neck and tease him to let her go, since he was
more apt than Aunt Gen to be easygoing about such things.

She was standing like that, pouting and pouring out her com-
plaints in a high child's voice, snuggled up against Uncle Will's chore
coat which smelled (but not unpleasantly) of grain and rain and animals, when Aunt Gen came into the kitchen. Her calm expression
changed to what – disgust? Jealousy? Surely not jealousy. She said,
"Joy, you're getting to be too big a girl to act so babyish. Get up to
your room, now, and quit whining and carrying on."

That was all, and it was nothing more than a reprimand like a
hundred others. But it gave Joyce a queer, self-conscious feeling. She
had never sat on Uncle Will's lap again, or kissed him good night.
No, you certainly couldn't tell Aunt Gen any of the crazy things that
had happened in the past months.

Now that it was too late, she also wished she could talk to Mary
Jean. Mary Jean might know how to bring this sort of affair to an
end. In the first days of her enchantment, Joyce hadn't understood
that this thing had happened to other people. Of course there had
to be some; Edith's story of her tragic first love showed that, but
she thought of them as rare and exceptional. As far as she could tell,

nobody she knew was like that. She couldn't have opened her mouth to talk to anybody about it, least of all a girl like Mary Jean, who was sophisticated and could design her own clothes and had had an abortion.

She knew now that it happened to a great many people. The men-women and women-men at Anitra Schultz's party had opened her eyes, and the habitués of Club Marie were only shabbier, dingier examples of the same thing. There were bars and clubs and magazines that catered to these people and enabled them to find each other. Famous scientists had written books about them. It was true there weren't any of these books in the college library – but the college library didn't even have a copy of Kinsey.

So perhaps Mary Jean could have given her some good advice. The trouble was that she couldn't ask. The quarrel between them had simmered down to a kind of politeness. They spoke now when they met in the hall. You couldn't avoid anyone on a campus as small and chummy as this one, and in any case Joyce had never learned to stay angry. But the old closeness was destroyed, and couldn't be built up again.

Even if she could think of a good excuse to get Mary Jean off by herself for a few minutes, it wasn't a subject you could jump into. It needed the darkness and leisure of late night, after other things were talked out. But Mary Jean was rooming with Bitsy now, and their light was out by eleven.

If only something would *happen.*

All her days were up and down. When she was memorizing lists of conjugations, or sticking gummed labels with the owner's name and address under borrowed armchairs, or losing herself in Degas and his tulle-skirted girls, she felt at home and easy in her mind. When she passed Edith in the hall, or counted the days since they had been in each other's arms, she wanted to lie down and die.

Chapter Twenty

"So I went over to his house and told him I was sorry," John said. He smeared mustard on his hamburger, put the thick slice of onion back in place, and closed the bun. Then he laid the whole thing back on his plate and sat looking at it, shaking his head. "Hardest damn thing I ever did in my whole life. He was nice about it, though."

"Well –"

"He's a good guy, you know that? I don't think I ever appreciated him before. I didn't change my mind about what he does." John interrupted himself to say, "I still think it's a stinking thing to do. But other ways. He didn't defend himself."

"What could he say?"

"Well, there are arguments. He's sorry for the girls, he could say. If he didn't do it some quack would and they'd be worse off. I read it in some magazine; one pregnancy out of every six in this country ends in abortion." He scowled. "That's what they figure; of course you can't get accurate statistics on it."

Joyce shivered. It was cold in the diner; the manager-cook had gone to the bank to deposit his Saturday take, leaving John in charge. No other customers came in and John had opened the door to clear out the smoke from the grill. "I haven't really thought it through. I'm figuring it for myself right now," John went on. He stirred his coffee and put in more sugar. "What I mean, basically he's a decent guy. Not the hero I used to think. Maybe there aren't any heroes."

"Yes," Joyce said. She was thinking about Mimi and Edith, and in her thoughts they were somehow the same person, and she felt a new compassion for them.

"You have to grow up some time and learn to make allowances for people." Introspection didn't have any effect on John's appetite. He bit a half-moon out of his sandwich and sat chewing, frowning with thought. "If he didn't do it, they'd go someplace else. Someone who wouldn't boil the instruments. Your girlfriend was all right, wasn't she?"

"She was fine. He did take a chance coming out to see her, too." John shook his head. "It's not so simple."

Chill touched her heart. She reached a hand to him, then pulled it back. "You wouldn't do it, though. Would you?"

"No. But I'm glad I made it up with the old man, though."

She got up and filled his cup from the glass pot. It was as though, having made up his mind to tell her, he wanted to get it over with. I know how he feels, she thought with a sudden flash of insight. I felt the same way with him. She flashed him a startled look. He caught her thought. "Good at spilling to each other, aren't we? Maybe it saves a couple other fellows from being bored with us."

"I'm not bored."

They sat drinking coffee in a companionable silence. She sensed that he was through with what he wanted to say. But she asked, "Will you go back there?"

He shook his head. "It didn't come up. I don't think I would anyhow. Something's gone out of it." She knew that feeling too. "Thing is, I'm going back to school after Christmas. I've saved almost four hundred bucks from the cannery and I've got the promise of a good lab job at school for the second semester. So there wouldn't be any point in my going back for such a short time anyhow."

"I'll miss you."

"Will you write?"

"I don't now. There wouldn't be much use, would there?"

"How do you mean?"

"Well – look. Men don't mean anything to me, in a romantic way

188 | *Whisper Their Love*

I mean. I'm never going to fall in love or get married or anything like that, so why go through the motions?"

"Uncle Doc told me once," John said, "that about forty percent of the girls who go to doctors for marriage-license examinations are virgins. Forty percent – that's less than half. Do you think the other sixty should stay single and not have kids, or anything, on account of a little membrane being ruptured?"

"That's not what I mean," Joyce said. She looked intently at her coffee cup. The rim was chipped; the place was rougher and lighter in color than the cup. "I haven't got any feelings. I'm frozen solid inside."

"Oh, crap," John said. He finished his sandwich with a gulp and wiped his mouth on his paper napkin. "I didn't eat any supper," he said. "I was walking around planning what I was going to tell you. Want another?"

"No thanks."

"I do." He went around behind the counter, took a patty of meat out of the freezer and removed the two squares of waxed paper. "Joe ought to give me a quantity discount." He laid the meat on the grill. It sizzled appetizingly. He bent to look beneath the counter for a fresh carton of buns. "There's nothing the matter with you," he said. "You're going through a tough time and naturally you don't feel like yourself."

"You think you know so much." Joyce stood up. "I've got to get home; it's getting late –"

"No, wait." He turned around and flipped the hamburger over. John wasn't a man to get rattled or lose his head; she guessed he would make a good doctor. He came back and laid a hand on her arm. "Don't go yet. We don't have any business getting mad at each other, we're too close."

"That's what I keep trying and trying to tell you. I don't want to be close to anybody."

"I'd as soon put it off a couple years myself," John admitted.

"But it's already happened; we can't change that." He switched off the grill. The wires glowed and darkened. "You know," he said casually, "maybe a sample of the real thing would help straighten you out. You want another hamburger?"

"No…. What are you talking about?"

"I was thinking," John said. He looked embarrassed; you couldn't imagine him being embarrassed, but he was. She liked it in him. "You could go to bed with me if it would help any. This isn't just a new kind of proposition. You've got to start some time, you know, making a woman out of yourself. I figure on our getting married some day anyhow. So it might as well be me you learn on."

Joyce stared at him.

"Shut your mouth before a fly walks in." He bit thickly into his sandwich. "Want to try?"

"You're crazy."

"Not at all. I've laid a girl or two in my time. Those diagrams in the medical books help, too."

"Oh, be serious." There were tears in her eyes; she blinked them back. "I tell you my troubles, and all you do is make corny jokes."

"Never more serious in my life." He came around the counter and sat down beside her, still eating. "Analyze it. You're not happy in the half-sexed deal you've got, are you?"

"Oh God," Joyce said, "why do you think I told you all that stuff? Sometimes I think I'm going crazy."

"Same time, you've got this silly idea there's something the matter with you –"

"I know there is."

"You know why women are frigid? They don't love their husbands, or their mothers scared them when they were kids, or they're afraid of getting pregnant or something." He patted her knee. "It doesn't come built in. Okay, go to bed with me tonight and we'll see. You don't have to be afraid; I'll take care of you."

He meant it. Realization filtered in slowly. Why not? She

thought. It might be the thing she was hoping for, a definite step. It might somehow break the web of confusion that held her in its sticky meshes. Even if it weren't an answer it might be a clue. Maybe, she thought, if she tried love with a man and it didn't repel her – she didn't expect to enjoy it, of course – it might prove something. She wasn't sure. "I don't see what good it would do," she objected.

"Prove you're a normal female capable of normal feelings," John said. "Not tied down to something you've already outgrown. Sure, I'd like it for my own benefit. If I didn't enjoy it, I wouldn't be any good to you. But that's not it, this isn't a scheme to get you in bed. I'm not that clumsy with women. I can get a girl the usual way."

Joyce looked at him. He looked so everyday and ordinary she couldn't imagine being afraid of him. "All right, I'll do it."

He waved at her plate. "Eat your sandwich first. Making love's hungry work."

"Later. I'll eat something later. If we're going to do it I want to do it right now, before I lose my nerve."

"Okay. Soon as the boss-man gets back."

She stood out on the sidewalk, coat collar turned up and her hands in the deep pockets. Mimi had sent her this coat, a soft fleece in pale yellow, and she hadn't written yet to thank her. Never mind. Through the glass of the diner she saw John and the boss arguing – apparently John wanted to pay for all the food he had eaten and Bruno was saying with hands and shoulders and eyebrows, no, it's on the house. John swung the door open and was beside her. "A motel's the best. Cheap, and nobody asks questions. Do you want to take a cab or should I borrow a car?"

The thought of Scotty raised the fine little hairs at the back of her neck. There was no reason why a taxi would be driven by Scotty, but she felt, unreasonably, that it would be. "Please, let's get the car."

There seemed to be a lot of waiting involved in this: outside the drugstore, while John went in – she saw him standing at the counter, thin and redheaded and serious, and marveled again at how matter-of-fact some people were about things she had always considered shameful, under a tree at the corner near his friend's house, a square yellow layer on a square brown layer, like a cake. It looked so respectable and middle-class she was afraid he might change his mind and not come out again. She walked around a little, with short nervous steps. Now that her mind was made up, she wanted to get it over with. The memory of Edith's hands woke in her muscles, and another memory, brutal and terrifying. I won't think about that, she promised herself. This is different. He's doing it to help me; an act of kindness, not love.

All the way out to the edge-of-town motel they were quiet. John drove fast, but well. His profile looked stern. She was a little afraid of him. When he parked he didn't speak to her, but came around silently and held her door open.

A neon sign said VA ANCY; one bulb was burnt out. She saw a curving row of neat little white-painted houses on a gravel drive, like doll houses with colored shutters. She stood outside the office with her bare left hand shoved down in her pocket, another interval of waiting, while John signed the register. When he came out he was smiling. "That's one good thing about being a Smith or a Jones. It saves you trouble making one up."

"Have you done this a lot?"

"Every night since I was thirteen," John said, "and twice on Sunday."

"In other words, mind my own business."

He took her fingers in his. His hand was cold. He's scared too, she thought, and then dismissed the idea because he couldn't possibly be scared. Somebody has to be calm and grown-up about this. She wrapped her fingers around his thumb. "Come on. Let's go in."

Chapter Twenty-one

The cabin was bright and light, decorated with western decals on every possible surface. Cowboys and Indians, bucking broncos, Davy Crocketts with terrific coonskin caps. She had pictured a tacky place like Stella's cabin, but this was modern and streamlined.

"Can we turn the light off?"

"If you want. It's better with it on, though."

"Any way you say."

"That's my girl."

They undressed quickly. She was glad she looked all right with her clothes off. She fought back a silly impulse to put her hand in front of her. John said, "Scared?" and she said, "No."

"You lie in your teeth."

"All right, I'm scared."

He was no boy now, but a man. He moved against her, and his arms were tight and strong around her. She felt the hard solidity of his muscular body. No boy. He said softly, "Come to bed, honey."

The sheets were smooth and cold. When she felt his body stretched out beside hers she began to tremble. It was silly, she hadn't expected it, but she couldn't help it. "I won't hurt you," he promised.

She thought: he expects me to be a virgin, he doesn't know about.... Her teeth chattered. He stroked her arms and shoulders gently, leaning over her, propped on one elbow. She relaxed a little. But then his hand moved down and stopped. She started to shake again. "I can't. Oh, don't make me."

"You'll feel better after. I was scared the first time, too."

"What was your first girl like?"

He considered, wrinkling his forehead. "Oh, just a girl. You know how a boy is at sixteen or seventeen, with hot pants. Doesn't mean anything after it's over."

Her heart was banging. She could see it thump under her smooth skin. The pulse in her throat pounded. She shut her eyes. "Okay. Go ahead."

"Not till you are ready. It's no good for you this way."

She lay stiff and still while he caressed her. The warmth didn't go deeper than her skin. "Please, let's not."

"You know, you're holding out on me." She could feel him looking at her, though her eyes were shut. "All that stuff you told me – that's not the whole story, is it? There's something you're keeping back."

"No. Not anything that matters." He rolled over and lay on his back, arms under his head. She turned away from him, face to the wall. "Please."

"Why not?"

She didn't know. Want was growing in her, not only for the relief of having at last done something definite but in some deeper way that was rooted in her own body. Yet she couldn't go ahead with it, could not let him enter her. She pressed her legs together, trembling so that the bed shook.

"Okay. We won't do it." John sat up on the edge of the bed, smiling a little. He looked self-conscious, and it occurred to her that she had hurt his feelings.

She said timidly, "I'm sorry."

He got up without answering and went into the little bathroom. She heard water running and the gurgling noise of the toilet being flushed. She raised her arm; the flesh was dotted with goose pimples. She pulled the blanket up to her chin.

"Everything okay?"

"John, are you mad at me?"

"No. Look, why don't you take a little nap? I'll lie right here and keep you warm. Put your head on my shoulder. I won't make any passes or anything."

His skin was warm and smooth. He smelled a little of sweat and some odor that was vaguely male, not unpleasant. Her head fitted right into the hollow of his shoulder. Timidly, she moved against him. He put an arm around her. Her tense muscles began to thaw out. Being married must be like this, she thought; after the sex part's over you'd feel real close and cozy together, never lonesome or scared any more.

When his watch showed him that it was after midnight, he had to shake her to get her awake. She rolled over, sighing. For a moment she couldn't remember where she was or why she was lying here naked with a man's body pressed against hers. Her neck was stiff. She pulled away from him and sat up, beginning to be scared again.

"Some honeymoon," John said. He sat on the edge of the bed, pulling on his shorts. "You got a good nap, anyway."

"I wasn't asleep."

"Then why were you snoring?"

"Oh."

"I felt you relax," John said. "It was nice."

Her lips shook. "I'm so sorry. About everything."

"It's okay." He bent over to pick a sock off the floor. All she could see was his back, the muscles stretched. "Maybe it's better to wait till we're married. You were brought up old-fashioned."

"I don't want to get married," Joyce said. It was hard to sound prim and hook her bra at the same time. She felt the circumstances weren't exactly suited to arguing.

"You will. It'll take time, that's all."

She gave up. You couldn't tell him anything.

He was the one who tidied the room, putting everything back in place, turning down the sheets so they could be changed for the next couple. He raised the window shades to halfway and set the straight chair against the wall. She stood looking around the neat little room. Silly as it was, she hated to leave it. Tenderness had been here, and a feeling of security. She leaned against John, trying to hide her sudden tears in the front of his shirt. He kissed the top of her head. "It's all right, kid. We've got plenty of time. C'mon, time to go."

A car was pulling out as he turned the key in the lock. The head-lights swept across the drive, the front of the cabin, the bent back of the young man trying the doorknob and Joyce's erect figure as she waited for him. She blinked in the sudden glare. Then the car backed out of the parking space, turned, and rushed down the highway toward town. The sky was dark and the air quiet except for traffic and someone's faraway radio.

They walked across the grass to where the borrowed car stood parked. Their shadows went ahead of them, immensely tall and far apart, an empty space between them.

Chapter Twenty-two

Mary Jean stopped her in the hall after breakfast. "I have to see you," she said. She laid her books on the newel post at the top of the stairs and leaned back against the wall, gripping the knob of the post with a white-knuckled hand. Her eyes, deeply shadowed, were fixed on Joyce's face.

She knows, Joyce thought. "I'm busy." It was partly the quick defense of one caught unprepared, partly the mean pleasure of getting even. I really am busy, she thought. Practice at ten, last one before dress rehearsal, and an Art exam after that. She smiled thinly, feeling the muscles of her face stretch. "Whatever it is, it'll have to wait."

Mary Jean's face was like that of a slapped child. It had been white; now the white turned a sick gray. "It's all right," she said in a low voice. She hesitated a moment, then picked up her books and walked away, her soft moccasins making a dragging sound on the hall rug. Joyce stood looking after her. She wanted to run after her and call: come back, I'll listen, you can tell me. But she stood there with a set face, and then a group of girls came out of the bathroom and shut Mary Jean out of her sight.

She went down feeling guilty and ashamed for no reason. Probably wasn't anything, she comforted herself. Probably wanted to borrow a dollar or a pair of shoes. But the feeling didn't go away, or the conviction that Mary Jean knew about the motel.

She might have been there herself. I wouldn't put it past her.

The auditorium was a scramble of girls in jeans and dirty shirts, milling around, moving extension cords that writhed across the floor like rubber snakes, scraping chairs. The floor in front of the stage was littered with lipstick-smeared cigarette butts, although it was against the rules to smoke anywhere in the building. Molly Andrews was down on her knees painting flats, with gilt in her hair and a cerise smear across the seat of her pants. Ellin, as the blasé English divorcee, sat hunched over in a folding chair gabbling lines she should have known two weeks before. Joyce felt it was an almost professional mess, with all of the racket meaning something. She fished the prop list out of her skirt pocket and went backstage, more to be a part of the clatter back there than because there was any more doubt about where things belonged.

She was tired. In eighteen years she couldn't remember ever having been this tired before. There was the time the girl from Derwent High socked her during the second quarter of a baseball game, and she finished the game and then went to the nurse and had two cracked ribs taped up. There was the summer she worked detasseling hyrid corn; the second morning she'd been so stiff she couldn't walk, had crawled to the bathroom and soaked in a tub of hot water till her locked muscles loosened. But those were physical things. This was an all over fatigue that left her feeling heavy, dead and blank. "I feel blah," she thought. She must have said it out loud because Linda Garrick slapped her on the back and said, "It's the cheap liquor that does it."

Either all of her props were where they belonged, or she was too gone to know the difference. She went down again and sat on the edge of a folding chair, right in front of the stage. There were regular theater-type chairs with arms between, used for compulsory chapel and whatever outside entertainment the college could book, but it was supposed to be more knowing to sit well forward and criticize the performance, or pull a funeral-parlor chair to the back of the auditorium and test the acoustics. Today she kept losing the thread, although she'd sat in on so many practices that she knew most of the parts. She got up and walked out in the middle of the love scene, restless in spite of her fatigue.

198 | *Whisper Their Love*

Something was wrong. You don't ask help from someone you've quarreled with, not if you can help it. She looked sick, too. I'll find her the first thing after Art, Joyce decided, and see what's the matter. The decision made her feel better; it answered some demand in her. She headed for the semi-basement, full of good nature. I won't hold anything against her; I'll do what I can to help her.

Perhaps it was the virtuous feeling that made the test so easy in spite of her fatigue. Her headache was going away, too. The pen scurried over the pages of the Blue Book, her mind picked the right answer out of the air. Manet, Monet, Seurat, Renoir, picking answers for mix-match.

She finished the second book and sat looking out the window, waiting for someone who didn't mind being an eager beaver to turn in her test first.

The hall telephone rang. Miss Wilkes got up quietly and went to answer it, leaving the door open so she could at least hear what was going on. Our girls are refined and well-bred, Miss Wilkes reminded herself with grim pleasure, our girls do not cheat in examinations. Not unless they sit more than one row from the front and the teacher's near-sighted.

Molly Andrews stopped chewing her pencil and copied briskly from her neighbor's book, word for word and X for X. There was paint across her knuckles.

Miss Wilkes came back on rubber soles. She looked sharply over all the meek, bent heads – light, dark, red, with little chiffon bows tied into the ponytails or jeweled pins set among the curls, this season's fad. The innocent little darlings, she thought grimly. She walked flat-footed to Joyce's chair. "Will you report to the dean at once? You can finish your test later."

"Oh – I'm done." Joyce handed in her book and left. There was a little buzz. Eyebrows were raised and smiles spread over faces.

"Quiet, please," Miss Wilkes said. She had been young once herself. She was only forty-two now, she sometimes reminded her reflection in the bathroom mirror, and forty-two isn't dead by a long shot. There was a man back home, department manager in a store, she was keeping reserve. "Anyone I see talking will fail this test," Miss Wilkes said, rapping her desk with a pencil.

Edith Bannister was standing in the middle of the study, tapping one foot like a woman who's tired of waiting. Her face was a mask Joyce had never seen before. Narrow vertical wrinkles between her eyes matched the thin pinched lines at the corners of her mouth. Her lipstick was blurred at the edges and a bit of hair hung down over her forehead. "Where were you last night?" she demanded.

Joyce had to stop and think. Between last night and this morning there was a great gulf, a stretch of not-sleeping followed by restless, half-conscious sleep. Already the hours with John had the unchanging fixed look of something that is over and past. She lifted her eyes carefully to Edith's face, and what she was there warned her to be careful. "I went downtown with a boy I know, a town boy. We had hamburgers and coffee."

Edith said nothing.

"It was Dr. Prince's nephew," Joyce said nervously. "You know Dr. Prince, he gave the typhoid shots last fall." You're talking too much, she warned herself.

"I know Dr. Prince, all right," Edith said. "I asked you where you were last night."

"Did I forget to sign out? If I did, I'm sorry. You're always saying I should go out with boys because it keeps people from getting suspicious."

"Oh, shut up!"

Joyce had never heard Edith shout before. She stepped back.

Edith leaned ahead, her neck stretched out – she had a skinny neck, Joyce thought – her lips fixed in a dreadful smile. "Do you want me to tell you where you were last night, you cheap little sneak? You were at the Sunset Motel with this doctor or whatever he's supposed to be, and you were there from around eight till almost one this morning. One of the board members saw you leaving and phoned me this morning." What in hell was he doing there? Joyce thought; as if I didn't know.

"A blonde in a yellow coat, he said, and you've got the only yellow coat in school."

Joyce put her hands behind her and watched Edith's face intently, afraid to look away.

"Till one o'clock, my God, in a cheap motel, with a man, like a common whore. Oh no, you don't have to tell me what you were doing. I know what you were up to all right. It's been three weeks –" Her voice cracked. Joyce took another step back, measuring the distance to the door. The air was charged with danger.

"No wonder you haven't wanted me lately! No wonder you looked down your snooty little nose at Anitra and her friends, after she welcomed you into her house! I saw you making fun and acting superior. You haven't got the guts for a real honest relationship." Her hand groped toward the desk. Joyce watched, fascinated. "No, oh, no, you have to go to bed with men. Any man that comes along, I suppose. You're no better than a common streetwalker."

"That's a lie."

Edith's smile broadened. Her teeth glittered. There was saliva on the edge of her lower lip; she wiped it off on her sleeve and that was the most shocking thing she could have done. "You'll catch a disease. You'll get in trouble and have to have an operation like your nymphomaniac friend. And then I'll laugh at you, do you hear me, I'll laugh at you."

She's crazy, Joyce thought. The walls of the room seemed to shrink, penning her in. She reached behind her for the doorknob. The crystal ashtray whizzed past her head. She felt the air stir her hair, and then there was a crash and a thump as the ashtray hit the door and fell to the floor.

A hot, reviving anger poured through her. She took two long steps and slapped Edith across the cheek.

Edith burst into tears.

"Oh God," Joyce said. She looked at this disheveled wreck of a woman standing with her hand to her red and smarting face, and there was neither fear nor love left in her, but only a deep strength. I hope to God nobody's out in the hall listening to this rumpus, she thought; they're sure hearing plenty if they are. The assurance that swelled her chest was like the feeling that had gripped her at Mary Jean's crisis. She could do anything she had to do. Somebody had to take hold and straighten things around. It was Aunt Gen's phrase. Her voice was like Aunt Gen's too, sure and quiet. "Oh, stop it. You're making a fool of yourself. It's none of your business where I go or what I do. You're not my mother."

The words hung on the air of the room. It's true, she thought wonderingly. "I don't need a mother any more," she said. "I've grown up."

Edith bent her head. "It's only that – I love you."

"I guess maybe you do," Joyce admitted. "I thought I loved you too, but I didn't. I'm sorry. I never meant to lie to you, though."

"You –"

"You want me to tell you where I was last night? I was out at the Sunset Motel with John Jones. I thought maybe if I acted like a normal decent person just once, if I went to bed with a man the way I'm supposed to, maybe I'd understand things better. It wasn't any good, though."

"You did that!"

"Yes. It wasn't any good. I couldn't do it." Joyce reached out and picked up the African figure. Full sagging breasts, distended belly, full thighs. Woman, unthinking and fulfilled. She stroked it absently. "I'm one of those frigid females you read about. I haven't got it in me to love anyone."

Edith lifted her head. Her shoulders straightened. "I could make trouble for you," she said. A thin smile touched her lips. "I can get you expelled. All I have to do is tell everybody what you are, what you've been. A pervert. They'd make it really bad for you." Her lips curled back so the teeth showed. The red patch on her cheek glowed dully. "There's nothing people enjoy more than hurting someone different. I could fix it up so you'd never get a job or an education, either."

"I guess you could." The warmth still upheld her, and a mind not her own had taken over. She felt clearheaded; she felt fine. "Of course that works two ways. I can talk too. In court if it comes to that. I was eighteen when I came here," she pointed out, "a young girl from the country, and you taught me all those things. That would look fine in the papers, wouldn't it?"

"Joy –"

"Everybody knows about you. The girls." She didn't know where that piece of information came from, but she had no doubts about it. "There must have been others. I wouldn't make any charges, if I were you, or even start any gossip."

Edith's knees caved in. She stumbled backward and landed on the desk chair, staring at Joyce with her mouth open.

"Do anything you want to," Joyce said. "Tell anybody you please. It doesn't matter any more. I'm getting out of here."

"Where?"

She shrugged. A gesture borrowed from Mary Jean, who used it to mean many things. "It doesn't matter. Nothing matters. Can I go now?"

"Joyce, for heaven's sake!"

Joyce went out quietly, shutting the door without a sound. Her knees felt stiff. She realized that she was holding her breath, and exhaled deeply. She felt hollow, like someone who has borne up bravely under a long illness in the family and now, the funeral over, has to go back to an empty house.

Hungry, too. She remembered not eating anything last night, and this morning she'd skipped breakfast. I'll go and wash up, she thought, then beat it downtown and have a sandwich and find out about train times. Maybe looking at schedules will give me an idea where to go. I'll get my money from the bursar's office. She hadn't known she had any plans, but there they were, all shaped and ready to be put into action. This is the time. Get a job in a store – no, an office. Find a room. Maybe if I can be alone for a while....

One sure thing, she thought climbing the stairs, I can't go back to the farm. Can't face the folks till I get this worked out. Aunt Gen would never forgive me. Aunt Gen's face rose in her mind, the forehead knit in disapproval, the lips thin. No mercy there for anyone who transgressed her unchanging code of right and wrong. No, Joyce thought, I have to do this for myself. Nobody else can help me with it.

The need for confession was urgent. Telephone John? No; he was probably hating me already. She felt, suddenly, a sharp realization of loss. There's nobody I can talk to any more. It was crazy, it didn't make sense, but already John had come to be that rare thing – a friend who could be counted on.

Have to get the trunk out of storage; thank goodness I have enough clothes for a long time, she thought. She mounted the stairs, feeling at once competent and bereaved.

The bathroom door was shut. Why, this time of day? She pushed it open and went in.

A cold wind funneled through the room. She stepped forward to shut the window, and stopped.

The blood in the bottom of the bathtub was dark-red and sticky-looking, but what lay on the sides, splashed up in uneven scallops, was thinner and lighter. As if, finally, Mary Jean had bled herself dry – as if this was the last thin drainings of her life. The white of her bare arms was streaked with runnels of blood and there were flecks of it on her pink housecoat. Her fingers hung down, helpless. How could

204 | *Whisper Their Love*

you push a blade through all the vein and gristle of a human wrist, and where had she found the old-fashioned straight razor that lay on the floor beside the tub?

Soap and towel lay there too, stained. She had bathed, she had made herself clean for the final rite.

A single fly buzzed at the edge of the viscous red pool, lifting its jointed legs daintily out of the wet.

Mary Jean's eyes were open, looking at her.

Joyce screamed. She could hear herself screaming. The sound echoed inside her head and she knew she was making it, but she couldn't stop. She went on screaming until feet pounded on the stairs. Then Mrs. Abbott was in the door, a black whale with staring eyeballs, and Mrs. Abbott's rings were biting into her shoulders and the room was going around in slow sickening circles. Then nothing at all.

Chapter Twenty-three

Some things figure out the same, anywhere you go. Death is one. Everywhere on earth there are special taboos and rites associated with death, ceremonies to celebrate the good qualities of the departed or protect the living against evil spirits and unknown perils. Whether old hymns are sung or tribal dances performed, wreaths ordered from a florist or bowls of food set out on the burial mound, widows draped in black and given a handkerchief for their tears or bound hand and foot and burned on the funeral pyre, for a little while people set aside their own affairs and think with wonder of the life that has ended and the loss to those left behind.

Even on battlefields, where man falls by his brother's hand, the chaplain says a prayer.

So the folk rituals of Ferndell held, here on the campus, and classes were dismissed for three days. Two hundred girls were milling around, vaguely uneasy, with nothing to do. Not that there was any lack of activity. Two white-coated orderlies came and took Mary Jean away in a long wicker basket, steering it neatly around the bend in the stairs, and there were whispers and arguments. Autopsy. Yes, but what do they really do? The law, when somebody commits suicide. At the thought of Mary Jean's drained body subjected to knife and scalpel, Joyce's scalp prickled and she looked around wildly, feeling that the walls were closing in. As if Mary Jean could be hurt any more....

The students, at a loose end, felt constrained to behave in a manner suitable to a house of mourning. Suddenly the campus became

Mary Jean's home, everybody living on it a member of her family. Girls who felt like playing canasta or giving each other home permanents did so quietly and furtively, as if they owed it to their dead friend to be above such everyday pastimes. Meals were sketchy, and served with less ceremony than usual. That was partly because Mrs. Abbott, usually so quick to rebuke the heavyhanded and slow of foot, had delegated herself chief mourner and was going around sniffling into a wad of handkerchief. She talked about Mary Jean to girls who stood glassy-eyed and unanswering, wishing they were somewhere else. That beautiful talented young girl, Abbott kept insisting in a mournful voice that made Joyce want to push her face in, why would she do such a dreadful thing when she had everything in the world to live for?

The police came with notebooks, and asked questions. Reporters, too, a young man from the local paper, and the fluttery old girl who did the Woman's Page, and a tired-looking man from St. Louis, from the *Post-Dispatch*. News photographers came and took pictures of buildings and teachers, but especially girls. Girls going to class with armfuls of books, and playing basketball in the gym, and toasting marshmallows in the lounge fireplace. They picked out the most photogenic students for this, and there was some feeling among those who weren't asked to pose.

The story was printed the next day in the papers Joyce had never even heard of, in Dallas and Birmingham and Raleigh, and there were five telegrams and a barrage of long-distance calls ordering people home at once. Nancy Freeman refused to go, and her father took time off being a sugar tycoon and came after her in a blue Cadillac a block long.

Plumbers came. They tramped upstairs with hammers and wrenches and took away the tub in which Mary Jean had bled to death. Even then, the girls at that end of the hall refused to use the room; they kept the door shut and sidled past. It created a rush-hour problem, everyone using the bathroom at the other end of the hall, but

Lissa expressed the general feeling when she said, "You wouldn't get me to take a bath in there even if I stayed dirty the rest of my life."

Miss Edith Bannister, that cool and competent woman, shut herself into her room for an afternoon and came out only a little paler than usual, with every hair in place and no trace of agitation. She refused to look at the body, but then, some people thought that showed her good sense. She called up the girl's father and they agreed that under the circumstances it would be best to hold the service at the school.

"She's wonderful," Mrs. Abbott said fervently of Miss Bannister, and you had to admit that she was.

Wayne Allston came, as the only resident trustee. He wore the uneasy look of a hearty man thrown into sudden contact with death. He had taken a couple of drinks before he left the office, and now he found himself needing another. Nothing you could do for the girl, poor kid, and Ede seemed to have everything under control. He found her sitting at her desk, staring at the blank plastered wall, doing nothing. He cleared his throat. "This is an awful thing. Anything I can do, you just let me know and I'll see to it."

She didn't answer for a moment. She looked at him absently, as if she had met him somewhere but couldn't quite remember him. "Thank you. That's good of you."

"Well, I thought flowers. It's tough on you. Nobody could blame you for anything, though."

She was silent.

Dr. Prince stood washing his hands over and over, although the wet slipperiness of the skin and his awareness of time's passing told him they were clean. Crazy damn kid. Hysterical type, going off half-cocked before she could be sure. He frowned, remembering that the beautiful mutilated body had been under his hands before, and wishing he didn't have to remember. She had behaved well that time, ready to explode with pain and nervous tension, but standing it better than most. A pretty kid, the sort any boy would fall for.

No question about why she did it. Five to six weeks, he guessed, far enough along for easy diagnosis. She hadn't wasted any time getting in trouble again. The question was, why? He remembered the faces of other girls sharp with repulsion, voices shrill in protest. Not me, doctor, I'll never look at another man. Sometimes, God and their perplexed young husbands knew, they kept on feeling that way after you'd expect time to work its healing miracle.

This one had been looking for trouble. Some kind of a mental twist, he guessed. He stepped on the hot-air dryer, glad he was a man. Women have it tough. A hell of a business to be mixed up in. Yeah, but if you don't do it, someone else will, and there are the payments on the house.

For one crazy moment he wondered if there was some way to falsify the records, and knew there wasn't. Hide anything, fake anything around a hospital? Somebody always knew.

Joyce moved through the buzzing and the silences in a kind of stupor. I wish I could cry, she thought, watching Lissa and Holly wipe their eyes and blow their swollen noses. It must be a relief. Her mouth tasty tinny and her throat ached, her stomach pinched with hunger, but the smell of food made her sick, and when she tried to swallow her chest hurt. She sat in her room with the door shut, wondering what they were doing at the hospital. In her mind, autopsy was confused with dissection; she had a blurry image of medical students under a glaring light, which dissolved into a picture of the undertaking parlors downtown. Embalming. Or sometimes they cremate you instead; that didn't seem so bad, clean and final. Holly said they took all the blood out when a person was going to be buried, and put some chemical in. But Mary Jean didn't have any blood left.

She remembered that slender lovely body drawn up in the convulsions of cramps, and later, sprawled out in a doped sleep. Quarrel or no quarrel – oh, God, how silly that seemed now – she had taken care of Mary Jean intimately. The thought of any further indignity to her was unbearable.

She thought, I won't look at her when they bring her back. I can't.

Ought to be packing. She was jumpy with impatience to be gone from this place, could hardly wait for the funeral to be over so she could leave, yet the thought of actually making plans paralyzed her. She went to the closet and stood looking at the double row of dresses and blouses.

Bitsy came in without knocking. "I have to see you alone," she said imperatively. "Come on down to the kitchen and have some coffee."

"I don't think we are supposed to go there."

"Rules are made to be broken," Bitsy said primly. "Sometimes it's necessary to use your head."

The kitchen was at the back of the basement, reached by a narrow cement-paved corridor that gave on dark mysterious storerooms, fruit cellars and coal bins. Joyce had never been there before, and in spite of fatigue and grief she was curious. Visitors were never shown through this part of the building, which was run by the servants under Mrs. Abbott's direction, and Mrs. Abbott was ladylike enough to ignore what she couldn't change. As a result, there was no regard for glamour here and not too much attempt at sanitation, either. The Home Ec classes had a lab kitchen and dining room in the Administration Building, and Joyce had assumed that the food she ate came from some place as white-enameled, as glittering with stainless steel. Now she realized the substructure of her meals was shabby to the point of slovenliness.

The stove here was gas, black and thick with spattered grease. There was a wood range alongside for winter use; a fire crackled in it, and red showed around the lids. A line over the stove held drying towels, some smeared and stained with food. A fat cockroach ran across the toe of Joyce's loafer and vanished in a shadowy corner.

The stout motherly waitress was slumped down, stocking-footed in a straight chair, drinking coffee. Bitsy reached for the enamel pot and tipped it carefully, pouring into a couple of thick white cups such as farm wives use for threshers. She handed one to Joyce. The waitress sat unmoving, cup in hand, until Bitsy smiled at her and sat down. Then her eyes met the girls' with liking and acceptance.

"Nothing like hot coffee, a time like this."

"Sure isn't."

Joyce had drunk so much of the stuff in the last few days that it tasted like water, but at least the heat relaxed her throat. Maybe if I could get some sleep I'd be able to eat, she thought. She looked at Bitsy, sitting quietly erect. Bitsy wore a dark skirt and white blouse, as though bright colors would be an affront to a house of death. Her ponytail was slicked into a neat bun; her face looked sharp and sober, the freckles prominent. Joyce envied her. Bitsy would always know what she was doing, and would always do the right thing. If trouble came to her, it wouldn't be the outcome of her own foolishness.

Bitsy intercepted her look. She set her cup down on the table, moving a sticky spoon, and took a piece of paper out of her blouse pocket. "What do you make of this?"

The waitress drained her cup and left, tactfully.

The paper was wrinkled with folding and unfolding. Mary Jean's big loopy handwriting, three or four words to a line. "Joyce. Maybe God will forgive me now. I know I've been bad but I can't take any more of this." Joyce's hand shook so that the sheet rattled. Bitsy's eyes were sharp on her face. The kitchen was warm and stuffy; for a moment she thought she was going to faint. She looked at the far wall, where a cobweb swayed slowly.

"I have to know," Bitsy said. "It was under my pillow – thank the Lord I found it before anybody else did."

There was no evading those gimlet eyes. Joyce looked at the floor. "She was in trouble," she said, low. "The time we went away. She had an operation – you know, operation."

"I thought it was something like that," Bitsy said. She sighed. "That was good of you, to stick with her. It wouldn't have been so nice if anybody found out."

Shame flooded Joyce. "I threw it up to her," she said. "I wouldn't even listen when she wanted to talk to me – the day she did it." It seemed long ago. "Maybe if I had, she wouldn't have."

"It's too late now," Bitsy said sensibly. Oh, a sensible girl, the kind who gives you aspirin and hot tea for a broken heart. It now occurred to Joyce that maybe tea and aspirin would be help, too. "Do you think –"

"She was afraid of it happening again. That was what we fought about, partly."

But was it, really? She shut her eyes, seeing how snarled and twisted the whole thing was, how the strands of her life and Mary Jean's were interwoven with half a dozen other lives. Nobody could ever unravel this tangle; nobody could say what was true or false, or who was to blame. She would never know.

Bitsy's eyes were bright. "Whoever does the autopsy will know," she said. "That's the first thing they always think about when a single girl kills herself. It'll be on the record. Seems to me what we have to worry about is, will the doctor tell? Gossip, I mean."

"No. Because he's the one –"

"Ah," Bitsy said in disgust. "Her father's coming," she said, taking hold of the matter as Aunt Gen would have, by the practical end. "We'll simply have to work up a good story and stick to it, and hope Prince keeps his mouth shut. It was Prince?" Joyce nodded. "He's probably scared too."

"Cancer. You can't pick up a magazine without reading some article about cancer," Joyce said hopefully. "It's supposed to make you go to the doctor and find out, but *I* think all it does is scare people."

"Mind, you suspected all the time. Back me up on it, though, or so help me, I'll –" Their eyes met.

Bitsy was little and wiry. She would have made a good pioneer, swinging an ax in forests infested with hostile Indians. Joyce followed her straight narrow back out of that slovenly kitchen, feeling a little better to know that Bitsy was helping carry this load.

This try, she got a suitcase of clothes sorted and packed. Then she went over to the bursar's office to draw out the money so carelessly deposited, now precious because it would be the tool of her escape. The florid middle-aged woman looked at her suspiciously but asked no questions, and she offered no information. A new doubt assailed her: a woman controls her own money at eighteen, but can she leave school without permission from somebody? Worry about that later. Her account had grown to one hundred and thirty-two dollars. She felt safer when she had stuffed the bills into the zipper compartment of her Sunday purse. I'll think about plans after the funeral, she promised herself.

In the dorm, everybody was cranky and short-tempered. Nobody had had enough sleep; there was an unsettled feeling in the air that kept the girls up late, playing cards, making coffee, eating, visiting back and forth from room to room. A few who had taken aspirin or Phenobarbital to induce naps complained of feeling let down and heavy. Dinner was late, and the potatoes au gratin were scorched enough so that cheese sauce didn't help. Mrs. Abbott and Bitsy left for St. Louis, to meet the Reverend Kennedy's plane. Nobody reminded the dining-room girl to change the tablecloths, and the untidiness added to the general feeling of disaster and disorder. Joyce left the table before dessert, without making any excuse, because she felt that she couldn't sit still another minute.

Mary Jean's father was a tall solid man with quirky eyebrows like hers and iron-gray hair that had probably been black, too. He wore a businessman's gray suit, but his rimless glasses and black oxfords were ministerial, and so was his handshake. Joyce saw him walking down the hall after dinner, with Mrs. Abbott on one side and Bitsy on the other, like a large and a small tug convoying the liner. His head was bent to Mrs. Abbott's unending talk, but his eyes were remote.

Joyce guessed that Mrs. Abbott was telling him, like a stuck needle, what a wonderful girl Mary Jean had been, so pretty and talented. She hoped he wasn't listening. He looked like a man who had been talked at a lot in his time.

Bitsy wasn't saying anything. She had one good walloping lie that would ease his mind if anything could, insofar as it gave Mary Jean a sound reason for doing what she did. Bitsy would bring out her story if the right time came, hoping that Dr. Prince was enough involved to cover himself and Mary Jean at the same time. Now she let Mrs. Abbott go on and on, wiping the tears away before they could roll down and spoil her makeup.

Joyce thought that Mr. Kennedy looked like a good man and a strong one, regardless of what his religious beliefs might be. She hoped his faith would hold up under this. She didn't think he would sleep very well in the guest-room bed. He would get through the night hours somehow, remembering his wife's desertion and the short years of his daughter's life, and tomorrow he would take Mary Jean's body back to Charlotte on the train (more fitting, more dignified somehow than by plane) and start learning to live without her. He looked like a man who, having helped other people through their troubles, would bear his own sorrow well and not cry out against it or expect anyone to share it with him.

She woke up thinking about him, at two in the morning. You can't ever really help anybody, she thought confusedly, turning on the reading lamp and reaching for the closest book. The printed words didn't make sense, and she couldn't even remember afterwards what the story was about, but it helped to pass the time until the sky turned light.

Chapter Twenty-four

The next day was endless. Holly Roberston got hold of a fifth of rye and she and three of her best friends shut themselves into her room for a while and came out looking happier. Lunch was sandwiches and coffee; nobody was hungry. Several people found small errands to do and signed out for town, coming back more or less reluctantly in time for the service scheduled at two. Joyce, sitting alone in the room where so much talk had echoed, counted her money one more time to make sure it was still there. She didn't know yet what she was going to do, except that she was leaving. Even if I have to run away in the middle of the night, she thought. I can't stand this place one more day.

A minister showed up from somewhere. She had never seen him before; he wasn't one of the oldish men who usually spoke at Sunday chapel, but young and hearty, with a booming bass voice and toothy smile. He shook hands with Mary Jean's father, who looked noncommittal, and mounted the platform with an air of being at home there. Joyce didn't like him much. It bothered her, because she had been brought up to have respect for all the appurtenances of religion.

The heavy purple-velvet curtains were parted on the stage of the auditorium-chapel. Tomorrow night, Joyce thought, was the freshman play. She wondered if they would have it, and who would take back all the borrowed chairs and tables, the ostrich plumes and fans and furs. But it didn't matter. She wasn't going to be here. Already she felt separate from her surroundings, as if she had already gone and was looking back on her three months of college from a far place.

There was a heavy silver-colored box on the platform, with pink and white carnations spraying out from a stiff silver bow on the lid. Mary Jean was in there. Joyce looked away. She sat up straight, trying not to listen to the organ playing "Rock of Ages." That song was tied up in her mind with way too many funerals and revival meetings, it made her feel weepy, and she was in no state of mind to shed tears.

A hat felt unfamiliar on her head. She looked down and saw that she'd put on her good gray suit, the one she had worn to Chicago. She didn't remember changing her clothes, but apparently she had, because she had on nylons, high heels, even gloves.

The organist changed keys and went into "The Beautiful Garden of Prayer." That was better, that one was so sentimental you could feel scornful about it. There was a little scuffle in the back of the room. People half-turned to look, trying not to act curious but not wanting to miss anything either. Three young men sat down in the back row. The middle one was Bill. His face was white and there was a dab of adhesive on his chin. He had been drinking. Somebody had got him into a dark-blue suit and a tie. He looked like an insurance salesman after a binge. His eyes were puffy from crying, or liquor, or both. He sat down carefully, looking straight ahead because his eyes wouldn't focus and he was probably sick at his stomach. Joyce wondered if he knew why Mary Jean had done it. She guessed he had a pretty good idea, anyway. Likely, scared as she was, she had gone to him and told him, maybe begged him to marry her this time. And if he knew, the sober, wary-looking boys flanking him knew too. It would be a miracle if the story didn't go farther. His friends sat looking at him, not at the casket or the Reverend Mr. Sampson.

She looked at Mary Jean's father, sitting with his face composed and his hands folded, down in the front row. Let him get away from here without finding out, she prayed. It was a real prayer, the first she'd made in a long time, the first since she was a little kid down in the Primary Department, believing there was a God up in the sky who spent all his time listening to people and giving them what they asked for.

216 | *Whisper Their Love*

The minister had never seen Mary Jean, but he talked about her just the same, saying the same things Abbott had been saying for the last two days. They might have let Abbott give the sermon and saved him the trip, she thought. For one fleeting moment she had a picture of Mary Jean lying naked on the bed, chewing on an apple and reading French grammar. She'd get an awful wallop out of this, Joyce thought, she'd think it was funny as anything. She grinned.

In the middle of the eulogy, Bill tried to say something. She knew it was Bill, because nobody else would have done it. She turned around a little but couldn't see him. The voice ended all at once, as if somebody had put a hand over his mouth and the thick half-coherent words tapered off into sobs. Sitting there and crying, she thought, the big bum. But there was no life in it. There was no room for any feeling in her, she couldn't hate anybody or even remember how it felt to hate. She sat looking at the purple curtain with the tarnished silver "H" and wreath in the middle of it, seeing every little detail of the fabric and not thinking about anything else because there was nothing else that would bear thinking about right then.

Finally it was over. Her watch said twenty minutes from start to finish, but she knew better. She had been sitting there forever. Benediction, sonorous, with the hand upraised, but falling flat without a choir's amen as on Sunday mornings. Now people could get up and go out, not pushing or talking as they would have at a play or commencement exercise, but quietly. Everybody knows how to behave at a funeral, how to put on humility and stand back and let others go first. Quite a few town people were there, relatives of local girls who had been students or storekeepers who made money from the place. In the corridor they stopped to exchange greetings, the women's voices regaining normal pitch while their husbands waited, looking less funereal and more normal. Their expressions said: pretty soon we can get home and take off our ties, have a drink, go back to the office for a couple hours and clear up those accounts, call up a girl or maybe get the wife into bed for a while. Somebody else was dead, but they were going to be alive for a while yet.

The Reverend Mr. Sampson came out with Mary Jean's father and Bitsy beside him. She guessed Bitsy represented family, a sort of proxy for aunts and cousins who would attend the interment in Charlotte. This is the time when you need your own folks, if you have any. Or maybe Bitsy was still on guard. Joyce didn't doubt that some of the girls guessed what the matter was, since living in a college dormitory is like living in a goldfish bowl, but they wouldn't talk. They probably all know about me, too.

It didn't matter. But she felt chilly.

Miss Ryan went by, flat feet slapping down hard, looking more masculine in a skirt and jacket than in her gym romper, with a hat on her bird's-nest hair. Scotty went by, raffish in a pretty good suit and a sunburst necktie. Genuine hand-painted glows in the dark. He looked at Joyce, lowering one eyelid a trifle. She looked the other way. I'll never have to see him again.

There was only one person she wanted to see, and he wasn't there. She felt clearheaded now, and she knew why she had looked at everyone so closely, coming in and going out of the auditorium. No man was there with high cheekbones and shrewd, kind eyes, eyes that knew everything before you could even make up your mind to tell him.

Some day you'll need me. Some day you'll be ready to tell me.

The telephones on this floor were all out in the hall on little tables, handy for teachers. It was impossible to get any privacy here. But in the basement there was a pay booth in a little glass cage, the one Edith Bannister had called from to pull her out of art class. She didn't know yet what she was going to say, what excuse she would make, but it wasn't important. She was already headed for the stairs.

After counting that money a dozen times, waking in the night to feel the envelope in her purse and be sure it was still there because it was the key to her escape, she had left it lying on her bed along with – she remembered now – her tweed skirt and blue sweater. She thrust

218 | Whisper Their Love

her hands into her pockets. A piece of Kleenex and a gum wrapper in the left one; in the right, down in the dusty-feeling seam, a dime. It was a sign. She clutched it in her palm and ran down the stairs, pushing the last of the mourners aside without apology or explanation.

Edith Bannister walked past, erect and pale in a charcoal suit that was almost, but not quite, mourning. Their eyes met. Edith looked away without a flicker of recognition. Holly Robertson was walking beside her, and though her voice was soft and her walk decorous, there was a glitter of interest in Holly's eyes and an alertness about her. I hope she knows what she's getting into, Joyce thought, pushing open the door of the telephone booth. In the moment between taking down the receiver and dropping in her dime, she felt a flicker of remote and impersonal pity.

Chapter Twenty-five

Joyce looked at him across the table. They were probably going through time and eternity sitting across tables from each other or side by side at drugstore counters. In a city of fifteen thousand, buildings thick all around them, there wasn't any other place where two people could find even halfway privacy.

"I wish we had a place to go," she said.

"We might try another motel." That wasn't as funny as it was supposed to be. She knew one thing now about this man who was still a stranger to her, but a stranger she couldn't feel complete without: he was funny when he was hurt or worried. Serious, everything was all right. The last motel had been disastrous in so many ways that she couldn't even find a token smile for him, but she looked at him with affection and an unexpected longing to comfort him. "Forget it," he said, "I'm sorry I said it. We'll have a house of our own some time. Lock the door and shut everybody else out."

He had this crazy idea and she couldn't talk him out of it. Sure, she had to see him, but this was the last time. It had to be. She said, "Look, I'm frigid. I'm never going to live with anybody."

"Sure, but you won't always feel like that."

She gave up. Stubborn, bullheaded, impossible to convince.

"Our own house – even if we have to rent it. We'll sit around and talk all over the place. Gab, gab, all day long. Kitchen, bathroom, bedroom – no, I guess we'll have better things to do in the bedroom, won't we? We could use the living room for nothing but talking; anyhow, no television. I'm not so crazy about television anyhow."

"Will you be serious?"

"Do I have to?"

She had to drag his attention back to the original problem, the thing she had gotten him down here to talk about. Confession before she went away to make a new life. This was the last time. She would never see him again. The thought hurt like a fist in the stomach. "You can see the whole horrible mess was my fault," she said.

"Sure. Some of it, anyhow."

She didn't want this calm agreement. What she wanted was someone to make her feel better. "Edith Bannister doesn't care," she said rather sulkily. "She's got her next girl picked out already. I hate her."

"What business do you have, hating somebody that loved you?"

"It wasn't love."

"It was a crazy screwed-up kind of love," John said. "Don't be snooty. I'm sorry for her."

"Oh, how can you be?"

"Well, what does she get out of it? And getting older all the time." His eyes narrowed, his mouth sad, he looked down the chilling vista of the years.

It was true, but she brushed it away. "If I'd listened to Mary Jean she'd be alive now."

John pushed his plate back, with half a ham sandwich on it. She had never seen him waste food before. "Mary Jean wanted to die. She could have taken precautions like anybody else – hell, you said she used to, before she got all wound up. Or she could have quit the boy, even if she'd been married to him she could have quit him if she wanted to." Her own argument, but hearing it from him made her angry. "A normal reaction from a girl who'd been through all that pain and worry would be to freeze over for a while, leave men alone. Instead of being extra careful she jumped right back into the mess again."

"An accident. She was terrified of its happening."

"Accident, hell. She's afraid of being run over by a train so she goes out and stands on the track. Look, kid, the need for self-destruction is in all of us. People feel guilty all the time, they punish themselves in all kinds of nutty ways – sure, most folks don't take a razor, they eat too much or drink too much and work too hard." He was somber. "It's in all of us. We have to fight it all the time."

Joyce's mouth trembled. "It's still my fault."

"Sure. Now you gotta learn to live with it."

"I must say you're a big help."

He looked at her. "You want me to lie to you?"

Sure she did. She wanted him to take her in his arms, in a platonic sort of way, and tell her she wasn't to blame for anything. The finality of separation from Edith had begun to penetrate her cortex of not-feeling. "Why does it hurt so much to have her not want me, when I was the one that wanted to end it?" She had asked him in bewilderment, and he'd answered. "It always hurts to be rejected. Hurts your pride, at least." That sounded uncomfortable enough to be true.

"Look," John said, "nobody has a perfect life. I was in Korea. I don't know if I killed anybody or not, but that doesn't really matter. I was part of an organization set up for killing and the guilt's there. Call 'em Communists, they were still human beings." He stopped and thought as he so often did. "I'm no pacifist. I haven't got any plan for ending wars. All I know is, I have blood on my hands and every once in a while I wake up and think about it, when I've had a bad dream or something. I can't change it. All a person can do is go on from where he's at."

"I can't."

"You have to. You're an adult now."

"Then being adult is for the birds."

"You can't become a child again." He put out his cigarette, not grinding it down in his coffee cup like most young men, but pulling the lumpy ashtray to him. He had good hands, doctor's hands. She thought again: he'll make a good doctor.

"I don't know what to do," she said in a voice that was one degree short of tears.

He shook his head. "I don't know either. That's what we've got each other for, I guess. Finding out together."

She pushed her plate away. He had ordered milk toast for her, of all things, and it was the first thing she had been able to eat for a couple of days. She was grateful for his knowledge and care. But she certainly wasn't going to marry him. "I am certainly not going to marry you," she told him. Nothing was going to lessen the burden of her guilt. All right, skip it. But she had to get this one thing straightened out before she went away and never saw him again. "I'm not going to marry *anybody*. I don't even want you to touch me."

"Sure about that?"

His hand was light and warm on hers. It felt good. "I don't mean like that. You know perfectly well what I mean. Sure I'd like to have you for a friend; that's not what I'm talking about."

"Well, you poor ignorant little goon," John said, admiringly. "If you had the sense God gave jellyfish you'd know being married is being friends. The closest kind of friends there is. Fighting and having kids together and worrying about the house payments and all that stuff. Did you think it was all jumping into bed together?"

"That's what most of them get married for."

"Yeah, and that's why most of them are unhappy, too. Look," he said, "it's like being hungry for a long time. You get so nothing matters but food. But then when you're getting three squares a day, you're free to think about other things. Or like the winter I was overseas, I couldn't think about anything but getting warm again. Frostbit my feet. Now I take being warm for granted. Went around all last summer griping about the goddamn hot weather." His smile recognized his own stupidity. "You don't know ABC about anything, Joy. The sex part is a thing you learn, the more you do it the better it gets, and it's vital, but there're other things."

She was very angry with him. Her lips trembled – with anger.

"I don't know why I love you like this," John said. "Looks like I'm stuck with you, though."

She said, "You ought to be real happy, then, because I'm going away tomorrow. For good. This is the last time you'll ever see me."

"Where do you think you're going?"

"I don't know. Anywhere I can get a job."

"Well," John said comfortably, "I'm going away too. I was going to wait till after Christmas, but I guess there's no real reason to put it off that long. We could get married in three days – have to take a blood test – and have a real cheap honeymoon. Go out to the farm and see your folks, maybe?" Later she remembered that she took his assessment of Aunt Gen and Uncle Will as her folks quite for granted; that was a switch in viewpoint she hadn't been aware of while it was happening, but he was right, they were her next of kin. She could never tell Uncle Will about these last months; his countryman's knowledge of life held no acceptance of abnormality. She could certainly never tell Aunt Gen, whose unswerving standard of morality had been handed down from Sinai by way of the Reformation. But she was old enough now to know that they were her family, even while her path in life branched away from theirs.

"Maybe if we're real lucky we can get married students' housing on campus next term," John said hopefully. "Nice little barracks with oil stoves and no plumbing."

"You're making all this up."

"No I'm not. Of course I can't support a wife," he said. "You'll have to work. College and pre-med and then on and on while I build up a practice."

He was serious. She stared at him, beginning to feel trapped. Panic rose in her. The first thing I know, she thought, I'm going to find myself standing up in front of a preacher with this man. "You've got to listen to me. I can't marry you. Or anybody."

John looked around. The drugstore was empty except for the pharmacist, who was making entries in his record book, back in his little glass cage. The girl who had waited on them was in the kitchen behind the fountain. Through the half-open door John could see her leaning against the counter, drinking a glass of milk. He nodded. "Of course you're still holding out on me. There's something you're scared to tell. Well, I'm not in any hurry – any time'll do, whenever you feel like it."

"All right, I will." She took a deep breath. "I'll tell you. I was – I had an experience with a man. It was horrible."

"Really horrible? You didn't like it at all?"

"Oh!"

His face lit up. The expression of polite attention (bedside manner?) broadened into cheerfulness. "Good. Shows you have all the instincts of a normal female. Curiosity and a desire to be dominated by the male. I'm going to be dominating as all hell. Wait till I get you in bed once." She was making strangling noises. He ignored them. "Tell me honestly, didn't you enjoy it at all?"

She let him have it. "I did, if you want to know. While it was happening."

"Sure. After, you were scared silly. I don't suppose he took any precautions either. You dumb clunk, you crazy, did you think you were the first person it ever happened to? Lots of girls react the same way to their wedding night."

"You haven't heard the worst yet. It was my mother's husband."

"So naturally you're going to feel funny about it till you see him again. I bet he isn't looking forward to it with any pleasure either, poor guy. Is he a pretty repulsive type?"

"I liked him at first."

"And of course you didn't encourage him, or anything like that."

If she could have laid her hand on something heavy, she'd have thrown it at him. She'd dragged out her darkest and most terrible secret – betrayed herself, she thought furiously – and he acted as if it were a thing that could happen to anybody. As if he'd listened to millions of case histories. She was damned if she was going to be a case history. "If you knew how I hate you!" she said.

He considered that. His thin face fell into tragic lines. He stood up. "I guess you do. But never mind, you won't ever have to see me again. I did think I loved you." With a deep sigh. "I guess it's a good thing, though; marriage would be a mistake for both of us." He stood looking down at her for a moment, ignoring the way her mouth had dropped open. "Goodbye, darling," he said sadly. He was into his jacket and out of the store before she even knew he was going.

But this is *John*.

He can't do this to me. Oh God, if he gets away!

She didn't wait for her coat. He was halfway down the block before she could get the door open; he fingers were clumsy with fright and haste and the knob kept slipping. He was walking along like an old man, with his head down and shoulders hunched, not looking back. She ran, shoving aside a startled man who was loaded with grocery packages; stumbling a little, her ankles turning on high heels. One shoe flew off and she didn't have time to stop and put it back on. She flew along limping, not even stopping to kick off the other pump. She yelled, "John Jones!"

"Did I forget something?"

"You damn fool!"

"You forgot something," he pointed. "Your shoe. I bet you forgot to pay the drugstore man too. I don't know why I should go around buying food for women who aren't any relation to me."

"Oh, shut up." His arms were around her, and that was all that mattered. She was being kissed in the middle of Main Street, right in the middle of broad daylight – well, practically broad daylight, it was a winter five o'clock. This kiss lasted, stirring up feelings she'd sensed vaguely before, but with something added. A warm glow started in her back, where the scratchy sleeve of his jacket held her, and spread all through her body. "Don't you ever do that to me again," she said when he finally came up for air.

"I thought I did pretty well. Maybe I ought to take up the drama as a side line."

There were cars going by. One beeped at them. John waved gaily.

"This is Thursday," Joyce said. "We can be married Sunday."

"I have news for you," John said. "We can be married tomorrow. At least I think Uncle Doc would make out the certificates for us and date 'em back a couple days."

She hid her face bashfully against his coat. "I'm not sure," she said, "but I think maybe I have news for you too."

"Don't tell me, let me guess."

They began smiling like idiots.

They walked back to the drugstore. At least, he walked. She hopped, glad for an excuse to lean close against him. Her shoe was lying on its side in the gutter but she ignored it. The pharmacist was out in front, locking up the store. "Close at five," he said crossly. John pulled out his billfold. "We forgot to pay you," he said.

"That's all right. Come in tomorrow."

He probably thinks we're both drunk, Joyce thought. She giggled. John said, "We're getting married tomorrow."

"Oh hell, forget it then. Wedding present."

They stood on the corner, a cold wind whistling around them. Bits of rubbish blew along the gutters. John's jacket was almost big enough to go around both of them. "Aren't people good?" she said.

"Sure are."

"We're crazy."

"For better or for worse," John said. "Sink or swim, come hell or high water. I'm betting on us."

She put her foot on top of his, for warmth. A good thing; the kiss lasted quite a while. Finally he shoved her away. "Come on, let's go and get you some clothes. Damned if I'm going to marry any girl in her stocking feet." He grinned. "Beat it while you're still a virgin. All brides are virgins, don't you know that?"

It's true, Joyce thought, we'll be all right. We'll learn. She slipped her hand under the lapel of his jacket and stood still for a moment, feeling his heart beat in rhythm with her own. "I never thought it would end like this," she whispered.

"Stupid," John said, "this isn't the end. This is only the beginning."

Appendices

An Interview with Valerie Taylor
by Irene Wolt
from *The Lesbian Review of Books*, Vol. 14, No. 3, Spring 1998

On July 24, 1995, Irene Wolt conducted a telephone interview with Valerie Taylor in which she talked about her life, her work, and the history of lesbian writing in the twentieth century. This is a transcript of that interview.

I: We might as well start at the beginning. How did you get started as a writer?

V: I always did it. I've been writing stories since I was 8. I began by publishing poetry. I didn't have any prose published, except in short magazine articles, until I was over 30, but I had become known as a writer of verse. I fused my maiden name with my middle name – Nacella Young.

I: Where were your poems published?

V: I published in a lot of religious magazines, a Mormon magazine and a number of Catholic magazines, and in some of the women's magazines. It was a good way to make five dollars when you were absolutely flat broke. The best pay I ever had for poetry was from *Good Housekeeping*, which paid five dollars a line. I sold them an 18-line poem and got paid 90 dollars. I couldn't believe it. Mostly you got from three to ten dollars for a poem. I also published in poetry magazines. There were a lot of them in the '40s and '50s.

I: What year did you first get a novel published?

V: It was about 1952. I had a book published, not a lesbian book, called *Hired Girl*.

I: How did you get started writing lesbian stories?

V: When lesbian books were first published, around 1950, I realized that they were very unrealistic. Someone said to write about lesbians who are also human beings, real people with families and jobs and allergies, who went to the laundromat and so on. A lot of the ones that were then being published were written by men under women's names. They were fantastically bad. So I wrote some and sent the first one (*Whisper Their Love*) to Fawcett, a very good publishing company. Leona Hedler, the editor at Fawcett, thought I had something to be said and she took it. They did three books of mine.

I: Were they doing other lesbian fiction at the time?

V: They were doing a few. They had published *Trio* by Dorothy Baker, which has become something of a classic. They were very fussy about what they took. They took *Whisper Their Love*, which was a ridiculous title. I called it something else. They also published *The Girls in 3-B*, which I still think is a good book. That's never been reprinted, and *Stranger on Lesbos*, which started me off on the Erika books, although Erika wasn't in it. Then I went to Midwood Tower, which was printing a great deal of lesbian and gay material, and they did *Return to Lesbos*, *A World Without Men*, *Unlike Others*, and another. I had known Barbara Grier [of Naiad Press] through *The Ladder*, when she was doing book reviews as Gene Damon. We used to correspond. So I began sending her books. *The Ladder* was the only lesbian publication in this country at the time. They made a great thing about arriving in a plain wrapper so that the neighbors wouldn't see.

I: How did you find out about *The Ladder*?

V: I'm not sure. I didn't have a close circle of lesbian friends, but I did have lesbian friends. I was in Chicago then. I suppose someone told me about it. And then we organized a chapter of the Daughters of Bilitis, the D.O.B., of which I was a member for a long time.

I: What year was that, when you became involved?

V: Sometime in the late '50s.

I: Did you know other lesbian writers when you were writing in the '50s?

V: Jeanette Foster, who was the grandmother of all lesbian poets. She was writing lesbian poetry before the First World War. She wrote *Sex Variant Women in Literature*, and now it's a college course. She had been Kinsey's librarian for a year or two. She said Kinsey was a slave driver and the pay was very low, but she had access to all of his materials, including a huge amount of hitherto unpublished material in many languages. She learned Italian so she could read some of them.

I: How did you know her?

V: I think through *The Ladder*. She had published in *The Ladder* under two or three different names. One was Abigail Stanford; I don't remember the others. I had read her poetry and we started corresponding. When she came to Chicago, we got acquainted. And later Marie Kuda published Jeannette's and my poems, calling it *Two Women: The Poetry of Jeannette Foster & Valerie Taylor*. Jeannette was a very good poet and a remarkable woman. I was also writing at that time to Elsa Gidlow. She's magnificent. I'd like to see all her work reprinted.

I: Did you write for *The Ladder*, as well?

V: I had a few things in *The Ladder*, some verse and a number of letters. That's how I first knew about Del [Martin] and Phyllis [Lyon]. And also Mari Sandoz, who is the daughter of Ann Mary Sandoz, who wrote *Old Jewel* and *Capitol City*, classics in their time. She was an editor at *The Ladder*.

I: So you connected with these women through *The Ladder*?

V: It was all we had. Then when I began getting books published, women would write to me. They'd say, "Hi, I'm the only lesbian in this town of 40,000 people. How do I meet another one, if there's another one?" I used to tell them to get a copy of *The Well of Loneliness* and sit in the drugstore and drink coffee until somebody comes along and asks you what you're reading. And, of course, everyone was afraid of being fired.

I: Did you have any lesbian writers as models in those days?

V: Of course the usual. I think I knew very early on that May Sarton was a lesbian. I had never met her, but we corresponded a bit. She was my idea of a really dedicated writer. And of course I had read Colette and all those people, and Gertrude Stein.

I: Did you feel you were part of a lesbian writers community?

V: I didn't think of it as a community, but I felt related. I'd read Compton Mackenzie's *Extraordinary Women* and Rosamund Lehman's *The Ballad and the Source* and we knew those were lesbians. And after I'd read Jeannette's *Sex Variant Women in Literature* I realized that I'd always suspected some of the others. You find a little inkling in some quite old and innocent books.

I: Were you "out" as a lesbian when you were writing your novels?

V: I was out to my publisher and a number of other people. It was a very strange situation because, except for D.O.B., which kept rising and falling in membership, there was nothing you could belong to. You could go to the bars, but some of the women's bars were very tough. And also they were constantly being raided. A guy in plain clothes would come in and go into the washroom and leave out the window, and a few minutes later another guy in plain clothes would come in and everybody would be arrested. It was a real setup, and then the *Chicago Tribune* used to print the names of all the arrested people on the front page. They'd ask your name and where you worked, in case your employer missed the story. So everybody was very cautious. And everything was very imitative of heterosexuals.

I: Were there ever any problems from the publishers?

V: No, I don't think so. I think they welcomed us. An amazing number of publishers were lesbians, too.

I: Why do you think they welcomed you?

V: They wanted something that was readable for people who didn't just want trash. A couple of the books had been translated and reprinted in other countries. And some time during this period, all of my work was banned in South Africa, which I regarded as a great honor.

I: How were your books distributed and marketed?

V: A lot of them through drugstores. People would read them and then pass them around. At that time drugstores were going all out for gay literature, men's as well as women's. There was a man in Chicago, I think he called himself Sylvia Sharon, who said he'd sold 500 gay novels, a lot of them to Midwood Tower, which was my gay publisher. When I was in New York for my job, I asked the Midwood Tower people if that were true and they said, "Yes, but what he does is outline a plot and send it to us and then we fill it in." I never did anything like that. Everything I've ever sold was my own, to the last comma.

I: I read that you did your writing the "old-fashioned" way, where you started at the beginning...

V: ...and told the story right through. Right. That's the form I've always followed. And I never sold the book until I had the whole book. If I have something to sell, I want it to be in the shape to be published in case they might like to keep it. Once or twice I thought I had sold a book and then the changes the publishers wanted were so extensive that I took it back, and, of course, made no money. Writing lesbian novels doesn't pay very much, anyway. I've never made more than a thousand dollars a year writing.

I: How well did your books sell?

V: They sold very well. Of course the royalties are very small and the readership is small, too, when you consider the general population. When I was writing for professionals, for trade publishers, they sold better because sometimes people would pick them up in the drugstore just by chance. But when I began publishing with a lesbian firm, it was not very profitable. It never has been.

I: I read that one of your books sold more than two million copies.

V: That was one of those first ones form Fawcett. It was *Whisper Their Love*, the very first one. It went through two large printings. Fawcett paid on print order. Most of them pay on copies sold, so you get something like 1.5% on print orders. If they didn't sell them all, you still got paid for them. I got the whole thing from Fawcett. I remember how joyful I was. Then they sold it in Canada and that was another payment. I had borrowed $500 from a friend to pay my living expenses, so the first thing I did when that $2,000 came in on the first printing was pay back that $500.

I: Were you doing other work to support yourself?

V: Oh, sure. I always had a job – sometimes two jobs. I've raised three kids without any support payments. When I began publishing, I worked in the office of a paper box factory, running the switchboard. That's when I get my divorce. Later I worked at a very stuffy, stodgy publishing outfit. It would have shocked them if they'd known what I was doing.

I: How did you make time to write?

V: I don't know. You just do it. I wrote whenever I had the chance, at the same time I was also writing *True Confessions* magazine stories at night and selling those. That was regular formula stuff: "He kissed me passionately and, boy, was I sorry afterwards." Many years later, after I made a reputation as a lesbian writer, I tried to do a few *Con-*

fessions again, but they'd completely changed their format from the "good old days." They're much more sophisticated than they were.

I: Some of the lesbian books you wrote had some pretty racy scenes. Was that common in lesbian novels in those days?

V: Yes.

I: And you also wrote some non-gay books?

V: I wrote a non-gay book under the name of Francine Davenport, a Gothic romance called *The Secret of the Bayou*. It had everything in it, including a woman who practices witchcraft who was killed with a silver bullet.

I: Why did you use a pseudonym for that?

V: I was making a reputation as Valerie Taylor, which was not my birth name, and I didn't want it to be confused with what I was writing.

I: Was there a difference between writing that book and writing the lesbian books?

V: I don't think so. You just picked out your plot, one you hadn't worked on yet. I had been in the hospital and needed to make some money in a hurry, so I wrote a Gothic. I'd always read a lot of them just for fun. It was with one of the commercial paperback houses. I don't remember which one at this point.

I: I read that you were told to rewrite the ending to *Stranger on Lesbos*, to give it a sad ending.

V: No, that's they way I conceived that book. People felt *Whisper Their Love* had a sad ending. The girl ends up with a nice young man and she really is not a lesbian. She's a young girl looking for a mother image.

I: Was that the way you intended to end it?

V: That was the way I intended it to be from the start. I didn't think of it, at the time, as a lesbian story because the lesbian was something of a villain. There was a lot of flack about it, because they thought she should have remained a lesbian.

I: You got that when the book first came out?

V: Yeah.

I: Were there any taboos, or areas where publishers changed material?

V: I'm sure there was for many people, but I didn't get much of it. My work was much more sedate than some.

I: In an article that you wrote more than 30 years ago in the *Mattachine Review*, you said that one of your books was rejected because of the age of the characters and that a publisher changed another one – *The Girls in 3-B* – because there was some incest involved.

V: Yes, the woman character had been raped by her father, or stepfather. It sounds a little strange now, with all the publicity that subject has had, but I was told I had to make it someone not related to her, that people don't rape their relatives.

I: So you rewrote it?

V: I just changed the person to a next-door neighbor, or someone of that sort. What I wanted was some reason for this woman not to like men particularly. She was one lesbian among the three girls of the story. The other two were both hetero.

I: You also mentioned in that article, in 1961, that a novel of yours was rejected because the heroine was 40.

V: I don't remember what book that was, but it's quite possible. Forty was old in those days.

I: I read somewhere that you felt the emergence of lesbian paperbacks was the best thing to happen to lesbians.

V: I think it's been one of the best things. Reading helped to form our viewpoints. For a while when a lesbian book came out, you would buy it no matter how bad it was. I'd always thought *The Well of Loneliness* was a rather bad book – all this nonsense about being predisposed before birth because your father wanted a son. I don't regard a lesbian as an imitation of a man, either. Women are women, thank God.

I: Do you still identify yourself as a lesbian feminist?

V: Yes. I see both lesbianism and feminism as part of a much larger thing, which is a cause of justice and peace in the whole world. I'm a very strong anti-war activist. I'm a Quaker. And an old-fashioned Eugene Debs Socialist, probably the last surviving one.

I: Do you think your writing has reflected this?

V: I think so. My last book, *Rice and Beans*, had a lot of little bits of socialism in it. In the book Althea says a lot. Many of her views are mine – the way men treat women, the way people treat women in general, and the whole peace and war situation. I see all of this as part of the same struggle.

I: As a lesbian writer of lesbian fiction, how do you think things have changed?

V: Well, we're much more open and, in many ways, much more secure and accepted. But being a gay person in society is rather like being a black person in the North. I've heard black women say, "It was better down South because we knew where we were. We knew they were going to stomp on us. Up here everybody is supposed to be equal, and then suddenly you find out you're not equal." I think that's the situation we're in right now. There's a lot more acceptance of gays, but we haven't won all the battles yet. There's still a great deal of prejudice, and some of it is fairly overt. It may always be that way. Of course, there's prejudice against old people, too.

I: I have some information about a first annual lesbian writers conference that you attended in 1975. How did that come about?

V: I got to help organize it. Marie Kuda, such a ball of fire and so persistant, called me one day and said, "What we need here is a lesbian writers conference." I said, "Fine. Come to my house and we'll talk about it." So four or five of us met at my northside apartment in Chicago. It was Spring of 1974, a very cold, windy day, and I had come home from a health food store bringing a great big loaf of rye bread, which we ate up before we ended. The five of us laid out all the plans for the conference. They asked me to speak at it. I said, "Sure, I will." And we said, "If we're lucky, maybe five more people will come." So we got a church to lend us a room and got over 200 women to come.

I: How did you publicize it?

V: We put notices in newspapers and in the Mattachine newsletter, of which I was the editor. I was also editing a newsletter for the Women's International for Peace and Freedom at the same time. Marie printed my remarks in a little booklet called "To my Granddaughters." I probably have the last surviving copy. We held the conference for five years, 1974 to 1977. During that time, I moved out of Chicago and into Margaretville, New York, but I came back for the conferences. And they were really terrific. Alma Routsong, who is really Isabel Miller, who wrote *Patience & Sarah* and *The Love of a Good Woman* – one of the best books I've ever read, by the way – was the second keynote speaker, I think. I had met her the year before, when she and a friend came to Margaretville to meet me. I recommended her for next year's keynote speaker. Then we had Barbara Grier and her partner.

I: Did you do other speaking engagements at that time?

V: I'd always done some speaking. In Chicago we had the first Gay Pride Speech – it must have been about '71 or '72 – and I was the keynote speaker for that, under Picasso's statue. And somebody threw an egg at me. It missed me, luckily. I had done a lot of speaking and I'd been on the radio and TV in Chicago. Nobody seemed to mind. I was working, and by that time I had left for Spain for a year. I was working for a trade journal, doing direct selling. I was head of the advertising department, writing ads on how to sell products. I used my writing name, which is Taylor. I was working under my legal one. But I don't think they cared, at the journal. Once in a while somebody I knew would call up and say, "I heard you on the TV last night."

I: A 1979 piece quotes you as saying that "lesbian writers have always been about three steps ahead of straight women writers because they don't have to worry about what some man thinks about their writing."

V: That's right.

I: Do you still think that?

V: This is a very sweeping statement. It would depend on which lesbian writers, which straight writers, and which men. But I think at that time that male publishers, male editors, were more likely to be punitive. We became very brave and we were out, very pushy, as we needed to be.

I: What time period are you referring to?

V: From about 1960 until about now.

I: Who do you mean by "we"?

V: I mean lesbians who have some communication with the public.

I: During the '60s, you wrote your Erika Frohman series. How did those come about?

V: I had written *A World Without Men* (1963) about Kate, who was an alcoholic. I had invented Erika to solve Kate's problem. Kate was the one I was interested in. But I very quickly fell in love with Erika. Then I published the other Erika book, *Return to Lesbos*. And at that point I brought in Frances from *Stranger on Lesbos* (1960). That was the first time she and Erika had met.

I: How did you come up with a character who had been in a concentration camp?

V: I don't know. I was interested in concentration camps. I was grown up when they were happening, and I knew people who had been through the Holocaust. She appeared to me. And she seemed to be the right person for Fran. Then, eventually, I wrote another book about her, called *Ripening*. *Ripening* is what happens after the women are in middle age and come out to Tucson. That was published by an entirely different company. I sent it to Barbara Grier, at Naiad, who had published the previous ones. I thought she'd want this one, but she didn't. I had gotten acquainted with Benjamin Aiken at Banned Books in Austin, Texas, through the mail. I sent it to him and he liked it.

I: Naiad had published your previous book, *Prism*, which also had mature characters. Did you have any difficulty getting that published?

V: None whatsoever. Barbara was crazy about it and hardly changed a syllable. I wrote *Prism* after I retired and moved to Margaretville, in New York State. Abigail, NY [fictional site of the novel] is actually Margaretville. I didn't have an apartment over the drugstore, but somebody I knew did.

I: What kind of response did you get?

V: I've had some very good mail, especially from older women. I was very amused by one letter I got from a woman who said she was so glad I had written *Prism*. She said she was afraid she would never have another lover and how she's learned old age is no handicap. At the end of the letter she mentioned she was 36.

I: How did it feel to have Naiad reprinting some of your earlier books?

V: I was very happy about it. They did quite a bit to push them, but I guess they lost money on them. The books were sort of seen as historical novels, the way I'd feel if I suddenly met Harriet Beecher Stowe.

I: Do you think lesbian writing has changed since when you started?

V: I don't think so. I think there's as many kinds of writing as there were. We have a lot bigger frame of reference now. We don't feel we have to write only about lesbian subjects. We can write about anything.

I: Any other changes?

V: They give respectable reviews in highly respectable publications, which they didn't used to do. There's a great proliferation of publications now.

I: Are you working on anything now?

V: I started a book about 12 years ago about a young girl in the Midwest in 1923. I'm trying to finish it now, but it's not coming very well. I may not write it. At 81, you never know what you might be doing tomorrow. You might be dead.

I: I read that you're a cross between the resident writer and resident grandmother at a gay private club.

V: The club dissolved in the early '80s, but the same people own the building. I have half of their guest house and they live on the next street. They're the most wonderful women and charge me only token rent.

I: Do you have contact with other lesbian writers?

V: Not so much with writers. They gave me membership in Wing-span, a local club which has a nice headquarters down on 4th Avenue, which is our answer to Greenwich Village. When I was first injured, in the spring of '93, Lee Lynch – probably the best we have today – started a fund for me, and numerous people sent money. I knew my sisters wouldn't let me down, but I didn't know it was going to be like this. Every day the checks were coming in, for weeks. It was handled by the women's bookstore there, Antigone. There really is a lesbian community all over the place. It's invisible. It's like the congregation of saints that religious people talk about, I think we don't realize how much there is of it. It really does exist, and I wish all those women could know how much I love them.

Poems
by Valerie Taylor
from *Two Women Revisited: The Poetry of Jeanette Foster and Valerie Taylor* (Austin: Banned Books, 1991)

FOOTNOTES TO LOVE

1.
Cunt
sounds like a ripe melon,
tastes like it too.
Well, she said, don't just lie there.
Cut yourself a slice.

2.
They were so lonely
next day,
I put on a net-lined bra.

Now I know what Gertrude meant by
Tender Buttons.

3.
Morphology, that's the
study of shapes.
Your finger, a stem without a flower,
seeks the blossom of pleasure.

4.
All things in nature
have their counterpart.
The heart-shaped leaf
will heal the heart's distress.

Here for a promise
is the hot dark wet
cave of my mouth.

5.

Kiss not for courtesy, nor any reason
Save need of kissing. This twice-wounded breast
Will grow a thickened cortex in its season,
Will greet the assassin as a common guest.
So much I know, who lay abed and strengthened
Another time: this anguish will depart
Unless the time of suffering is lengthened
By turning of the knife within my heart.

A final grace I ask, since I am frightened
To see these wounds spring open, newly red.
Forbear to touch my hurts till they have whitened.
The gentlest hand is heavy since I bled.
Some way or other, healing will be found.
Having dealt the blow, forbear to touch the wound.

AFTER

Impossible to get closer
than the smell of you on my hand
after the bed is made,
towels tossed in the hamper.
Moving around the kitchen
sniff
remembered excitement

EACH CELL GLITTERING

I should like to tiptoe to your bed
and wake you with love
while the disregarded sun rises to zenith.

I must compose my face
and walk among others,
at least in the daytime.

I put on my office dress
and turned the key in the front door.

The air crackled with autumn,
The sidewalks and trees and houses had all been
   laundered and starched.

Sitting at the lunch counter
while my coffee grew cold
I looked back at myself
from the placarded mirror.

The others were sleepy
and did not see
your face reflected to me
from each of my pupils.

The Sweet Little Old Grey-Haired Lady in Sneakers

I am a woman,
a lesbian,
a creative spirit,
a worker,
a handicapped person,
a peace worker,
an Indian,
over sixty.

An eight-time loser,
how can I not be
a revolutionary?

How can I not see my sister in every woman,
my brother in every man,
my child to cherish in every child?

When they dragged Jane Kennedy into solitary
that was my arm
the pigs were twisting.

When they dropped napalm on the rice paddies
that was my blood
running out red and sticky,
that was my skin on fire.

Give me eight kinds of strength
to fight back.

City Homecoming

Twilight over the city – the brick school, the railroad yard
   where noisy trains are switching;
Breeze from the river, cool with spring, ruffles my hair; I
   pull off my hat and carry it in my hand.
Two schoolgirls on roller skates swoop down upon me, separate
   with shrieks, clatter past.
A young mother joggles the carriage back and forth as she
   gossips.
Here are our steps. Key in hand I reach for the railing
And turn. You are hurrying down the sidewalk, a bag of
   groceries in your arms, your eyes bright over the top of it.
Now above the snorting and chugging of locomotives come the
   faint sweet strains of distant music,
The sidewalk blossoms under my feet, and stars flash out to
   spangle the smoky sky.

STANDSTILL

I am too old. She looked across the water;
I, at the sand littered with yesterday's joys:
Bright towels, beer cans and a wrack of toys.
We are too old, though you could be my daughter,
With work to do and bills to pay.
                                        Removing
Bifocals from my tired eyes, I nodded,
Knowing how many an aging heart is prodded
By the sharp stick of desperate last-ditch loving.

Let us be friends, be cautious; oh, clutch reason,
Hold to this friendship, for the time of kissing
Has passed us by. We both have known love's blessing,
Though not together, in youth's flowery season.

She touched my hand – mouth firm, and eyes grown colder.
A fork of lightning raced from nail to shoulder.

MEMO TO FREUD

I lost a word.
Needed it, I thought,
to make a poem.
Chased it for days,
salt shaker in hand,
seeing its tail feathers whisk around corners,
elusive, maddening.

Yesterday, talking to a girl
with a wrench in her hand,
leaning against a smashed-up car,
I found the word perched on my head.

Androgyne.

Now I have the word
and the girl's phone number
but the poem has gone somewhere else.

Uncle Sig,
how do you explain this?

MORNING GLORIES

Blue
as a lustre pitcher,
blue
as the skies of a long-ago October
are my morning glories.
No garden blooms for your deft arranging
or florist's offering in cellophane and slick green ribbon,
I bring them in my hand this summer day.
When they fade, throw them on the ground.

So I brought you my first love,
carelessly in my hand.
Already the wind is ominous of winter,
the heart-shaped leaves of the morning glories are
    shaking in the wind.

"Valerie Taylor: Writing Since the 1950s and Still Going Strong"
from *Happy Endings: Lesbian Writers Talk About their Lives and Work* by Kate Brandt (Tallahassee, FL: Naiad Press, 1993)

Mention Valerie Taylor's name to a lesbian reader whose library (or interest) predates gay liberation, and one response that you might provoke is "She's a 'pulp' writer," because of Taylor's paperback novels such as *Whisper Their Love* and *The Girls in 3-B* (1958 and 1959; both now out of print). But ask Taylor *her* opinion of that label, and she declares, "I rather resent being thought of as a pulp novelist."

To Taylor, a pulp novel is "a little more melodramatic than real life, the characters not being as fully developed as they are in a really good book." And that definition contradicts Taylor's reason for writing lesbian fiction in the first place: "I thought that we should have some books about lesbians who acted like human beings."

Taylor "began writing when I was very young – romantic stories of boarding school life. And I began writing lesbian stories in the late 1950s partly because I wanted to get some money, of course – had I known how little money is in it, I might have tried something else – but there's been a great deal of satisfaction in it.

"At that time, there was a great upsurge of lesbian fiction, and it was very trashy. Most of it was written by men under romantic-sounding female names. So I thought it would be nice to write some stories about people who acted human, who had problems, and families, and allergies, and jobs, and so on. Those [other] early books were full of people who did nothing but leap in and out of beds, and stayed out long enough to send the sheets to the laundry."

Taylor's first lesbian novel was called *Whisper Their Love* – "a disgusting title," according to Taylor – one that was chosen by her publisher. "I called it *The Heart Takes Many Paths*, and I started it with an old Arabic proverb, 'The heart takes many paths in search of love' – I was the old Arab, of course, who invented the proverb – but [the publisher] changed it, and called it *Whisper Their Love*. That was the style at that time."

In another convention of the time, the book "had a little [blurb] by a 'reputed psychologist' – I figure he was probably the office boy –" Taylor notes wryly, "saying, in effect, 'Parents, buy this book; it will keep your daughters from succumbing to the temptations of lesbiansim.'" The protagonist of *Whisper Their Love* did "succumb to the temptations," but only briefly, much to the dismay of some of Taylor's readers. "I was given a great deal of abuse from people writing in later, because the girl ended up in a pure love with a man," Taylor admits. "That was almost required [at that time]; either she [killed] herself, like the woman in [Lillian Hellman's play] *The Children's Hour*, or she fell in love with a man."

But expectations for lesbian novels changed as the market changed. Taylor explains, "There were people who were interested in something besides love-'em-and-leave-'em stories, and who wanted to read something a little more realistic. And people came along like Ann Bannon, for example, and [publishers] revived some of the oldies like Gale Wilhelm. The audience was *there*. The readership was *there*. And then the *Ladder* popped up during that time and published people's short stories."

During this time (the early 1960s), Taylor continued to write lesbian fiction. Her novels of this period followed three characters through what became a related series of books. "I wrote a book called *Stranger on Lesbos* [1960; now out of print]," Taylor recounts, "about this middle-class woman [Frances] who discovers she's a lesbian. Then, I wrote a book called *A World Without Men* [1963], which is basically about a woman named Kate who is an alcoholic and a lesbian, and Kate becomes involved with Erika Frohmann. Then, I did *Return to Lesbos* [1963], in which Frances and Erika get together.

"And then somebody at [my publisher] Midwood Tower, which was struggling to stay alive, said, 'Why don't you do a book about Erika as a teenager, when she first became a lesbian?' Teenage books were very popular then. So I did *Journey to Fulfillment* [1964], because by this time, I had filled in, in my own mind, all of Erika's back history."

Three of these books were reprinted in the 1980s. But although Frances was the focus of the first and last books of the original series, the three reissued volumes were reprinted as "The Erika Frohmann Series," with *Journey to Fulfillment*, the story of Erika's early years, as the first book, followed by *A World Without Men* and *Return to Lesbos*.

Erika first appeared in Taylor's books as Kate's lover in *A World Without Men*. But when Taylor decided to continue Erika's story, she "killed off" Kate and brought back Frances as Erika's lover. "I was sort of entranced with Erika. I know every little detail about her. Maybe I knew her in some other life – assuming we do get 'recycled.' Makes more sense than anything else," Taylor adds drolly.

"But I was through with Kate when I was through with that one book. It was like a mystery, and once you solved the puzzle, it wasn't very interesting. I liked Kate, and I was very sorry for Kate, but I just was through with her. It just turned out I wasn't through with Erika; I didn't know that at the time."

Taylor certainly was not through with Erika, as it turned out, since she and Frances reappeared over twenty years later in a sequel to the series titled *Ripening*, published in 1988. "It isn't as good a book as the others, I think," Taylor admits, "but it sort of rounds off the series."

But what is most remarkable about *Ripening* is its place in Valerie Taylor's *second* career as a lesbian writer. After spending most of the 1960s "working all day and writing 'confession' stories [for romance magazines] at night" to support her three children as a single mother, Taylor "was ready to do something else. So I wrote a book called *Love Image* [now out of print], which wasn't terribly serious. It's kind of a readable book, about a fifteen-year-old child star in Hollywood being groomed for adult stardom who discovers that she's gay, and, in order to join her first lover, has to run away."

Love Image was followed by *Prism* in 1981, then *Ripening* in 1988, and *Rice and Beans* in 1989. In discussing her reborn career, Taylor offers an unusual explanation for her literary inspiration. "I have had books, I think, given to me by the Goddess," she explains. "I'm not superstitious, but I can't account for it any toher way."

Of the idea for *Prism*, a story of late-life lesbian love, Taylor relates, "I was going to bed at a friend's house in the Catskills [in upstate New York], and while I was getting ready for bed, this whole book came into my head: characters, plot, people's names, setting, everything. All the details. And I thought, ah, well, you know, it's like dreaming a book; when you wake up in the morning, it's gone. So I went to bed thinking little of it, and when I woke up in the morning, I still had it. So I wrote it."

Of *Rice and Beans*, a story of working-class life in Tucson, Arizona, where Taylor now lives, she says, "[A few] years ago, I went to apply for food stamps – having a reputation as a writer doesn't necessarily mean you have any money in your pocket – and the food stamp situation was excessively [desperate]. I suppose it is everywhere, but in the Southwest, where many food stamp recipients and applicants are minority-race people, they are treated with very little respect. And it's very difficult to get any kind of government aid.

"Anyway, I didn't get the food stamps, and I was pretty concerned about it. And the next morning, again, when I woke up, on a hot hot summer day, I had been given another book, which turned out to be *Rice and Beans*. That book, I feel, also was given to me completely, you know, with all its finger- and toenails."

In addition to such inspiration, Taylor draws on her own life to provide background for her stories. In *Prism*, "the town of Abigail is partially Margaretville, New York, where I was living," Taylor explains. "I kept trying to rearrange the town; I kept trying to put the cemetery, for example, at the other end of town, and it kept hopping back to where it was. [But] the people are totally imaginary. Well, some of the minor characters are not – the people she meets at the senior center, for example. But the woman who's the love interest, Eldora, is completely imaginary. The same in *Rice and Beans*," Taylor continues. "The people in the food stamps place are exact descriptions of the people who were there when I was there."

And in *Return to Lesbos*, Erika and Vince belong to a discussion group of gay men and lesbians that is modeled after the early homophile group, the Mattachine Society. "I was one of the organizers of Mattachine Midwest," Taylor recalls. "I was the only woman on the board for a long time. Daughters of Bilitis was the [lesbian organization], but they had very small groups. We had a DOB group in Chicago and it averaged about five people. But Mattachine was both men and women."

Although Taylor draws on real-life experience to create her stories, she points out that "all my important people are imaginary," and adds, "I like my characters. The people I write about are not great heroes, or heroines, of any kind. They're quite ordinary people. But they do try to do their best, most of them. I always feel that my main characters are people that maybe you'd really like to know. I feel very empathetic, for example, to Marty and Thea of *Rice and Beans*. They're not drawn from anybody I acutally know. But I think they're good people. And the same in *Prism*. I can empathize with Ann – I am not Ann, at all – but I can certainly empathize with Ann all the way through, and Eldora, too."

Another part of Taylor's life that appears in her stories is her love of books, particularly those by and about lesbians. "I'm a reading person," Taylor declares, adding, "There are always books in my books." For example, in *Rice and Beans*, Thea says that she knows about lesbianism from a book she's read, *Beebo Brinker* (a novel by Ann Bannon). In *Ripening*, in a scene set in 1980, Taylor describes the books by lesbian authors on Erika's bookshelves. And in *Return to Lesbos*, Frances first becomes acquainted with Erika when she buys Kate's collection of lesbian books, which Erika has donated to her friend Vince's used bookstore. As a whimsical in-joke, Taylor includes herself as one of the authors whose books Frances purchases and reads. "Yes, well, my books get a little inbred sometimes," Taylor admits with a laugh.

Taylor goes on to explain the roots of her characters' love of books. "I like literate people," she states. "My parents [were readers]. Small-town people were often very civilized, quite middle-class people. You know, you read some [books] that give the impression that an American farmer around the turn of the century was a peasant! They were never peasants! They were very self-respecting people. I think people should know their ancestors were not ignorant people.

"We don't know very much about what's happened [in earlier times]," Taylor continues. "Kids don't get stories from their grandparents anymore. We had word-of-mouth connection. My grandmother – I could tell you everything that was in my grandmother's trousseau when she married my grandfather. She sent to Boston, if you please, for fine white flannel to make her wedding petticoat."

This acknowledgment and honoring of the past is a perspective that is important to Taylor. "The young [lesbians] take [today's relative freedom] for granted," she remarks. "You can go to a bar now, and you're safe; you're not going to be busted – probably. And you have some foundation for keeping a job, even if you're out. In the old days, the *Chicago Tribune* used to print, on the front page, the names, addresses, and places of employment of everybody who was in a bar raid. Just in case your boss happened to miss it, you know, the name of his company would pop up at him.

"I think [today] we take it for granted that we can go to the local bar and visit with friends. But in the old days, you were sort of taking your life in your hands. And I think the young ones [today] take [their freedom] for granted. You fire somebody for being a lesbian, and chances are she'll haul you off to court. She may not win the case, but she's going to try."

But it is not only "the young ones" who express their convictions with such feisty dignity. Born in 1913, Taylor has a long history of speaking out for her beliefs. She recalls a time in the early 1950s when the women's magazine *Ladies' Home Journal* "used to have a very good department called 'How America Lives.' Every month they would go and visit a family – one would be a black sharecropper's family, one would be a married student and his wife living in student housing, or there would be a successful businessman and his family – so [there were] all different kinds of representative families. And I wrote [to the magazine] and said, 'Why do you not do a lesbian household?' And they were very upset, and said 'We don't think our readers would [approve].' So I wrote again and said, 'One American woman in every ten is lesbian, and I'm sure some of them read *Ladies' Home Journal.*'"

Today, Taylor is an eloquent representative for older women. "It's a terrible youth culture!" she exclaims. "I don't think that older women have had, by and large, a fair reputation in current lesbian literature." But as a still-active novelist, Valerie Taylor helps to improve the image of women of all ages with her sympathetic portraits of lesbian life, based on one simple criterion: "I like to write about the kind of people I like to know."